ALSO BY HILARY MANTEL

Every Day Is Mother's Day

Fludd

A Place of Greater Safety

Eight Months on Ghazzah Street

A Change of Climate

An Experiment in Love

The Giant, O'Brien

VACANT
POSSESSION

VACANT
POSSESSION

HILARY MANTEL

An Owl Book
Henry Holt and Company
New York

Henry Holt and Company, LLC
Publishers since 1866
115 West 18th Street
New York, New York 10011

Henry Holt® is a registered trademark of
Henry Holt and Company, LLC.

First published in hardcover in the United Kingdom
in 1986 by Chatto & Windus

Library of Congress Cataloging-in-Publication Data
Mantel, Hilary, date.
Vacant possession.—1st Owl Books ed.
p.   cm.
"An Owl book."
ISBN 0-8050-6271-8
I. Title.
PR6063.A438V33   2000   99-33536
823'.914—dc21   CIP

Henry Holt books are available for special
promotions and premiums. For details contact:
Director, Special Markets.

First Owl Books Edition 2000

Designed by Paula Russell Szafranski

Printed in the United States of America

1   3   5   7   9   10   8   6   4   2

To Gerald

". . . and that is what one does, one does not get better but different and older and that is always a pleasure."

GERTRUDE STEIN

"Can these bones live?"

EZEKIEL 37:3

VACANT
POSSESSION

It was ten o'clock in the evening; raining and very dark. A man was walking along the road whistling "Santa Lucia."

Muriel Axon stood alone at the window of her room; a square plain woman, forty-four years old. She was wrapped in an eiderdown, and in the palm of her hand she held the boiled egg she was eating for supper. The glow of the streetlamps showed her wet slate roofs, the long lit curve of the motorway outside the town, and a bristling cat in the shadow of a wall; beyond these, the spines of black hills.

Cradling the warm egg, Muriel dug in her fingernails to crush the shell. She did not go in for table manners; they wasted time. She began to peel the skin, wincing a little as she did so. She put her tongue into the salted gelid hollow and probed gently. The room behind her was dark, and full of the minute crackling her fingers made. She sucked, thought. Most of Muriel's thoughts were quite unlike other people's.

Down below, she heard the front door opening. A dim light shone onto the path, and a second later her landlord appeared, Mr. Kowalski, shuffling the few paces to the gate. He looked up and down the road. No one. He stood for a moment, his bullet head shrinking into his shoulders; turned, grunting to himself, and slowly made his way back. She heard the front door slam. It was ten-fifteen. Mr. Kowalski was drawing the bolts, turning the key, putting the chain on the door.

CHAPTER 1

"I wonder who will be the new Poet Laureate?" said Colin Sidney, coming down to breakfast. There was no reply from the other residents at number 2, Buckingham Avenue. He paused on the half-landing, looking out of the little window. He saw the roof of his garage, and his neighbour's garden. "Well, who?" he muttered. There was nothing in view but a scudding 8:00 A.M. sky, a promise of weak sunshine, a vista of close, green, dripping trees. Mid-summer. Colin went down, twitching his tie.

Behind him, the three younger children were preparing for their day. He heard shrieks and curses, the kicking and slamming of doors. The radio was on, and they were playing records too; Acid Raine and the Oncogenes were shaking the walls with their current hit single. "Ted Hughes?" Colin asked. "Larkin?"

There would be perhaps ten minutes' grace before the children erupted down the stairs to fall on their breakfasts and begin their daily round of feuding amongst themselves and insulting their parents. Colin examined himself in the mirror at the bottom of the stairs. He wished that Sylvia would move it, so that he did not have to begin every day with a confrontation. Perhaps he could ask her. He did not think of moving it himself. He had his spheres of action; this was not one of them.

He saw a man of forty-three, with bright blue eyes, thinning hair, and what he described to himself as faded good looks. But no, he thought; courtesans are faded, schoolmasters are merely worn. He saw a kind of helplessness, in the face of family and wider society; a lack of fibre, both moral and dietary. Listening to the racket above, he solaced himself with a quotation: "They fuck you up, your mum and dad / They may not mean to, but they do."

Sylvia was in the kitchen already. He thought he could hear her special muesli mix cascading like a rockfall into a dish. But instead he found her in the middle of the room, head tipped back, gazing upwards.

"What a mess," she said. The entire ceiling and the upper third of the walls were coated with the black smeary deposit from yesterday's fire. Lizzie, the daily, had opened the door from the hall, and there it was, stinking smoke billowing everywhere. Lucky she had presence of mind, or it would have been far more serious.

"I can't see why it's so greasy," Sylvia said. "It isn't as if we ever fry anything." She gave a little hitch to the pants of her tracksuit. "The whole room'll need repainting. Probably the hall as well."

"Yes, all right," Colin said, going to the table. He was sick of hearing about the fire. "Can I have an egg?"

"Well, be it on your own head," Sylvia said. "You've had two this week. You know what the doctor said."

"I think I'll be reckless for once." Colin opened the fridge. "Was young Alistair at home when this fire started?"

"If he was, he won't admit it."

"He's the source of most of the calamities round here, isn't he? And I can tell you now—" He broke off. "Where's a pan for this egg?"

"Where it always is, Colin."

"I can tell you now I'm not doing the repainting." He ran the tap. "Either Alistair does it—for a fee, if necessary—or we get somebody in."

Sylvia picked up an orange from a straw basket on the worktop. "I don't see why you can't do it." She tossed the orange into her left hand, and it slapped against her palm. "It's the end of term soon."

"True. I have one day's summer holiday and then I start on next year's timetable."

Sylvia's eyes followed him as he moved about the kitchen. "Are you having bread?" she asked, her tone incredulous.

Striding about in her bright blue tracksuit, Sylvia would never have been taken for a mother of four. Suzanne, the eldest, was eighteen now; her mother was waiting hopefully for the day when someone would mistake them for sisters. It was mysterious, this matter of Sylvia's age. At twenty, she had looked forty; all the girls on her street wanted to look like their mothers. The Youth Cult passed her by; at thirty she looked forty still, square and deep-bosomed, with her hair bleached and lacquered in the way she had worn it on the day she was married.

Then at some stage—Colin couldn't pinpoint it—she had stopped getting older. She took herself in hand. She bought a leotard, and went timidly to a class at the church hall; she stood watching, her hands splayed self-consciously to hide her pannier thighs. The next week she bought a tape of disco music, and started dancing. She clumped over the fitted carpets, making the glass shelves tinkle in the china cabinet that had been her mother's. She threw out the china cabinet, and got some pine shelves instead.

These days she wore her brown hair in a short curly perm, which her hairdresser, Shane, believed would soften her firm, rather harsh features. Her body was lean now, dieted and disciplined, capriciously nourished and not too much: as far as her brain was concerned, she was taking a course at the Open University. Now that she had lost so much weight, she was always in pursuit of new clothes, little tee shirts and cotton skirts which were bright, cheap, and casual; she picked up her ideas on the same plan. It seemed to Colin that she had chosen, among current fads and notions, all those designed to diminish his self-respect and make him most uncomfortable.

How nice it would be if she had a job, Colin thought. He was a

Deputy Head; they scraped along. There were even luxuries, like Lizzie Blank the daily woman (Tuesdays and Thursdays). But the children ate so much, and left the lights on and the taps running; they needed outfits and treats, and dinner money and bus money and more money, they insisted, for day-glo paint and handcuffs and all the other stuff you wore to an Acid Raine concert. They wanted special diets and school trips, and a tent so they could sleep in the garden in summer; they wanted video nasties, and Claire—it was reassuring, he supposed—wanted a new Brownie uniform. Every whim cost cash down. For all he knew, they might be maintaining a heroin habit. It couldn't have cost more. When he opened his bank statements he felt as if he were being eaten away, month by month, from the inside out.

But unfortunately, there were no jobs; not for anybody really, and certainly not for Sylvia. She was not qualified for anything. She was educated now, but not trained. The old Sylvia showed through too often. She became emotional when their opinions differed. Under pressure, she was always regressing to the received wisdom of the cooked meats factory where she had worked before they were married.

Colin found a plate for his bread and took it to the table. "So . . ." he said. "What are you up to today?"

"Citizens Advice Bureau, ten till twelve." Sylvia peeled her orange. "Then later on there's this committee meeting. We're thinking about setting up a women's refuge."

There was something bubbling and thwarted in Sylvia that only meddling in other people's business would satisfy. Before the birth of their youngest child Claire, when they had lived on a large housing estate, there had been plenty of time for gossip; some of it idle, some of it manipulative. Buckingham Avenue had repressed her, with its absence of tittle-tattle, its well-kept fences, its elderly residents leading sedate and private lives. Good fences make good neighbours, he used to say, when they moved in, nine years ago. Sylvia didn't agree. In her fortieth year, Sylvia discovered social concern. She discovered community action, and protest, and steering committees. If Alistair's blossoming delinquencies didn't spoil her chances, she'd probably end up a JP. This was a big change; but it was not unaccountable. The children no longer needed her, and the marriage was not worthy of sustained attention. It just ran on, taking care of itself. After twenty years you can't expect passion. It's enough if you're barely civil.

Colin stood over the cooker and looked down at his egg, bobbing dizzily in a froth of leaking white. As if alive, it flew about and tapped itself against the side of the pan. He picked up a teaspoon and dabbed at it, scalding his fingers in the steam. He could feel Sylvia watching him. By her standards, he had no common sense: he had never laid claim to it. But he was a clever man, and capable in his own line. His face wore a habitual expression of strained tolerance, of goodwill and anxiety, uneasily mixed.

"We're still marking exams," he said. He dipped for his egg with a tea strainer, which he had found by chance in a drawer. "I've got three hundred reports to sign. And the union blokes are coming in to see me this morning. You'd think they'd let it rest till after the holidays. But no."

"Strike?"

"Well, they're talking about it."

"I've every sympathy."

"So have I, I want a pay rise too, but it makes it bloody difficult to run a school." He sighed, and went about with his egg.

"What are you doing?" Sylvia asked. "Why don't you put it in an egg cup and sit down with it? Or are you going to race off with it down Lauderdale Road?"

Colin sat down with his ovoid ruin and picked up the newspaper. The day had brightened and the pleasant morning sun shone through his double glazing. "I always think of *Gulliver's Travels* when I eat an egg," he told his wife. "You see—" He broke off, gaped, put down his egg spoon, and seized up the newspaper. "Good God, Sylvia. York Minster's burned down. Look at this." He thrust the newspaper at her. The front page bore the headline NIGHT SKY LIT UP BY GOTHIC GLORY ABLAZE and a four-column picture of the Minster's south transept wreathed in smoke and flame.

"It never rains but it pours," Sylvia remarked, glancing at the kitchen ceiling. She tilted her yoghurt carton and scraped it out delicately with her teaspoon. "Funny, Lizzie was off to York yesterday on a day trip. I wonder if she saw it."

"It happened at half two in the morning."

"What a pity. She doesn't like to miss anything."

"Good God, it's not a tourist attraction," Colin said. "It's a national tragedy. Four million pounds' worth of damage." He groaned.

"Don't take it so personally."

" 'The fire took almost three hours to contain,' " Colin read out loud. " 'Although it was stopped from spreading to the central tower, or from seriously damaging the Minster's famous collection of stained-glass windows, it left the transept's ancient roof beams and plastered vaults a smouldering mass on the floor below.' "

"Your egg's going cold," Sylvia said. "I'd have thought you'd eat it, after you went to such trouble to get it."

"I've lost my appetite. You don't seem to appreciate what a loss this is to our heritage."

"It's no loss to your arteries, anyway." Sylvia tossed her yoghurt carton into the wastebin. She opened one of the kitchen cupboards and began to take down the packets of the stuff the children ate. Amid Colin's disinterested grief he felt a sharp prickle of personal resentment: she still does things for them, but nothing at all for me. "How did it start?" she enquired.

"Lightning, they think. They quote a priest here who says it was divine intervention."

"Why should it be that?"

"Because of the Bishop of Durham. He was consecrated at the Minster last Friday. You know, all about his controversial views on the Resurrection. I thought that now you're so friendly with our vicar you'd be well up in all this."

"Francis doesn't talk about the Church much, he talks about community projects." Sylvia rummaged in the cutlery drawer. "If God didn't like the Bishop of Durham, why didn't He strike him personally? And do it promptly, on Saturday morning?"

"Well, I tend to agree with you," Colin said. "It can't be that, can it?" He turned to the back page for more news of the disaster. " 'The Lord was on our side as we battled the flames,' " he read. "By the way, how's the vicar's son? Has he come out of Youth Custody yet?"

"He's not in Youth Custody. He's having Intermediate Treatment. He's doing community service." Sylvia reached out for a piece of toast and picked up her knife. "Do you know what Francis says?"

"Watch it, that's butter you're eating," Colin said.

"Oh, so it is!" Looking thoughtful, she put the bread down on her plate. "He says that this business of Austin doing take-and-drive-away, it's a deep compulsion he has, a compulsion to find out his real identity by sampling and testing out various machines."

"You mean it's the vicar's fault for naming him after a car?"

"At some level, you see, Francis thinks he does believe that. By dumping the cars, he's trying to jettison the mechanistic fantasies that have taken him over, and affirm his survival as a human being. It's a form of acting out. Francis's real worry is that because he usually leaves the cars in such a wrecked-up condition, it may indicate suicidal tendencies."

"Lordy, lordy," Colin said. "I didn't know you could kill yourself by sniffing glue."

"It can damage your brain."

"How would they know?"

"Francis is very worried. He can't talk to Hermione. She thinks it's because they didn't send him to boarding school."

"I don't doubt he'll be boarded out soon enough, and at the taxpayers' expense. How he got off this time beats me."

"He didn't get off." Sylvia looked offended. "Community service is a very valid option."

"I'd rather he were in custody. Keep him away from our kids. How does a vicar's son turn out such a thug?"

There was no time to go into this, because the children rushed in: Karen and Claire in their school uniforms, and the boy in a kind of romper suit of sagging jersey fabric, with holes cut out of it here and there, exposing bits of flesh. The girls flung themselves into their chairs.

"Brownies tonight," Claire said: a chubby child, putting out her paws for everything edible within reach. "And I haven't got my new uniform yet, Mum."

"Okay, I'll see about it." She knew that the Brownies were a conformist outfit, pseudo-masculine if not paramilitary, but she suspected that they were more harmless than some of the things her children got up to.

"You ought to see her," Karen said. "She shouldn't grow so much, it's uncouth. Her skirt's up round her bum. It's child pornography."

"That will do," Colin said.

Claire stuffed a piece of toast into her mouth. "It's Brownie Tea-Making Fortnight soon. I have to make at least fifty cups of tea for family and friends. And every cup I make, they give it marks."

"If you make me any mouldy tea," Alistair said, "I'll pour it down the sink."

"I have these mark sheets," she went on. "You have to say what my tea is, Excellent, Very Good, or Good."

"What if it's witches' piss?" Alistair enquired.

"I wish you'd leave the table, Alistair, if you're going to talk like that."

"I'm not at the table, am I? I'm just stood here, watching you lot eating like pigs."

"Oh, let him starve," Karen said. "He's stunted, that's what he is. He's probably got rickets or sumfin."

"He certainly has not got rickets," Sylvia said.

"Well, he's so titchy. That's why he's such a rotten little bully. We done it in psychology."

"Perhaps he's a pygmy," Claire said. "He can't help it."

Alistair tore off a piece of kitchen roll, and blew his nose into it with great violence. He wadded it up in his palms and tossed it at Karen. It fell short, and lay on the cork tiles.

"Just watch it," Sylvia said. "Lizzie's not spending her time and my money cleaning up after you lot."

"I don't want her cleaning up after me," Alistair said. "You make sure you don't let her in my room."

"She can't get in, can she? You've always got the door locked."

"What do you do in there?" Colin asked.

"Black magic," Karen said. "Him and Austin. Austin nicks vestments and stuff from his dad, and they have Black Masses."

"I'd do a spell to give you spots," Alistair said. "Only you haven't got room for any more."

"So is that what you're going to do today? Lock yourself in and have a Black Mass?"

"Yeah," Alistair said. "And miss all the lovely sunshine." He slouched out of the room. Sylvia's eyes followed him.

"I do worry," she said.

Colin flapped over a page of the newspaper. "It's better than him joining the Young Conservatives," he said.

"You never take things seriously."

"Oh, I do." He glanced up from the news of the inferno. "I know a lot of kids. So I don't get alarmed."

"Yes, but Alistair's your own."

"Now that does alarm me. At times." But he knew a hundred children as bad as Alistair, a hundred worse; antisocial truants from broken homes. Theirs was not broken; only creaking a bit under the strain. The kids passed through his office every day, en route from brief rebellion to a lifetime's acceptance of their lot. They had silly hairstyles; beneath them, dull conformist little brains.

"I wish you'd keep them in school till the end of term," Sylvia said. "I wish he weren't leaving."

"What would he do if he stayed on? Take Oxbridge by storm with his two CSEs?"

"Off again," said Sylvia, stirring her muesli. She was training herself to eat slowly, putting down her spoon between mouthfuls, and the action gave her words a quite spurious consequence. "Off again with your little schoolmaster's sarcasms."

"Does it make you cross?"

"It makes me bored."

"We've nothing else for protection, now the LEA have abolished flogging."

"I don't think you really value education, Colin. You had too much of it."

"I had enough," he conceded.

"Alistair used to be so bright."

"That's what all the parents say."

Sylvia stood up and began carrying dishes to the sink. Her orange peel lay abandoned on the tabletop, a long strip dropped neatly from practised dieter's fingers. Colin looked at it with interest. You can do divination with orange peel, he thought. The future was there, in homely things, for anyone who wanted to know it; door keys, tea leaves. There are letters in orange peel, which tell you who will be important in your life. He could make out quite clearly a capital "I."

At once, a certain thought came into his mind. He examined it, and found it unwelcome. He would not entertain it; he kicked it out. His pulse rate rose a fraction; he dropped his eyes, put down his coffee cup. The thought rolled back, in a leisurely way, and closed around his attention like a loop of string. For a few months in his long marriage, he had been unfaithful to Sylvia. His affair with Isabel Field had been finished for years—it was years since he'd seen her—but the body has its own set of memories, and the mind hangs on to nagging superstitions. An initial leaps out from the table; horoscopes are read. A retreating stranger stops the heart on a station platform.

That part of life was over, of course. Isabel had been young and intense, full of devouring schemes. She'd been a social worker, full of tutored emotions; always nagging away about the inner meaning of things. He remembered, when he thought about her now, her gloom, her scruples, the problems she'd had with her clients; and the shock of contact, skin against skin, mouth against mouth, her quickening breath in the darkness of a parked car.

He'd had nothing to offer her; only what she could have got from any man, and in greater comfort too. Sylvia hadn't known about it. She hadn't noticed, he thought, the struggle that was going on inside him.

Just as well. Her ignorant body had done the battling for her. Christmas Day, 1974, she'd told him she was pregnant again. He'd given up Isabel so that Claire could be born, and grow up plump and cheeky, and get Brownie badges.

That had been a bad year; the guilt, the deception, the hopeless months that follow the end of an affair. Lately, and unwillingly, he'd begun to think about Isabel again. Change was in the air, an undercurrent of disturbance. He couldn't account for it.

"You're miles away," Sylvia said, clattering at the sink. She crossed to the table and scooped the orange peel into her palm, and dropped it in the bin. "You'll be late if you sit about any longer."

Colin looked at his watch. "Good God, twenty past eight." He threw the paper down. "Have a look at it, about the Minster. It's awful." He snatched up his jacket, made for the door. "Come on, you kids. Take care, see you about six."

What I should do, Isabel thought; what I should do is, I should start writing it down. I'd like to write down everything that worries me, about my life ten years ago. I'd like to write it. But I can't find a pen.

Isabel's brain moves slowly these days. She's only thirty-four. She shouldn't find thinking such an effort, and she shouldn't look such a wreck. Perhaps a sense of foreboding dogs her. That must be it.

If she had any paper, she wouldn't have a pen. When she was a social worker, she always had pens. She was organised; to a degree.

She was not organised now; she had just moved house, not unpacked yet. Here I am again, she said to herself, where I grew up and began my professional career; and had my first love affair. If that is what you call it.

It's not fair, she thought. I never wanted to come back here. I might meet Colin in the supermarket. I might meet his sister, Florence. Then again, I might meet Sylvia. I've never seen Sylvia, but I feel I'd know her at once. Instinct, if you like. Women who have shared a man can probably scent each other out.

What about this shopping list? She turned it over. She could write on the back, why not? Just to get started was the main thing, to get some relief from the thoughts going round and round in her head. A good search through her handbag turned up a biro. She sat down at the kitchen table. She took a deep breath. Yes, I might meet the Sidneys *en famille*, she thought. Then again, I might meet my old client, Muriel Axon. That would be worse.

"Ten years ago, I lived in this town, I was with Social Services, I was seeing Colin. I lived at home with my father; that was all of my life. But I had this case, and this is the case I want to write about. Muriel Axon, No. III/73/0059. Everything about this case bothered me. It still does.

"Muriel Axon and her old mother Evelyn lived at number 2, Buckingham Avenue, in that part of town where people have big gardens and keep to themselves. Next door to them, but round the corner on Lauderdale Road, lived Colin's sister Florence Sidney. We didn't make that connection until the end. Why should we? When I met Colin—sneaking off to some pub somewhere, hoping we wouldn't meet anyone we knew—we didn't talk about his sister, and where she lived, or my clients and where they lived. But if I had known, I might have been able to ask Florence Sidney about her neighbours. Get some sort of—clarification.

"Then again, I don't know if I wanted clarification. I was afraid to find out what was really going on in the Axon household. Later, when it was all over, and Muriel's mother was dead and Muriel herself had been put in hospital, their house came on the market and Colin bought it. He wanted a big house, and to live next door to his sister. He got it cheap.

"I did warn him against it. I saw him at the inquest, and I told him I wouldn't care to live there. I tried to convey to him that horrible things had happened in that house. He wouldn't take a hint. I couldn't do more than hint. I really didn't know. I couldn't expose my imaginings. I would have sounded superstitious, unbalanced, and he already thought I was that. By that time, everything was over between us.

"After all, it's just a house. Just an empty shell, when the people are taken away.

"I expect I'll find out how Colin's getting on. This is a small town. They're all around, I'm sure; old colleagues, old clients, old lovers. Of course there was always a risk, with Jim moving about for the sake of his career. If you're in banking and you want to get to be a manager quite young you have to be prepared to move about. I'd rather have stayed in Manchester.

"But I couldn't produce any good reasons why we shouldn't come back. Not reasons that convinced Jim. He doesn't take much notice of my opinions. That's understandable. I'm always crying, you see, bursting into tears, and falling over, and losing things. I was in banking too when we got married—I thought it would be restful and uncomplicated—but now I just sit about at home.

"I'm not fit for anything, Jim says. He wonders what's the matter with me. I spend my days thinking.

"So I thought I could write a book, you see, about the Axon case and all that, and when it was done I could send it to the Sunday papers, and then everyone would know how social workers operate and why things go so badly wrong. How you get cases you can't handle, and how clients conspire against you, and circumstances seem to conspire too. How it messes up your personal life. How you live with yourself afterwards; when disaster has occurred."

That will do for a preface, she thought. I can call it *Confessions of a Social Worker*, I suppose. She had long ago overflowed the shopping list and been forced to write on the piece of packing paper that had come around the teapot. The spout had got broken, but it didn't matter; there wasn't much call for tea. I'll buy a proper notebook later, she thought, on my way to the off-licence.

It was 12:30 P.M. when Sylvia came home from the CAB. In the hall she paused and called out, "Hello, Lizzie, all right are you?" A clattering from the kitchen told her that her daily woman was hard at work. What a comfort to have the basics taken care of, she thought. She told herself that she hated housework, though in fact for most of her married life it had been her pride, pleasure, and retreat.

Going up the stairs, dragging her feet in their striped trainers, she acknowledged that she felt tired. The wrangle at the breakfast table was always a strain, and now her head was buzzing with Social Security regulations and unanswered questions about the legal aid scheme. The house was quiet. She went into her bedroom, kicked off her shoes, and lay down on the bed. Her eyes closed; she dozed for five minutes, wrapped in the midday heat. Suddenly a shrill ringing brought her upright, shocked out of sleep. Damn that cooker timer, she thought, it's gone off by itself again. Why doesn't Lizzie stop it? Heart still racing, she padded over to the door. Opened it; the ringing stopped. She sighed. Better turn out those drawers, I suppose. Skip lunch. Don't need it, this weather.

She knew that if she began with the bottom drawer, she would find her photograph albums; and then she could sit on the bed and browse. It was something she'd not done in ages. She'd never had much time to herself. Lizzie's advent had been a blessing—even if she was a bit odd. You didn't engage a cleaner for her looks or fashion sense, or for her conversation; you just needed someone honest and with a bit of initiative. Lizzie always reminded her of how she'd come up in the world. She reminded her a little of someone she'd known before her marriage; one of the girls on the Pork Shoulder line.

She leaned back against the pillows. Wedding pictures, baby pictures; Suzanne grinning in her pram in the postage-stamp garden of their very first house. Suzanne had left home now, was studying geography at Manchester University. Then Alistair, scowling from under a woollen hat in the same pram. It was very like his present scowl, except that now he had more teeth. Here was Karen, two years old, digging in the garden of their house on the estate. Here she was again, a little older, mouth drooping, swinging on the rickety gate. Everything about that house had been rickety, leaky, or shoddy; it was a triumph of jerry-building. No wonder they'd been keen to move to Buckingham Avenue, despite its neglected and depressing condition.

The move had been a stroke of luck for them. With Claire on the way, they'd needed a bigger place; but how to afford it? Normally she'd never have considered the Lauderdale Road area—all those big detached houses, too gloomy and too expensive. Colin had grown up on Lauderdale Road, and his sister Florence, who had never got married, still occupied the family house; his father was dead, and Florence had put their mother in a home. Florence had called her up one day and said, "The Axon house is on the market, just round the corner, the one with the garden backing onto ours. You ought to enquire about it."

"What?" she'd said. "That place where those two peculiar women lived? It's falling down."

"It's going cheap," Florence had said. "Suit yourselves. But you could do it up."

Sylvia suspected Florence's motives, of course. She was possessive; she wanted her brother next door, on call for mending her fuses and unblocking her sink. But still . . . out of curiosity, Sylvia phoned the estate agent.

"It *is* in need of sympathetic renovation," the man confirmed, "but it's basically very sound. Of course, it's very well situated. Within easy reach of shops and schools—"

"I know where it is. Why is it so cheap?"

He'd dropped his voice, become confidential. "Can't say too much, bit of a sad case—old lady's died, and her daughter, she's not quite right, know what I mean? Gone into hospital."

"You mean they've put her away?"

"The old mother died suddenly, there was an inquest. It was in the paper, in the *Reporter*."

She didn't say, my husband was there when she died. That was irrelevant. But they'd wondered what had happened to the Axon girl. Not that they'd known the Axons, really; they were the kind of neighbours you didn't set eyes on from one year to the next. "What hospital has she gone to?"

"As to that, I couldn't say. You see what it was, madam, they were recluses. They didn't like other people in the house. So they didn't keep up with repairs. Well, two ladies, you don't expect it. But it's a lovely property."

"All right. When can we have the key?"

They'd been to see it together. Florence met them at the gate. "Well?" She was anxious that Colin's decision should not be coloured by the unpleasant episode that had taken place in the house a few weeks earlier. He'd called on Florence late one afternoon, fortunately as it turned out; plodding out through the twilit garden to inspect, at her request, a dubious bit of guttering, he'd noticed something very strange going on at the Axon house. At an upstairs window, a young woman was gesturing, calling for help; very odd, but Colin hadn't hesitated. Florence had watched amazed as he crashed through the shrubbery and pounded on the Axons' back door, ready to break it down. Once inside he'd raced up the stairs to let the girl out; Mrs. Axon had pursued him, only to meet with an accident. It came out later that she'd had a heart attack, as well as a fall. Colin had given artificial respiration; with no result. And the young woman? She was a social worker, making her calls; the old lady had tricked her into the spare bedroom and turned the key. God knows what else had been going on at number 2. Would Colin want it?

"Well," he'd said cautiously, "it's cheap. It needs work." But if the last occupants had left shadows, he thought he could dispel them. "We could cut some of these trees down," he said. "Let some light in."

"Yes," Sylvia had said. "Then Florence could see in our garden, couldn't she?" She was not enthusiastic about that. But the trees would have to go, and all the junk that the Axons had left behind them; and that little glasshouse that the agent had called a conservatory, with its cracked and grimy panes and its mound of cardboard and newspapers all festering and damp. What a clean-up job! But think of the possibilities . . .

So they had put down a holding deposit, and Colin had called the solicitor. Contracts were exchanged within weeks. Their married life had been full of upheavals; this was the only thing that had gone smoothly.

Sylvia turned back to her albums.

How the photographs improved, from shiny dog-eared scraps, faded brown with age, to the borderless silk prints of recent date. Here she stood before the front door of Buckingham Avenue, her arm through her husband's. Florence, she thought, must have taken the picture. Behind them, the house looked like the set of a Hammer Films production; that ugly stained glass in the front door, those great clumps of evergreens shading the paths. The woodwork was rotting, the downspouts were in a deplorable condition; and the two figures who stood before it were hardly in a better one. Colin must have been fourteen stone there, she thought. Look at his belly hanging over his belt. Look at the silly expression on his face.

Her own image offered little comfort. Her tight skirt—surely unfashionably short?—emphasised her large hips and stocky legs; she was still out of shape after her recent pregnancy. Here she was, holding the new baby, Claire, peeping at the camera with a simper above the infant's shawled bulk. Her hair had been bleached out to a strawlike mess. Had she not known that backcombing and lacquer would ruin it? Worse, had she not known that no one else had used them for years?

No doubt at the factory, she thought, we were behind the times. We didn't know any better. She accorded an indulgent smile to her teenaged self, making up for a Friday night out, scrubbing her fair skin until the aura of animal fat, sodium polyphosphates, and assembly-line sweat was completely wiped away and she moved in a mist of Yardley's cologne and heart-skipping expectation towards the weekly dance; off she went, a great big beautiful baby doll. Then, on the seven o'clock train, she had met Colin.

It was an awful photograph, why had she ever kept it? Quickly she detached it from the page and put it down on the bedside cabinet. There was a blank space now in the album, a testament to her vanity. There she was again, arms folded outside number 2. The garden had been dug over, and the house behind her had all its woodwork painted a gleaming white. It had been a gruelling year-long slog, up and down ladders with buckets of paste, back-breaking work; but it was a big house, and there was land at the side to accommodate the extension they had eventually built, giving them a fourth bedroom and a much bigger kitchen. That was the whole point about Buckingham Avenue, it offered such scope for improvement. How much easier it would have been if their removal had not coincided with the crisis in Colin's life. There had been a girlfriend, of course; he supposed she didn't know. His behaviour was odd and abstracted, even by his own standards. He had drunk too much, whenever he could get his hands on some alcohol; they could not afford, in those days, to keep a stock in the house. Their petrol bills had soared; where did he go? Finally, of course, he'd been breathalysed and banned from driving. His little affair had come to nothing. That was obvious, wasn't it? He was still here, she was still here; here they were.

Sylvia looked at her watch. Ten past one. She let the albums slip onto the bed, yawned, stretched, and peeled off her track-suit, dropping it into the laundry basket. She went into the bath-room, washed, and cleaned her teeth vigorously. Back in the bedroom, she averted her face to avoid the sight of herself half-naked in the dressing table mirror. Her thighs were going, her tummy had gone; after four pregnancies, what could you expect? If she had known then what she knew now . . . She pulled on her baggy cotton trousers, and took out of the drawer a tee shirt which said in big black letters NURSERY SCHOOLS ARE OUR RIGHT. Running a hand through her hair, she mooched off downstairs.

Lizzie Blank, the daily (a German name, Sylvia supposed), was standing at the sink wringing dirty water from a cloth. "All right, Lizzie?" Sylvia said.

"All right, Mrs. S.?"

Sylvia crossed to the fridge. She opened it, picked out a lettuce leaf, and stood nibbling it while she surveyed her domestic. She supposed that a survey of Lizzie Blank would be a comfort to any normal woman who was afraid of losing her looks. Weird was the only word for her.

Lizzie Blank was a woman of no age that could easily be determined. Her dumpling body, entirely without a waistline, was supported on peg-shaped legs. Her hair, platinum blond and matted, had a height and stiffness that Sylvia's in its heyday had never approached; two little squiggles, shaped like meat hooks, stood stiffly out by each ear. Her large face—rather blank in truth—was so caked with make-up that it was impossible to decide what it might look like naked, and her eyelids, outlined in thick black pencil, were painted a vivid teal blue. How many pairs of false eyelashes she wore, Sylvia could not take it upon herself to say. Her magenta lips bore no relation to her real mouth, but were overpainted greasily onto the skin, so that the merest twitch of her cheek muscles brought about a smile or a pout. The lips worked unceasingly; the eyes remained quite dead.

"How was your trip?" Sylvia asked.

"Okay. One of us thought there would be donkeys. We had them before, when we went on a day trip."

"I think you only get them at the seaside."

"I don't see why. Not as if they swim."

Sylvia was taken aback. "Tell me, Lizzie," she said, "do you wear a wig?"

Lizzie only smiled. Sylvia realised that her question was perhaps an intrusion. After all, she thought, if it is a wig, it's bound to slip about on her head from time to time. I could find out by observation alone.

Sylvia swung open the fridge door again, took out half a

cucumber, and cut an inch off it. She raised it to her lips. "By the way, you didn't try to clean Alistair's room, did you? I meant to tell you. I expect he's got the door locked."

"The spare room?" Lizzie looked at her; it might have been astonishment, but her face was so far from the human norm that it was always difficult to be sure what her expressions meant.

"Well, it's not really the spare room. Alistair's always had it, since we came."

"I call it the spare room."

"I daresay it was, before we moved here. Anyway, what I'm saying is—don't bother with it. His father will make him clean it up, when the school holidays start."

"Some rooms have no talent for cleaning. Some rooms will never be clean." Her tone was perhaps unnecessarily doom-laden, but Sylvia supposed she was devoted to her art. It was a good sign really.

"I was wondering, would you take on another lady?"

Lizzie was washing down the sink with bleach. She shook her head, without pausing in her work.

"Only, our vicar's wife is looking for somebody to do a few hours for her."

"Did you say you could recommend me?" Lizzie turned her full flat face towards her employer; her rouged cheeks glowed, ripely pink, in a waste of chalk-white powder.

"I mentioned your name. I didn't commit you."

"Not interested, Mrs. S."

"I did tell her, I didn't know how many other people you did for." Biting her cucumber: "You're a bit of an enigma, Lizzie."

"I can't take anything else on." Lizzie screwed the cap back on the bleach bottle. "I work at night."

She bent down to put the bleach away under the sink, presenting to Sylvia her large rear end. "Yes, well, I thought I'd ask. I'd better get off to my committee meeting. Can I give you a lift?"

Lizzie took off her large plastic apron and hung it behind the kitchen door. "Thank you kindly, Mrs. S. You're a good woman. An angel, I might add."

With a baffled smile, Sylvia went off to get her purse. Weird was the word. As it happened, though, Lizzie Blank was the only person who had answered her ad in the *Reporter*. The purplish, pinpoint, foreign-looking hand had prepared her for—well, a foreigner; a person of strange diction and eccentric ways of cleaning lavatories. Lizzie did not seem exactly foreign; but perhaps her parents were, perhaps she came from a funny background. She seemed a good-hearted soul, Sylvia thought, and willing enough; even if she was rather lavish with the cleaning materials.

She went back into the kitchen. Lizzie Blank was now in her outdoor garb; a dirndl skirt of red and blue, and a leopard-skin jacket. "I'm surprised you don't feel the heat," Sylvia said, counting out her money. "There you are, love." Lizzie's false nails flashed, and the notes vanished into one of her pockets.

"It's my pride and joy, this jacket," she said. "As my mother used to say, Pride must Abide."

Lizzie took out a chiffon scarf, pink shot through with gold, and went out into the hall. In front of the mirror, she adjusted it carefully over her coiffure. "Ready?" Sylvia said, swinging her car keys. "You'll have to give me directions."

Damn, she thought, I've been stuffing myself again; and I meant not to have any lunch.

They drove downhill towards the town centre. Right here, left here, said the charwoman, leading them into the maze of streets that still stood on the southern side of the motorway link. "All this will be coming down soon," Sylvia said. "You'll all be dumped over Hadleigh way in a high-rise. How do you feel about that?"

"All right."

"But it'll break up your community."

"Not my community. I wasn't born here."

"Oh, I see. But still, you won't like life in a towerblock."

"I shan't mind. You can throw things off the balconies."

Sylvia gave her a sideways look, then switched her attention back to the road. She slowed down. Small brown children played by the kerb, barelegged in the July heat, crouching in the gutter and darting out into the road. There was not a blade of grass for miles. Midsummer brought out the worst in it, baking the cracks in the pavements, raising a stench from the dustbins. The long ginnels that ran between the houses discharged a dim effulgence of stale sweat and stale spices; a thin ginger cat slept on a coal-shed roof, its scarred limbs splayed, its eyes screwed tight against the glare. Not a tree, not a patch of shade. "Displacing people from their environment," Sylvia said. "You'd think the lesson would be learned by now."

"Here it is. Eugene Terrace."

"Whereabouts?"

"This will do." Lizzie opened the car door and began to lever her bloated body out of the seat, swivelling sideways and kicking her feet over the kerb. Her ankle chain flashed in the sunlight. Out at last, she leaned down and stuck her face in at the passenger door. "Thanks a million, Mrs. S." Inside the leopard-skin jacket she was perspiring heavily, and patches of grease were breaking through her face powder; she gave a terrifying impression of imminent dissolution, as if fire had broken out at Madame Tussaud's.

Sylvia drew back from her grinning mouth and heavy scent. "Is this where you live, at this shop?"

"Over the top. It's temporary. I'm stopping with a friend, he's got lodgings here."

"See you Thursday then." She watched Lizzie, waddling towards the side door of the fly-blown corner grocery. I wonder what she means about working at night? Can she possibly be a prostitute? Surely not; she was too grotesque for anyone's taste. Lizzie stopped, ferreting in her bag for her door key. There was something unreal about her, as if she were a puppet, or an illustration loosed from the pages of a book. Suddenly, and with awful clarity, Sylvia understood her mingled repulsion and fascination, the prickling of kinship which had made her take the creature on. It was herself she was seeing, Sylvia Sidney of ten years back, the masklike maquillage, the jelly-flesh wobbling like a sow's; the great big beautiful baby doll. She felt suddenly sick. She groped for the gear lever.

Lizzie Blank, known otherwise as Muriel Axon, turned her key in the lock; and entered the dismal passageway of Mukerjee's All-Asia Emporium.

CHAPTER 2

The Mukerjees' stock in trade blocked most of the narrow passage: tinned cream of tomato soup in cartons of three dozen, boxes of pre-cooked rice and deodorant sprays, toothpicks, lavender furniture polish, and fancy bun cases. Muriel walked sideways between the boxes, holding her shopping bag across her chest, and went upstairs in the dark. She found she had forgotten the password again, so she booted the door until the sentiment "Christ is risen" came feebly from within.

The room was full of shadows and swirling dust, the sun kept out by a yellowing paper blind. Muriel walked to the window and released it; it shot up and out of her hand with a soft flurry like the exit of a family of rats. She looked out over the roofs of the outdoor privies and the coal sheds.

"Stir your stumps," she advised the man on the bed.

It was Emmanuel Crisp, her friend, her mentor, her old mucker from the long-stay hospital; it was Emmanuel Crisp, who liked to pretend he was a vicar, and who got put away for it. He'd been a troublesome sort of lunatic, always needing big injections; whereas she, whose antecedents were much worse, had given no bother at all; always neat, clean, and biddable, at least after the first few years.

Crisp flapped a hand over his eyes to shield them from the sun. "Hello there, Muriel. I thought it was you, kicking."

"I'm not Muriel. I'm Lizzie Blank."

"But you are Muriel really, aren't you?"

"Sometimes. But today I'm Lizzie Blank, because I've got my wig on, haven't I, and my make-up?"

Crisp studied her. "It's wonderful how you get transmogrified."

"I've got my job to do," she said grimly.

Emmanuel lay back on the bed. He was an exhausted man, with his greenish pallor and his high-pitched giggle. It was the day trip to York that had tired him. It had been their best get-together with old friends since they'd all been turfed out of Fulmers Moor Hospital, and left to fend for themselves.

"Sholto enjoyed it," Muriel said. "He didn't have a fit. It was only the excitement that made him sick."

Crisp's jaws worked around a yawn. He slid his long frame into a sitting position. "Do you have my press cuttings?"

Muriel took the newspapers out of her bag and tossed them onto the table. "It's hot in here." She pulled off her wig and dropped it by the *Daily Telegraph*; then, on second thoughts, arranged it on its stand, on the blank-faced head of white polystyrene that she kept on top of Crisp's chest of drawers. She didn't live here; she had a room of her own. But everything was arranged for her convenience.

"Well?" she asked Crisp.

Emmanuel looked up, gratified. "AN ACT OF GOD," he read. Muriel said, "Do you want me to go for some fish and chips?"

"I couldn't eat. I'm too excited."

"Suit yourself. I've had my lunch with my employers. They're not too pleased about the practice I had in their kitchen."

"They'll get it on their insurance," Crisp said, absorbed. "Heretics have no insurance." He smiled as he read. Muriel yawned, and scratched her itching scalp.

"I'm going to change," she said. "Don't watch me, Crisp."

She took off her leopard-skin jacket and hung it in the wardrobe, kicked off her shoes with a groan, and delved about under the bed for the flat open sandals that Muriel wore. She hauled up her skirt and released her black stockings from their suspenders. From under his eyelids Crisp watched her, rubbing with her fingertips at the indentations the suspenders had left in her blue-white flesh. Her blouse went over her head and onto the floor, and with a grunt she undid the fastening of her painful padded brassiere. Her own body, free from Lizzie's underpinnings, seemed flat and meagre. "Give me a towel," she said to Crisp. He watched her as she scrubbed off Lizzie's mouth, erased her lurid eyelids. After five minutes Muriel was back; her almost colourless eyes, her bland inexpressive features, her short dark hair now beginning to grey.

"Are you getting a multiple personality?" Crisp asked her.

She gave him a look. "I know who I am," she said.

She put on Muriel's skirt, and a limp cheesecloth blouse, embroidered on the bodice with blue flowers. She had a faraway look, Crisp thought; she was planning what she would do on the street. "Don't go," he said. "We could pass the afternoon in a study of the Psalms."

"Stuff that," Muriel said. "Where's my collecting box?"

"Bodily resurrection is a fact."

"I never said different. Don't go picking quarrels."

"Do you know, it's not the first fire at York Minster. Jonathan Martin, 1829, described as a lunatic. Emmanuel Crisp, 1984, right hand of the Lord."

"I hear you, talking like a nutter. Trying to get yourself readmitted."

"What if I am? We all pretend to be something we're not. Especially you, Muriel." She was heading for the door. "Don't leave me on my own. I feel jittery."

"Well, what is it you want to do then?"

"Stay with me a bit. You can talk to me if you like."

"What about?"

"About your life. I could give you absolution, Muriel."

She hesitated, came back into the room. "What's that?"

"Forgiveness for your sins."

"What's forgiving? It doesn't change anything. Anyway, I don't do sins."

"Your crimes, then. It's a nice point."

"But I don't like remembering, Crisp. It upsets me, thinking about my mother and all that. I'd like to oblige you. But it gives me a pain behind my eyes."

"Do you good to have a pain. You're a malicious old bat."

"What about you? Burning down churches?"

"I do it for God."

"I do it for me. I do it for fun. I do what I like."

But already the unwelcome process had begun. Her recall had nothing dim about it. Ten years ago, she had been a woman with a mother and a child. She'd had a lifetime of Mother, but the baby she'd only had for a few days. She had disposed of both of them: 1975. Only hours after the disposal, her life had changed completely; chance had shackled her in the long chain of events that brought her to where she was now. And they say crime doesn't pay! She was better off now than she'd ever been; it was only one of the things people said to comfort themselves. Before that dark February afternoon, with the social worker screaming in an upstairs room, she'd been nothing but a girl at home; a girl at home with her mother at 2, Buckingham Avenue, for thirty-four years.

Mother was not an easy woman. She was a landlord, a gaoler. She did a manoeuvre she called "keeping ourselves to ourselves." It involved close planning, bad manners; cowering in the back room if anyone came knocking at the door. It was not age that did this to Mother; it had always been her policy. When Muriel went to school, Mother waited for her by the gate. She took her by the neck and by the arm and hauled her home.

This was Muriel's life: days, whole weeks together, when Mother didn't let her out of the house in the mornings. She locked her in the bedroom, or hid her shoes. At St. David's School on Arlington Road, she was nothing but an object of remark. None of the remarks were flattering. She rocked on her chair, played with her fingers. She would not write, could not, had never learned, forgotten how. At the sound of a bell the children rushed out of the room and fought each other in an asphalt circus behind bars. She stood and watched the others, rubbing her arm above the elbow where Mother's fingers left her permanently bruised. She licked some rust from the railings; there was iron on her tongue, salt, ice. She laid about her with her fists. Soon this part of life was over; Mother kept her at home.

The streets, Mother said, were dangerous for a growing girl. There were attacks, impregnations, thefts. She could make your flesh crawl with her tales. By and by a man came to the house, making enquiries. His name was Mr. Hutchinson, and he was called an attendance officer. Mother dodged him for a month; finally she let him in. "Are you Mrs. Evelyn Axon?" he asked. He saw Muriel, sitting on a stool in the kitchen. He called her my dear. Mother sneered. Oh dear, my dear, she said, isn't it a gorgeous little cretin, a muttonhead, an oaf, and is it precisely what you want, sir, for your select conservatoire? Mr. Hutchinson had a cardboard file which he stored under his arm. He took a step backwards, away from Mother, holding the file across the breast of his fawn overcoat. It brought him up against the door of the lean-to; confused, he turned and fumbled for the handle, and found himself treading in the mulch of old cardboard and newspaper that was always underfoot in winter, breathing in the dank lean-to air. Cobwebs trailed across his glasses. From her stool, Muriel laughed out loud.

After Mr. Hutchinson had been retrieved from the lean-to and set on his way out of the front door, Mother had taken her aside and said: stupidity is the better part of valour. Doltishness is the best defence. After that, there had been similar visitors; meeting similar fates, if they got in at all. The Welfare, Mother called them. There had been a time when, just to keep them happy, Mother had let her go in a bus once a week to the handicapped class. She sat with other people in a room, four of them round each table. She cut out shapes in felt and sewed them with great tough stitches onto other felt. She got thin strips of cane and bent them up into baskets; and while she did this she spoke to no one, keeping her lips closed and preserving her eyes behind the thick glasses that the Welfare had got for her. Presently the materials were taken away, and they were given tea and biscuits.

A few months passed, and the results of freedom were visible. Mother kept her at home again. For decades she had sat imprisoned in the house; now she sat in the house behind the bulk of her pregnant belly. How did you get in that condition? her friend Sholto had once asked her. She had thought back, leaning on the hospital fence, looking over it into the world. I gave them the slip, she said. Mother took me to the door, down the path I went, round the corner, where I saw the dog lying on the path, the fox-terrier dog that lay there every Thursday afternoon; and I gave it a kick. I walked on, and I stood, and when I saw that little bus coming, I just turned myself round and went the other way.

I gave them the slip, she said. I went for a go in the park, looking in the litter bins, going in the summer house, getting on those swings. I should have been at my class doing basket weaving and community singing but I went for this go in the park instead. And your beau, Sholto asked; he had a little fiddle? He was a professional man, Muriel said; he had a lovely tweed coat, and some credit cards.

So it came about, she said sonorously to Sholto.

Sholto could keep a secret. He rolled her a cigarette, she smoked it leaning on the fence, and then they went in for their dinner. They had just got the cafeteria system. They took a tray and stood in a line and got brown baked beans and white fish pie. A few people arranged it into patterns, but Muriel had no heart for it. Talking about the past upset her: the cold and discomfort, Mother's bullying, the lack of proper food, the musty unlit rooms inside the house, and the screen of dark trees outside. Buckingham Avenue was so silent you could hear the dust move, and Mother's dying thoughts rustle through her skull; Christmas 1974, mice in the kitchen cupboards, two seasonal envelopes coming through the door. Miss Florence Sidney, their neighbour, came with a plate full of warm mince pies. Muriel was shut up; their fragrance, wafting up the staircase, made her jaws ache. Mother put Miss Sidney in her place. She forced raw whisky on her, bawled out "Merry Christmas," and booted her out in short order. One of Miss Sidney's pies leaped from the plate as she scurried down the hall, and smashed and opened itself on the dusty parquet floor. Muriel came down; she put her finger into its steaming golden insides and tasted it. Evelyn shooed her off, pushed her into the back room. She told her to let it lie. Next day it was gone.

Mother had knocked over the paraffin heater. She had groaned in the wet weather when her knees and hips gave her pain. She had taken away Muriel's cards from the Welfare and burned them, and forbidden her to play in the garden for fear that the neighbours might see her and report on her state. Mother was afraid of the neighbours. She was afraid of ghosts, of changelings. She complained that as she walked down the hallway little claws pulled at her skirt, little devil's crabs with no bodies, sliding noiselessly away from under her feet.

At one time, her trade had been giving seances for the neighbours. Mrs. Sidney, the pie-maker's mother, had called in to speak to her late husband, and had got scared so badly at Mother's proficiency that she had turned funny, and shortly afterwards had been sent away. People had come from the other side of town; once a woman had come all the way from Crewe, bringing a parcel of sandwiches wrapped in greaseproof to sustain her during her trip on the train. Afternoons, Mother had spent in the front parlour; groaning, sweating, making the bleak monosyllabic conversations that the dead enjoy. Evening, money in her purse; she would snigger, and go and put the kettle on. One day, as she headed for the kitchen, a black wall of panic rose up in front of her and blocked her path. Muriel, lurking at the foot of the stairs, watched Mother's throat gaping for air, watched her raise a fist and first hammer, then claw at the wall; saw her lift her feet and tussle in the thick air, treading and weaving inside her big woollen cardigan like a dancing bear.

The episode passed. I had a black-out, Mother said. It's my age.

After that Mother had regretted her seances. The house was full of what she had conjured up; a three-bed two-reception property on a large corner plot, all jostled and crammed with the teeth-baring dead, stranded souls whistling in the cavity walls, half-animated corpses under the flagstones outside. One bedroom, which they called the spare room, had its special tenants. Without eyes and ears, they made themselves known by shuffling; by the soft sucking of their breath, in and out; but they had no lungs. They were malign intentions, Mother said, waiting to be joined to bodies; they were the notions of the dead, expecting flesh.

Mother was now seventy years old; tired, done for, blue stains under her eyes. She'd tried to make a living and now she was to be penalised. No one can help you, she said. No one ever will. They were on their own. They never went out, because they were afraid of what might happen in the house while they were away.

Muriel could see herself as she was then; her pudding face above her smock. Days went by when they never spoke.

She felt a movement inside her, very strange. Mother said, you're occupied. It would be another mute, an ugly, a ne'er-do-well. She felt it ready to burst out, and that she would die. She knew about death very well, believing that her little thoughts would empty out of her head, and roll round and round in the spare room, picking up the dust from the floor.

Mother got books from the public library, first aid. When the baby started to be born she got out her reading glasses. She fumbled around in the bedroom, cursing. She went round the house with a torch, shining into all the dark corners. Muriel had a pain, a private pain, and she felt that something was going to come of it.

Next day Mother was tired. She made no secret of it; she had entertained hopes that a better sort of infant would be forth-coming. It was an evil-smelling scrap, greedy, drinking up every-thing that it was offered; it gave evidence of an intemperate nature, of an agitating character. It had a strange face, unlike theirs. It cried incessantly, like an animal shut up in a shed. I'm afraid it's worse than I thought, Mother said.

On the third day she broke it to her: it's not human. It's a changeling, Muriel; you've been duped.

But Mother was never at a loss. She had a theory, and her theory was this: you take a firm line, stand no nonsense, and arrange to get a human child back. How?

You find some water, a river; but there was no river, not without taking the bus. Luckily there was the canal, and the canal would do. Float off the wastrel, the substitute; wait a bit, and the chances are you'll get another in return. It's the recommended method.

Hearing this theory, Muriel had laughed. The Welfare never told me that, she said, and you get to know things from the Welfare. Such as? Mother demanded. Such as supplementary benefit, rebate on your rent. Mother gave her a slap. It was tried and tested, she said. Desperate diseases require desperate remedies, is that a proverb with which you are unfamiliar? Muriel saw by the quivering of her mother's face that she was at the end of her tether. She was afraid of the changeling and would not have it in the house. I could telephone the authorities, she said, and have you both locked up.

Of course Mother knew more than she did; she had years of experience, with the living and the dead. "All right," Muriel said. She was persuaded.

And so the day came to try the substitution. It was a raw winter's day, with a smell of earth and water. They walked over the fields to the canal bank, meeting no one. They set the box carefully on the surface of the water, the cardboard box with the baby inside. "Sink or swim," Mother said. The baby had not made a sound; it had given up crying by then, and they had put a blanket over its face and folded over the flaps of the box. It was not cruelty, merely a precaution; Mother knew what she was doing and didn't want interference.

Below the water was a slimy substance which Muriel found interesting. She put her hand in, and brought it out dripping. Mother gave her a handkerchief to dry it on. They watched the cardboard box, growing soggy, bobbing in the water. There was no sign of the swap. The two babies were already confused in her mind; cold, stunted, condemned to the changeling life, their scant humanity draining away from them year by year. The box dipped in the water and was soon lost from view; the days were short, and there was not much light under the trees. Was it a boy or a girl? Sholto had asked her. I don't know, she replied; it was all so long ago. She had felt on the canal bank—or was it only later that she felt it?—a small gnawing inside that she called regret. It was all she had, and now it was drowning. It was true that her knowledge of matters was limited, but it was possible that everything, from her go in the park onwards, could have worked out differently. It was not regret for the infant she felt; after all, she hardly knew it. Perhaps it was for herself then; she wondered for a moment how she came to be alive, how it was that her old mother had not brought her here and floated her off one day in the hope of getting in exchange a human child. She brushed the thought away, rubbing her slimy hand down the sleeve of her winter coat. She was hungry. Mother said it had not worked. It was time to be getting home; darkness was closing in rapidly over the fields.

They returned home. It was only five o'clock, but it felt like the middle of the night. The lightbulb had gone in the hall. Her tummy was rumbling. When the knock came at the front door, Mother said, it's that gas man again, I suppose we'll have to let him in sooner or later. She gave Muriel a shove in the ribs, told her to stay in the back room. Make yourself scarce, she said.

But when Evelyn opened the front door it wasn't the gas man at all. It was Miss Isabel Field from the Welfare, the lady they had been keeping out for months.

Mother had dropped her guard, and she probably knew then that she was going to suffer for it. But first she tried to retrieve her error, smiling sweetly at the girl, leading her up the stairs. Muriel leaned against the door of the back room, breathing, listening. As soon as Mother had ushered Miss Field into the spare room, she turned the key on her. Muriel came out into the hall. She sat on the stairs, her knees drawn up to her chin, and listened to Miss Field suffering. How she screamed! How she hammered at the door! How she hammered on the window! She'd put her hand through the glass if she didn't take care.

When the banging started at the back of the house too, the devil got into Muriel; she said right, solve this one, Mother, but she didn't dare to say it out loud. The sound of the words and the sound of the hammering went round and round and reverberated in her head as she padded in her bedroom slippers towards the kitchen door.

And then came the invasion. A man burst in. He ran through the house, shouting. Mother came after, striving and yelling; white in the face, wrapped in her cardigan, as fast as she could caper. Up the stairs ran sweating man. After him went Mother. The next moment she lay in a heap on the floor at the bottom. Muriel, behind the front door, stood regarding her.

Assembled in the hall now were Miss Florence Sidney, who baked mince pies; Miss Sidney's brother Colin; and the welfare worker, Miss Isabel Field. Miss Field said she was leaving the profession. It was too much, she said, to be locked up in a bedroom by some type of madwoman when you were only trying to do a home visit. She was trembling, crying a little. Miss Sidney's brother got down on the floor and lay on top of Mother. He fastened his mouth voraciously over hers. Mother did not respond; it was ages since she'd had the attentions of a man. After a few minutes, Colin Sidney pushed himself upright, wiped his mouth, and looked down at Mother lying between his legs. He raised his fist and hit her chest a tremendous blow; two blows, then three. Muriel watched closely, sharing his disappointment that Mother seemed to feel nothing of all this. Presently he gave up on her. He lurched to his feet, talking, breathing heavily. She was hanging on to me, he said, as I tried to get upstairs; like a maniac, Miss Field, you were pounding on the bedroom door. I shrugged her off, shrugged is all I did; she slipped, she lost her footing. Now, Colin, said his sister, Florence, now, Colin, the ambulance is on its way, no one is blaming you. You did the right thing to rescue me, Miss Field said; locked in that room by myself I felt something pulling at my skirt. She shivered. Colin took off his jacket and put it round her shoulders. There you are, Miss Er, he said. Field, she told him. Victor of the Field, Muriel whispered. For a moment they stared at her; they were not sure if she had spoken or not.

When Miss Sidney was out doing her telephoning, the brother and the social worker turned to each other. They acted as if no one was there; not her in the bedroom slippers, not Mother in a heap. They were people who had met before; their eyes met, and then their hands. She would not be surprised if they had not met on a go in the park. She had a grievance against the social worker, with her trim waist and pale pretty face. She herself was still bloated from her pregnancy, but the girl did not know that. The baby was something they'd kept to themselves; a private trial, which they had faced in their own way.

Miss Sidney was back now. She turned to Muriel. Now, Muriel, she said, I don't want you to upset yourself, and what we could do with is a blanket to cover up your poor old mum. Let her shiver, Muriel thought, noticing that she did not. Already the grievances of a lifetime were rising up in her mind. Did other people live like this? She had no idea. The social worker said that the place was like a morgue. She bent over Mother, turning her head with her slim white hand. No one's blaming you, she said to Colin Sidney; she's had a heart attack. Mother's face was a strange mottled colour; its expression was one of astonishment.

In the last few moments of Mother's life, she, Muriel, had come up the stairs from the bottom. Whilst Mother was slipping, sliding, clutching with one hand at the banister and the other at her chest, she had knitted her fingers into the back of Mother's cardigan, she had taken her by the scruff and bounced her slam, slam, against the wall; and this was why, when Mother died, she looked so surprised.

There were now more people in the house than Muriel could ever remember; more, at any rate, than since Father's funeral. She had been only a child then; she had wondered why Clifford Axon couldn't be buried at the back, outside the lean-to, but her mother had said no, she wanted him off the premises. Thirty years had passed; life was going to alter. In the midst of her speculations, her stomach rumbled again quite audibly. Murder makes me famished, she thought. She took a final look at her mother, then went into the kitchen and cut herself a piece of bread. She rummaged in the cupboards and found a pot of some kind of red jam. The old cow, she thought, she was keeping this for herself. There was quite a lot left, three-quarters of the pot. She got a knife from the cutlery drawer and spread the jam carefully, very thick and right to the edges of the bread. When Colin Sidney came in she offered him a bite, but he did not seem interested. She could hear the social worker being sick again. Vehicles drew up outside, and uniformed men took Evelyn away.

Soon after these events, Muriel left home herself. She understood that she would be going away for some years, to recuperate from her time with her mother. A woman called Tidmarsh collected her. She put a plastic bag in the boot of the car, containing Muriel's personal effects; the two smocks that Mother had made for her out of a pair of old curtains, and a few other odds and ends she found in the drawers. Muriel looked back at the house where until now she had always lived. She felt a terrible sense of incompleteness, as if something that mattered to her had been abandoned in one of the rooms. She pawed at the woman's arm, trying to get her to turn back, but the woman shook herself free and yelled out that they would have an accident. How was Muriel to know? She had never been in a car before, only the minibus.

Mother had always threatened her that if she didn't do as she was told, she'd be rounded up with the other ne'er-do-wells, and taken off and gassed. It had happened once, Evelyn said; and the whole world profits by example. So was this it? She felt no emotion; she did not know what gassed would be like. She looked out at the factory walls as they passed, her head lolling against the glass, shaking with the vibrations of the car.

It was a mild spring day, but the women in the streets were still bundled into their heavy coats. They pushed children in trolleys, their heads bowed against the breeze. Sunlight dappled the glass of a bus shelter. The mill gates and little rows of shops gave way to an area of semi-detached houses with white painted fences and pretty flowering shrubs in the gardens. A red housing estate climbed up the side of a hill. Soon they were in the country. Miss Tidmarsh wound her window down, and the smell of fresh grass filled the car. They turned into a gateway, into a gravelled drive shaded by towering hedges. Clouds flew across the windscreen. The car nosed onwards, through the summer ahead; birds wheeled over the fields.

The house itself, a crumbling grey core, looked out over the fields and towards the road. Gravel paths ran away from it, with flower beds on either side. There were parked cars, an ambulance, a scatter of Nissen huts and sheds, and a colony of new buildings, made of metal and varnished wood and plate glass. Beyond these was a belt of dark trees, and more fields. There was a faint ground mist, and moisture in the air.

When the car stopped, Muriel scrambled out. "Hang on a minute," Miss Tidmarsh called. She took her by the elbow. It reminded her of Mother.

The paths were dotted with little signposts: Hunniford Ward, Greyshott Ward, Occupational Therapy. She did not have time to read them all, but she could read much better than they thought. She craned her neck, straining back over her shoulder. "Come on, my dear," the woman said. My dear; for the second time. Mother never said it, only "You useless lump." Useless lump or my dear, the meaning was the same.

Inside the big building the tiles were cold underfoot. Another woman came out, wearing a blue and white check garment. She had an elastic belt and a paper hat. "Oh hello, Miss Tidmarsh," she said. "And how are we today? Got another customer for us?"

She had a special way of looking at Muriel, as if she looked straight through her and around all the edges to assess her size and shape. She shifted from one foot to the other, a little self-consciously, and twanged at her elastic belt. "We're supposed to be going into mufti soon," she said. "What do you think of that?" The woman made some reply. Muriel looked around the entrance hall, up at the ceiling. The nurse asked, "How about a cup of tea?"

"That would be brilliant," Muriel said.

The nurse gave her a queer look. "Not you, dear. Patients' tea comes at ten-thirty, you've missed it."

"I'll have coffee," Muriel said. "Jam, ham, Spam, roast beef, cornflakes, and Ovaltine." Miss Tidmarsh laughed.

They followed the notices that said ADMISSIONS. The ward had thirty beds. This is your locker, this is your orange bedspread, this is your bedside mat, this is where you will live. "And then, dear, in a week or two, when Doctor has had a talk to us, we'll be moving on."

Muriel sat on her orange bedspread. "My head hurts," she said. The nurse took away her dress. She took away her knickers. She gave her a thin cotton gown.

"Don't you wear a bra?" she said. Muriel shook her head. The nurse smiled. "We don't want to droop, do we?"

"I don't know what we're talking about," Muriel said. "Our head hurts."

"We mustn't be cheeky. We'll learn that soon enough, dear. Haven't we got slippers?" Muriel shook her head again. "You'll have to get your visitors to bring you some."

"Will I get visitors?"

"You'll get your family, won't you, dear?"

Muriel thought this over. Baby: drip, drip. Mother. She closed her eyes tiredly. Mother always said she would haunt.

"Pay attention, dear," the nurse said sharply. Muriel slapped the palm of her hand against her head. "That won't help," the nurse said. "I can't give you any medication. Not till you've seen the doctor."

"When will that be?"

"That will be on the ward round. Tomorrow."

When Muriel was left alone, she sat on her bed and dangled her feet. She examined them, hanging there on the end of her legs, her fat red toes. She had done a lot of talking since Mother died. Before, days had gone by without speech; weeks, months. Except for rhymes. She'd not give up making those rhymes, she enjoyed them. They were all she remembered from St. David's School. Sing a song of headache, holler scream and cry, Four and twenty nurses, baked in a pie. She would not cry; she could not be bothered. She scratched her knee instead. A blind was drawn at the window, and the ward was in semi-darkness. She felt the walls close in on her; safe again. Back in the prison of her body, and back in the prison routine with its sights and smells and noises; rumbling tummy, creaking ankles, the steady beating of the heart.

The first person Muriel met was Sholto. He stood in the long corridor blocking her path, a sinister dirty little man with bow legs. "Are you mad, or stupid?" he enquired.

"Both," Muriel said promptly.

"Join the élite corps." Sholto sprang forward and pumped her hand.

Country life. The birds woke her up at four o'clock. She struggled out of her dreams and threw back the bedclothes. She put her feet on the cold floor; head down, she blundered to the window. It showed her a pale milky light and her own pale reflection; the features blurred, amorphous, underwater. She rubbed her right hand down her nightdress, thinking of the clinging green weed.

"Come on, dear, back to bed," said a voice behind her. "What are you doing up at this time? Didn't you have your pill?"

Muriel nodded. "I swallowed it."

Early morning waking, said the nurse to herself, a sign of clinical depression. "Back you go," she said.

"Those damn squeakies in the trees," Muriel muttered. She glared at the nurse.

"Six thirty you get up," the nurse said. "Not four. We've got to get ourself into a routine." She watched Muriel wiping her hand down her nightdress. Obsessive-compulsive behaviour, she said to herself. Tics.

In the country the medical care was under the supervision of Dr. Battachariya, a plump smiling little man; fat eyes, like disappointed raisins, were studded into his golden face. She screamed when he tried to examine her.

"You have had a baby, Muriel?" he said shrewdly. A rude, unmannerly man, prying about like that with his plastic gloves. "When was that?"

She mumbled something.

"Where is the little blighter?"

"With my mother," she said.

The first week passed. Now who was mad? Who was bad? Who was stupid?

If they had been florid, talkative, and lively with delusion, the long years of Largactil and dormitory wards had made them vacant and passive. If they had been blundering, inadequate, and lost, the passage of time had taught them cunning, the thousand expedients of institutional life. A breezy humorous disregard was their attitude to the doctors; the doctors sat with downcast eyes, their voices droning, their thought processes slowed.

Day room. People sit about on vinyl-covered armchairs. None of the furniture here has any resemblance to the furniture used outside. They are not things that people would have in their houses. Jaws move, champing on nothing. Cigarette smoke curls up. My mother died . . . I had this accident . . . I worried all night because I hadn't done my homework . . . I should never have got married. Hum, hum, hum. Questions are meaningless when you can't sit still in your chair. They are like bluebottles buzzing round your head: hum, hum, hum. I had no idea there was such filth in the world . . . At this point there was no food left in the house . . . I knew he had got a knife . . . I knew that if I allowed myself to go to sleep I should die during the night. Each night in the six o'clock news there is a special message for me. People stare at me whenever I set foot in the street. Someone had broken my glasses/ started a fire/informed on me, hum, hum, hum. Marilyn Monroe stole my giro. I went to the café till my money ran out.

Can you name ten cities? Can you tell me the name of the Prime Minister? Manic motion, impelled to tread, tread, tread along the corridors, hands flying about face and ears.

You must have some feelings about yourself? Stare. A slow shake of the head. Shoulders held rigid, gaze rigid, face and hair grey. A certain rigidity of posture, says the doctor. Seemingly negativistic. How long is it since we first saw you now? No reply.

An affective problem . . . semi-aggressive . . . schizophrenic excitement . . . marked thought disorder. What about a little injection? You aren't afraid of a little injection, are you?

These were Muriel's best friends: Sholto, and Emmanuel Crisp. There were a few hangers-on; Philip and Effie. At first she had been a lost soul, wandering around the day room washing her big red hands together. She had missed her mother, in strange ways; Evelyn with her chattering and her nagging and her little ruses to defeat persecutors and spies. It was a fair bet that Evelyn had taught her a thing or two, and unless in fact she were missing her it was impossible to account for the hollow feeling that she carried around inside. At the same time, she was growing a little garden of resentment and speculation, watering her weeds in the small hours when she lay staring into the darkness, wide-eyed despite her sleeping pill. The Welfare did things for people, she now learned, got them money so that they could live on the outside, got them gas fires and shoes. They had never got anything for her. Even when Evelyn let them in, she wheedled around them and said that everything possible was being done. Pretending to be sane was a great strain on Evelyn, and this strain was the origin of many of the stand-up fights they had after the Welfare had gone. Sometimes she said to herself, Mother should be here, not me, left in this homely home-from-home to pursue a career as a lunatic. She was told that in pursuance of the truth about her mother's life they had sliced open her body, peered into it, and pulled out her insides. She thought back on the process with satisfaction.

Now that she knew more about other people and their way of life, she often wondered if her crimes entitled her to some sort of record. She could read properly now; there was a book, in great request among her friends, which had records of everything under the sun, and most of these activities—county cricket, nonstop dancing—seemed less interesting than her own. Ought she to put pen to paper about it?

Sholto advised caution. Was the baby found? he asked. No; or she would be in a prison. Still in the canal then; sunk into the soft mud at the bottom, strangled by green weeds, trapped under the rusting wrecks of bedsprings and fridges. He offered to consult Emmanuel Crisp, who with his church connections was an expert on all matters charnel.

Emmanuel thought. A peat bog will preserve anything, he said. That is not in question. Mud; soft mud, still water. And, a canal: acid in the water, surely. There's not much to infant bones—"but what you have there, Muriel, is perhaps a skeleton."

Sholto asked more questions. Was she blamed for her Mother's demise? No. Foul play was not suspected, Crisp put in. Could she handle the scepticism her claims would provoke? They were pernickety, the publishers of this record book, they did not entertain idle claims, they might want her to repeat her feat under test conditions. You can get another child, said Sholto, winking lewdly so that she would grasp his meaning, but you cannot get another mother. Keep it to yourself, he advised. The fact is, Muriel, that you can't prove a thing.

"I could, though," she said. "If I found the bones."

Crisp was a tall man, pallid and spare. He had a precisian's lip, a cold eye; his hair was coiled about his dome like a woolly snake. Wherever did he get his wing collars, Sholto asked him.

"Charity," said Crisp briskly.

"Myself I have fits," Sholto explained. "Crisp's life has been different. He was the verger once at St. Peter's."

Crisp cleared his throat. "I left undone those things that ought to be done."

"What things?"

"My flies. Later, a gas tap."

"He is one of those people who do not know what came over them," Sholto said. "He lived to tell the tale, though he leaves me to tell it. They put it in the *Reporter*. SEX BEAST VERGER: VICAR SPEAKS."

"Have you ever heard of entrapment?" Emmanuel Crisp asked. "It was what they call an *agent provocateur*. She said she was from the Women's Institute. She wanted to go into the choir stalls, and see the organ."

"You know you took her wrong," Sholto said doggedly. "You did it on purpose."

"She touched my sleeve." He shuddered. "I often pray for her."

"The vicar never spoke up for him. He's left now."

"He's dead," Crisp said. "Or ought to be."

As a group, they got together in the day room. It was a new idea, to mix the boys and girls together. Autumn had come; but next year, Effie said, they would meet out of doors where there was more privacy. God willing, Philip added piously. Emmanuel led them in a verse or two of "The Church's One Foundation"; then they broke up for tea.

After this came a period of considerable longueurs. Winter closed in over the fields. She stood by the window of Greyshott Ward and watched the rain beating against it. It was a year before she was put into a charabanc and taken in a great herd of chattering fellow patients to the shops in town. The journey took thirty minutes, and the excitement mounted with every mile. They went into a sweet-shop, and into a hardware store where the patients looked at bread-bins and said which colour they would have if they had any bread of their own. She looked around and was very tempted, but she stole nothing at all. Afterwards, back on Greyshott, she was praised up for her good behaviour.

She had special clothes for the outing, given her out of a card-board box kept in the nurses' room: a blue frock with six buttons, and a mackintosh that was only a bit small. Back on Greyshott she was given her old smock again. A nurse stood over her waiting to take the outside clothes away. When she came to take her dress off, she could only account for five buttons. The nurse made the noise "tt–tt" and blew a little through her teeth. It was something only nurses should do; if patients did it they got shouted at. She scooped up the dress and the mackintosh and dropped them back into the box. "Come on, get dressed, you idle sod," she said. "I can't do it for you." Muriel saw the dress and the mackintosh dis-appearing, the box borne away.

She sat on the end of her bed, rebellious. "Tt–tt," she said, and wagged her head slowly, and cast her eyes to heaven. By watching other people, by stealing their expressions and practising them, she was adding to her repertoire. I was no one when I came here, she thought; but after a few years of this, there's no saying how many people I'll be.

Effie was often Her Majesty the Queen. They went along with her, lining up by the ward door. She wore a pink plastic shower cap that had been brought in from the outside by some long-forgotten visitor. She offered them each the tips of her fingers, and her very sweetest smile.

"And how long have you been at Fulmers Moor?"

"Ten years, Ma'am."

"Indeed? You must have seen many changes in your time?"

Between official engagements, Effie sat and looked at the wall a great deal. From time to time a ripple of emotion made her face quiver. She would put a hand up to stop it, and then she would leap up in a frenzied pursuit of the nearest nurse. "I want my Largactil," she would bleat, "I want my Modecate, I want my nice Fentazin syrup." Tranquillised, she would lean against the wall, her face serene again; only a blink of the eye, only a minute parkinsonian quiver of the extremities, to show that she was alive at all.

"I make no showing," Crisp said, petulant. "I'd better get a delusion. I hope to become a public man," he told Dr. Battachariya. "I hope to be appointed Ambassador to St. Petersburg. Or Governor of the Bank of England."

Dr. Battachariya sucked his pen. He questioned him closely. "What is the difference between a ladder and a staircase?" he asked him.

Crisp smiled. "A ladder is a series of portable gradations," he suggested, "of either metal or wood; sometimes rope. It consists of two uprights, with steps, called rungs, between them. It serves as a means of ascent, as does a staircase; but a staircase, designed on the same principle, is a fixed internal structure. Suppose for the sake of argument that you were a window cleaner—and some honester men than you or I, Battachariya, do in fact earn their living in that fashion—then taking stout cords, you could bind the ladder to your vehicle's roof, and thus transport it; which you could by no means do with a staircase."

Dr. Battachariya toyed with his ballpoint. He was determined to fault it. "Don't you think your explanation is rather over-elaborate?" he asked. Crisp smiled again; his dry, remote, ecclesiastical smile.

Muriel sought him out. "Crisp, give me a book," she said. "A book of sermons. Anything."

"What do you want a book for?"

"I want words. I've got to have more words. I was kept stupid on purpose. I want some like yours."

"Listen," Effie said sharply, "this is the bloody Savoy. Do you know what we had where I was last? No doors on the lavatories, pardon me. One toothmug per seventeen imbeciles. Crisp, you don't know you're born." Recovering herself, she added, "Balmoral is no better."

But next day Effie went on the rampage. She had a filthy tongue in her head when she wasn't giving regal addresses. She ran screaming and cursing down Greyshott Ward and out into the corridor.

"I don't need hospital," she shouted. "I don't need nurses. I'm not sick. I may be daft but I'm not sick. I don't need getting up at six-thirty every day, Christmas Day, birthday, Queen's official birthday and every bleeding Sunday. I need to get up when I want and make myself a little cup of tea."

Two stout male orderlies got Effie by the arms and brought her back to Greyshott. They argued with her as they dragged her along. "And how would we get your breakfast, if you got up any old time you felt like it?"

"I'm not here to have breakfasts. I could get my own."

"Go without is what you'd do. And if we didn't get you up, what's to say you'd ever get up at all? What's to stop you lying in bed all day?"

Sholto stood by, scratching his head and looking on.

"The patients for the shifts," he remarked, "or the shifts for the patients?"

Dumping Effie on her bed, reaching for the screens to pull

around her, the orderly stared at Sholto; his face crimson, his breathing heavy. "Get your frigging ugly face out of here, Sholto Marks," he bellowed.

Effie subsided. She began to cry, her chest heaving with the shock and horror of her outburst.

I've killed a psychiatrist . . . I pulled all the stuffing out of the doll . . . they put gunpowder through my letter box . . . they sang in the streets outside my house . . . a strange letter came, post-marked Scarborough.

Philip had the secret of perpetual motion. Chug, chug, chug. I am a tractor. I am a Centurion tank. I am a shiny red new Flymo. Otherwise sensible, Philip oils his moving parts each morning.

Crisp attributes it to the decline of faith. You may hear it, he says, as Philip garages himself for the night: the melancholy long withdrawing roar. In days gone by, Philip might have believed he was possessed by a devil, but the trend this century is to penetration by rays, bombs in the skull, and possession of men by machines.

I am the internal combustion engine, says Philip.

After a year or two Muriel became angry. She went to the end of the ward where the charge nurse sat in his little plastic cubicle. He was a fair-haired belligerent man, with a habit of sucking on his underlip. His biceps bulged pink and scrubbed beneath the short sleeves of his tunic. He was reading his racing paper.

When he saw Muriel he folded up his paper and put it down.

"Eh up, it's Jane Fonda," he said. Muriel did not know why he used this name, which he always did. He was looking amiable, but amiable was not his bent.

"I have a question," she said.

The charge nurse lit a cigarette. "Fire away."

"Can't I be treated like a normal person?"

I'm worried about everything. What things? The bomb. What do you think will happen to you? Stay in hospital; then I'll die. You got very drunk, didn't you? Why did you go to the pub, do you think? My sinful nature. When did you last eat, do you think? 1952.

I'm dead of misery. Dead inside. There are murderers in this place, murderers in the night. They used to wear uniforms so you knew them but now you don't know them any more. There are murderers in the night. Lizzie Borden. Ruth Ellis. Constance Kent.

Lizzie, thought Muriel. Later she couldn't recall the surname. Lizzie Blank.

How would you like a new life? they asked Muriel one day. How would you like a new life, with your needs met by the community instead of the institution?

When Muriel looked at herself in the mirror, she knew that she was changing. She was a woman of forty, a woman of almost forty-three. In repose, her face was empty and expressionless, but at a word of inner command she could set it to work, assuming expressions acceptable to the people around her. The grimaces, she called them. The nods and smiles, the frown of concentration, the puzzled stare; all these were within her scope nowadays.

If you knew the language and the logic, you could get into people's workings. You could press the right keys, get out the response you wanted. You have to appreciate their prejudices: good defeats evil and love conquers all. That two plus two equals four, that cause precedes effect. Remembering, all the time, that this is not really how the world works. Not at all.

The hospital was changing too. There were new nurses, milder in their ways; at least for the first month or so. The patients were left to their own devices, allowed to stroll about the grounds together while Crisp lectured them on eschatology. He looked forward to the day of a more immediate and worldly release.

There was so much to be done; the Church was in a parlous state, and the General Synod—than where you would not find a bigger collection of atheists—had quite lost its grip. There were dwindling congregations, rectories turned into guest houses and deans living in maisonettes; and a demand for women in the ministry. Can you imagine, he asked, can you imagine Effie, in a sacramental character?

Crisp's preoccupations were his own; but more and more, their thoughts were turning to the outside world. "I'm learning to make meals," Muriel said to Effie.

Effie laughed. "Get away. Meals come out of those big trays in the canteen."

"Oh, do they?" Muriel said passionately. "That shows your ignorance. When I was at home I used to get meals from my mother, eggs, vegetables, that sort of rubbish, peas out of a tin. Where do you think the nurses get meals when they go home?"

"They live here," Effie said. "Don't they? This is where we all live." She relapsed into silence, and took up the occupation of looking at the wall.

Emmanuel was the first to go. "Social Services will be responsive," the doctors said. Emmanuel made a little speech, thanking them for their support as a congregation over the years. They sang a few of his favourite hymns, and he shook hands all round. He would be returning, he said, by the road to town which had brought him here some ten years ago; as if Calvary had an exit route. He turned up his face. A stray shaft of autumn sunlight gilded the waxen tip of his nose.

"The heart's gone out of things," Sholto said. He kicked at a stone and dug his hands further into his pockets. "It will dull our wits, trying to pass for normal."

They were walking in the grounds, their numbers diminished. "Do you think you can pass?" Sholto asked her. He looked at her keenly. "You might, Muriel. I might pass, if I don't fall down and foam. Crisp will pass. But Effie—never."

"After all, Muriel," they said. "Look at all the stuff we've taught you. You know how to do your shopping. You can count your change. You can use the telephone." Muriel nodded. "We'll find you a place," they said. "A nice little flat with a warden. You'll be a free agent, you can come and go as you please." They patted her hand. "You'll have lots of support. The social worker will call and see you. And you know how to make your meals."

Muriel thought: When I get out I shall get out, just let those wardens try; Four and twenty social workers baked in a pie.

Sholto said: "When you get out of here your aim should be to get as far away as possible from all those people who are going to treat you as an abnormal person. You have to get away to where nobody knows your face. You don't want a pack of people around you who are going to say, oh, you know, you mustn't expect too much, she comes from *there*. You don't want people making loopy signs at every trifling embarrassment. You want to get right away. Get a fresh start. Get treated on your own merits.

"If you let the Welfare house you they'll tell all the neighbours that they're to keep an eye out. Is that any way to start life? Every-body makes mistakes, but as long as they're watching you all your mistakes will be put on file. You want equal treatment, don't you? You want to merge into the crowd. Not to be pointed out in the public library as that cove who has fits. Not people coming up *helping* you all the time. Stuff them, I say. If I want to lie in the gutter and foam at the mouth it should be my entitlement. What are gutters for?"

The odd letter came, here and there. Tales drifted back from the outside. "Crisp is walking the streets now," Sholto said bitterly.

"I thought you didn't want nothing from nobody, Sholto."

"No, he doesn't," Effie said timidly. "But he'd like a little residence."

"Philip got a council flat," someone said.

"How did he like it?"

"He hanged himself."

Sholto was a man of very good sense; wise and lucid, and ready for anything, except for the days when he sat on the floor, holding his head. "What they claim," he said, "is an ongoing beanfeast, flats, nurses, jobs, day centres. But if you want to avoid all that you'll have no trouble at all. There aren't enough to go around."

"They're going to close this place," Effie said. "What will happen to me? Where will I go? What will happen to my bedside mat? It's all I've got."

"You get money given you," Muriel said.

"Of course, I shall have the Civil List." Effie cheered up. "I'll see you right, everybody."

Hunniford Ward was closed. Effie got desperate, crying frenziedly and pulling at her hair. "Look, we'll all keep in touch," Sholto said. He wrung her hand. "Me and you, Muriel, the Reverend Crisp. We'll go on trips together. We'll have donkey rides and such. We'll hire a little bus and go to places of interest."

Effie blew her nose, consoled a little. The next day she came running up, her face alight; the greatest animation seen on her features since 1977, when she set fire to a cleaning lady. "Giuseppe is back," she said, "that was thrown off Hunniford. If you don't like it they take you back. Giuseppe didn't like it."

They went to see Giuseppe after he was dried out. "I went down London," he said. His podgy face was lemon-yellow; his fingers played tunes on the bedcovers. "I went in a hotel. There was women in that hotel," he crossed himself, "they was tarts. I never paid those women. A man come threatened me get out of that hotel. I went down the coach station. I went down the café. I went down the Sally Army."

"Five more minutes," the nurse said. "He's been poorly."

They smiled at her. The nurses liked it when you were poorly. They were kind to you. If you were sick in bed, they knew what you were up to and what they ought to be doing.

"I went up Camden Town," Giuseppe said. "I went down Bayswater. I went up Tottenham Court Road to see my grandmother, but she was dead. I went in the bed and breakfast. I went in the night shelter. I ask for an extra blanket but they say, no no, fat man." Giuseppe rubbed his side. "My chest hurts. I'm a tramp. I go to Clacton. It's winter. I get a lodging and I walk by the sea." He closed his eyes and screwed up his face. "Mother of God, it's so lonely in Clacton."

"Just remember your medication," they said to Sholto. "A community nurse will call and see you."

"Not if I see her first," Sholto said.

Sholto got out on a Thursday. He was all set for his sister Myra's house. He made his way along the street, carrying his navy-blue holdall, the yellow nylon straps wound around his wrist. When Myra saw him coming she locked the door.

Sholto walked on to the corner. When he turned off Adelaide Street, a terrible sight met his eyes. The whole district had been razed. Osborne Street was down, Spring Gardens had been flattened. The Primitive Methodist Chapel was boarded up and all the gravestones had been taken away. He tramped through the meadow of blight where the bones of Primitive Methodists had once rested; the ground was strewn with glass and broken pots. He squatted down, turning over the shards. The weather was damp; his holdall was smeared with yellow clay. From where he knelt he looked up and read a sign: MOTORWAY LINK BEGINS MAY 1983.

Where the Travellers' Call had been there was a field of rosebay willowherb and scrap metal. There were a few aimless piles of red brick, two feet high, and in places the earth was turned up, as if someone had begun to dig foundations here and then thought better of it. Only the Rifle Volunteer was still standing, at the corner of where Sicily Street used to be. It was eleven-thirty, and while he watched, the landlord put on the lights and came out to open the doors. He stooped ponderously to draw out the bolt, and stood gazing for a minute at the sky; then he looked across the wasteland, shading his eyes as if he were scanning the prairie. Sholto was the only human figure within his view. There was a rusting refrigerator lying on its back, a swastika spray-gunned on a wall; human faeces. Sholto felt the straps of his holdall cutting into his wrists. Picking his feet out of the mud, scraping his shoe on a handy brick, he began to make his way towards the Rifle Volunteer. I thought the war was over, Sholto said.

Miss Tidmarsh was nearly fifty now, and still going strong. Her shiny new car waited outside on the gravel. Muriel followed her; withered flanks inside a scarlet bib-and-brace. "Guess what!" Miss Tidmarsh said. "We think we've found you a job. Who's a lucky girl?"

She reached a hand across Muriel, pulled her seat belt, and snapped it fastened. They crunched off over the gravel. Even Miss Tidmarsh's style of driving seemed less mature than it had been. Muriel said, "Whatever happened to Miss Field?"

Miss Tidmarsh glanced at her sideways. "Fancy you remembering Miss Field! Was she your social worker?"

"Such a lovely person," Muriel said dotingly. It was an expression the nurses used, about lady doctors who did not snub them and relatives who did not pester.

"Did you think so? She left. Went to work in a bank, if I remember. I think she got married or something."

They shot out of the main gate and onto the road to town. Muriel didn't look back.

She started off as a cleaner, pulling a little trolley with her brush and her mop and her scouring powder and her special bucket. She had her name written on the trolley: MURIEL. She slopped her water about the corridors and under the tables in the canteen; she tipped her powder down the lavatories, and sang while she plied her mop. She learned to sing with a cigarette in her mouth, because cigarettes were what the factory made, and any worker was at liberty to pluck the finished article from the machines and puff away during the tea break and the half-hour for lunch.

At the end of the first week Maureen said to her: "Muriel, love, I don't know what to say. Look at your brush, it's all worn down to stumps. Have you been chewing it?" Maureen sighed heavily. "There's a wheel coming off MURIEL. You've got through as much powder as I use in three months. And look at your Eezi-wipes; they're all over the place."

Muriel stood looking down at her feet.

"No point putting your bottom lip out," Maureen said. "I don't know, where've you been all your life? I suppose some can clean and some can't, and that's all there is to it."

"Am I discharged then?"

"That's not up to me, duck. There's enough on the dole as it is. On your own at home, are you?"

"I am at the moment. But I'm expecting my mother."

"Ah, that's nice. Well, look, lovey, buck up now. Perhaps we can get you on Ripping."

That first weekend of freedom, Muriel paid a visit to her old home. It was quite a distance from the room that Miss Tidmarsh had found for her. She saw buses going about the streets, but she didn't know how to get one to go in the right direction. So she walked; she had nothing else to do.

Considering how many years had passed, the district hadn't changed much. She turned off Lauderdale Road, where she used to wait for the minibus. She paused for a few moments before the house where the fox terrier used to live, and took a good look. The stained glass and the net curtains had gone. The woodwork was painted white, and there was a panelled front door of polished wood, with a brass knocker in the shape of a lion's head; and a carriage lamp on the wall. It looked very smart. If the dog came out, I could kick it, she thought. She turned the corner. Buckingham Avenue had hardly altered at all. Each house stood set back from the road behind its neat privet hedge. Peering down between the houses, she saw the thick clumps of rhododendrons, the striped lawns, the trellised archways for climbing roses. At number 2, her home, there were big stone urns on either side of the door; flowering plants spilled out of them, and a hanging basket swung from the porch. The shrubs had been cleared from the side of the house, and they had put up a flat-roofed extension, bright red brick against the pebble-dash. The windows gleamed. She walked to the gate and traced the number with her finger. She would never have believed that her mother's house could look like this. She felt lonely.

She hung about for a while on the other side of the road, waiting to see if anyone would come out. Other people lived in the house, and she knew who; that monster of lust called Colin Sidney, who had seized his chance to buy it up cheap and move in next door to his scheming sister. What about the spare room, she wondered. Had there been an eviction, or were they still forced to keep the door locked?

Muriel waited for an hour. No one came in or out of number 2. Her feet hurt and she was thirsty. Presently she set off to walk back to her lodgings and sleep until it was time to go to the factory again. I can come again next week, she thought.

The Ripping Room had sixteen occupants, ranged at two long tables. Kieran came from the lift, pulling his trolley. "I'm a YOP," he told Muriel. "They get me cheap."

"What's a Yop?" Muriel asked.

"Don't you know? It's a Youth Opportunity." He added, "We get a lot of those."

"Kieran brings the boxes," Edna said. "Right? These are old cigarettes, right, off shop shelves what have gone out of date. On that trolley he's got two hundred thousand rotten old fags. You get your box, right? Take out the packets. Open the packets, right?" She looked around her. "Kieran, where's our boxes, where's our bloody stacking boxes, where's our Universal Containers?"

Kieran came sloping up. "I was putting me lipstick on," he said. "I'm entitled."

"Get on with it!" Edna said. "Empty the fags out, right? Fags to the left, foil to the right. Fags to the left, foil to the right. Got it?"

"Got it," Muriel said. Edna was an angry-looking woman, with varicose veins and black corkscrew curls. She wore an overall and white cap. "Away you go then," she said, and went off grumbling back to her own table.

"What happens to them all?" Muriel asked.

"Oh, they scrunch 'em all up and make 'em into new ones," Kieran said.

There were two tables, and Edna's got preferential treatment. When the Navy Issue came back in their tins, with the mould growing under the lids, it was never Edna's table that got them. They were Permanent Rippers. On the other table, the girls could be moved, as the work required, to the Making Room, to the Blender, or the Hogshead. Before the week was out, Muriel had learned to rip very nicely. She was never moved; nor was the elderly lady who worked opposite her.

This was a humble little woman, with a worn bony face, and eyes and nose and mouth so insignificant that to call them features was an inflation of the truth. A scant amount of iron-grey hair was pinned fiercely to her little skull. The skin of her neck was yellow, her shoulders were bowed, and her hands shook a little as she reached for her cigarette boxes. She hardly seemed to have the strength for ripping. Every morning, before Kieran brought his first trolleyload, she would take out her teeth and wrap them in tissue paper, and slide them into her handbag. She would snap the clasp and hold the bag to her for a moment, looking around her with an anxious little smile; then she would put on her overall, over her pinny, over her old polyester dress. She seldom spoke. Her eyes watered continuously. She walked with her knees bent, her head down; a soft silent creature of depressive aspect. From time to time—once a week perhaps—some word from one of the other girls would catch her fancy, some gossip or quip, and she would tip her head back, open her toothless mouth, and roar with silent laughter, wiping her eyes the while and trembling at her own temerity.

She'd had a hard life, Edna said. Her name was Sarah; but everybody called her Poor Mrs. Wilmot.

Muriel's second trip to Buckingham Avenue was more enlightening than the first. She had only been hanging around for five minutes when who should she see, coming up the road with her Saturday shopping, but Miss Florence Sidney?

Miss Sidney had put on weight, and her frizz of hair was now grey. She wore stout shoes, a check skirt, and a woollen scarf with bobbles on it, and she advanced along the street looking neither left nor right. As she passed number 2, going around the corner to her own gate, the front door flew open and a gang of screaming teenage children swarmed down the path and fanned out across the road. Miss Sidney was almost knocked into the hedge. Steadying herself against the gatepost, her face flushed, she called out after the children, "Alistair! For heaven's sake!"

"Eff off, you old cow," the boy called Alistair shouted back; wailing and yodelling, the gang careered around the corner into Lauderdale Road.

Miss Sidney put down her basket to recover herself. She steadied her breathing, allowed her flush to subside, and picked a few bits of privet from her cardigan. Looking up, she saw Muriel watching her from the other side of the road. Muriel smiled; there was no one she would rather see pushed into a hedge. Miss Sidney's eyes passed over her, as if she thought it was rude to stare; it was plain that she had no idea who Muriel was. She gave a half-smile, picked up her shopping, and trotted round the corner.

She doesn't expect me, Muriel thought. But she ought to expect me.

Muriel fished in her coat pocket, and brought out a piece of newspaper. She unwrapped it as she crossed the road, took out Mrs. Wilmot's teeth, and tossed them over the hedge into the Sidneys' front garden.

Just as she was rounding the corner, the front door of number 2 opened again. Colin Sidney came out and loped down the path towards his car; a big fair man, balding, lean and fit. She watched him jump into his car and shoot away from the kerb. He did not even notice her. She raised a hand after him; like someone giving a signal to a hangman.

Mrs. Wilmot was being retired. She had been at the factory for thirty years; today was her last day.

"Course," she said, in her usual dead little whisper, "I'll not get my pension, I'm not sixty. Course, I'll get my benefit. Course, I'll have to put in for it. Course, I don't really know." She picked up a corner of her overall and wiped her left eye.

"It's a bloody shame," Edna said. "Ripping's all she's got. Here, love, we'll give you a send-off."

"Course, they gave me a Teasmaid," Poor Mrs. Wilmot said. She wiped her other eye and sniffed.

"Bugger the Teasmaid, we've got a lovely presentation to give you. We'll give it you down the pub, it's Friday night, isn't it?"

"Course, the pot was broken," Mrs. Wilmot whimpered. "Course, I didn't complain."

"I wish you'd told me," Edna said, "I'd have complained all right. I don't know, this place is going down the drain, you can't leave anything about, people's teeth being nicked out of their own handbags, they want bloody hanging. You could do with a new set, you should have asked for one, you should get compensation."

"No point really," Mrs. Wilmot said dejectedly. "I have to get my cards. I have to go to the office. I don't like."

"What do you mean, you don't like?"

"Going to the office. I don't like."

"I'll get your stuff for you," Muriel offered.

"Oh, would you?" A tiny hope shone out of Poor Mrs. Wilmot. "Muriel, ask them for my wages as well, lovey." The next moment her situation overwhelmed her again; she looked away and sniffed, and soon the tears were coursing down her cheeks.

"Off again," Edna said. "Come on, duck, pull yourself together."

"Course, you can understand it," Poor Mrs. Wilmot said. "Course they don't like me coughing on the tobacco. I appreciate that. Course I do."

They arrived at the Swan of Avon just after opening time. Edna organised the moving of tables, commandeered extra chairs, and herded them into the Snug. "Let's have a kitty, girls," she called. The girls fumbled in their bags and tossed five-pound notes into the centre of the table. "No, not you, love," Edna said to Poor Mrs. Wilmot. "This is your day, duck. Come on now, wipe your eyes. That's it, give us a smile. Have a go on the Space Invaders." She bustled her way to the bar, shouting through an open doorway to some male cronies from the Hogshead who were ordering up their first weekend pints in the public bar.

"Eh up, Edna!" the men shouted; and other badinage. "All girls together, is it, all girls together? Room for one more, is there, room for one more?"

A warm beery miasma drifted over towards the noisy party in the Snug. The weekend free-issue was opened, and soon the air turned blue with smoke. "Give over, you cheeky monkeys," Edna yelled across the landlord's head. The men roared back at her. Edna trilled with laughter, waved her arms. Her eyebrows shot up, her face reddened. Muriel watched her from the pub door. Her every gesture was florid, packed with life; her voice was as commanding as the factory hooter.

Muriel came up behind her. "I've been to the office for Mrs. Wilmot's forms."

"Good lass!" Edna cried. "Have you got them?"

"Yes, and I gave her the wages."

"Righto then, you can help me carry." She thrust a tin tray crammed with dazzling drinks into Muriel's hands. "Here you go."

"Oh ho, Passion Cocktail," yelled the men from the Public, crowing in their mirth, and swaying backwards and forwards on the bar rail.

"Don't buckle my rail, lads," the landlord beseeched. Sweat started out of his forehead at the strain of keeping up with Edna's drinks order. "Can you make a Harvey Wallbanger?" Edna asked him.

There were more than thirty women now packed into the Snug, perched on each other's knees, flicking peanuts at each other, rocking and shrieking with laughter, and addressing the odd shout of encouragement to Poor Mrs. Wilmot. The younger women had stripped off their overalls and bundled them into their shopping bags, and were heading back from the Ladies; "Hutch up, hutch up," they cried. "Where's Edna with them drinks, I don't know, taken the kitty and run off to Monte Carlo!"

"Course," said Mrs. Wilmot under her breath, "it was good of Muriel to fetch me doings from the office. Course I'm not sure what I ought to have, I ought to have forms; course, I'm not sure."

"Cheer up," said Leslie-Anne, digging her hard in the ribs. "What are you mumbling on about now?"

Caught unawares, Mrs. Wilmot lurched forward and began to cough violently. With cries of alarm the women nearest to her slapped her on the back. "Here's Edna with them drinks," Maureen called, and Edna began to pass the order over their heads: "Six Pernods and blackcurrants, a port and lemon for Poor Mrs. Wilmot, seven Tía Marías and Cokes; and a Piña Colada for Yvonne."

The noise level rose, the blue fug thickened and drifted, cocktail cherries rolled gaily across the tables. All around Poor Mrs. Wilmot, her colleagues were swaying from side to side on their chairs and stools, singing "Y Viva España." As the debris around her accumulated, her timid little hand shot out and began to sort the cigarette packets, piling the cellophane and foil to one side; as the merriment grew, she looked about her, a swift glance from side to side; seeing herself unobserved, she seized up a packet, emptied it with one practised movement, and swept the cigarettes to the left of the table, while the papers went to the right. They had reached the third round of drinks by then, and her eyes were watering more than ever; never the centre of attention in her life before, she shook inwardly, her head nodded, she looked about her and showed her gums in a frequent wavering smile.

"Poor Mrs. Wilmot's enjoying herself," Leslie-Anne said, and returned to her argument with Edna; a friend from Dispatch had left to pursue matrimony full-time, and Edna said anyone was a flaming idiot who gave up a good packing job with three million out of work.

"Let's hope she gets something out of him," Edna said. "She got nothing out of the last one."

"She did. She got shag-pile carpets. You had to take your shoes off when you went in her house."

"Bugger that for a game of coconuts," Edna said, unconvinced; it was an expression much in vogue among the rippers. "She took on that Norman when he was a cripple, and he used to sit in his wheelchair and hit her with his stick. She's too soft-hearted. This'n'll give her the run-around. He started giving his first wife's stuff away before her body was out of the house. He went round after the funeral and proposed to Trudie Thorpe's daughter."

"He didn't!"

"He did! Anyway, he gave her a sideboard."

Muriel listened. This is how their affairs are managed, she thought. Lust, assault; the exchange of furniture. These women had life at their fingertips. She watched Edna, expostulating, tossing the fourth Export Lager down her throat. Her eyes shone, her cheeks shone, and even her bared teeth. I could practise Edna, Muriel thought, I could crack her in one night. She felt in her bag for Mrs. Wilmot's papers, for the documents that tied her colleague to the working world. It was six-thirty now, and some of the men were beginning to drift homewards, carried out into the wet blue street by the jeers of their mates; a game of darts was in progress, and the women never thought of moving. Their faces were flushed and their eyes alight; Raquel's mascara ran in black trails down her cheeks, and Leslie-Anne lurched from her chair and staggered into the Ladies to throw up. Edna came back from the bar with a handful of packets of crisps; she stuck another cigarette in her mouth. "Bugger these free-issue," she said to Maureen. "Have one of these Balkan Sobranie. I've ordered us all pie and peas."

Presently the pianist arrived. Freddo lurched through from the Public, a gangling Welshman with a solemn face and a loud check jacket. He leaned on the piano and somebody passed him up a pint. "I left my heart," he sang, "in San Francisco." Poor Mrs. Wilmot tipped back her head and laughed her stifled laugh. Suddenly she dived into her handbag and pulled out her wage packet; tore it open, and scattered its contents onto the table.

"Let it all go," she wheezed, "what does it matter? Let's enjoy ourselves while we can, girls! Let's have one of them Bacardis, and get one for Muriel!"

It was half-past eight before the party broke up. Muriel took care of her bag; she took care of the expressions on her face, and of a few ideas that were beginning to run through her head. Mrs. Wilmot was half carried through the doors, supported under her elbows by Maureen and the green-faced Leslie-Anne. Outside on the pavement, with a cry of "oh, blimey," Leslie-Anne dropped her and sped to the gutter, where she bent over and retched. It had been a lovely evening. Poor Mrs. Wilmot staggered back against the wall. Over her pinny she wore the long string of cultured pearls which her workmates had given her to remember them by. Her eyes closed. Her life was over, she thought: she was entirely slipping from view. She hummed softly to herself: "Where little cable cars, Climb halfway to the stars . . ." Soundless, she laughed.

As soon as she saw Mr. Kowalski and his house, Muriel knew it was where she must live. It was a big house, rambling and damp and dark; a permanent chill hung over the rooms. It had been condemned long ago, put on a schedule for demolition, but it seemed likely that before its turn came it would demolish itself, quietly crumbling and rotting away, with its wet rot and dry rot and its collection of parasites and moulds. There were only two lodgers, herself and a young girl, attracted by the card in the newsagent's window, by the low rent and by the faint spidery foreign hand setting out the terms in violet ink.

Two days went by, after Mrs. Wilmot's party. During those two days she practised; then she called on Mr. K.

She stood on the doorstep, presenting an altogether lacklustre appearance. "I hear you've got a room to rent," she said. "I could do with a room."

Mr. Kowalski stood inside the hallway. A low wattage but unshaded bulb cast upon his caller a mottled and flickering pattern of shadows. "Step where I can see you," he ordered.

The visitor complied, turning up her sunken face. Her hands were blue with the raw autumn cold. Her mouse-coloured coat with its shawl collar reached almost to her ankles; her feet stuck out, monstrously huge in holey bedroom slippers.

"Here's me stuff," she said faintly. She indicated a bundle behind her, a battered old suitcase tied up with a plastic clothesline.

Mr. K. appraised her. His eyes were suspicious, sunk into a roll of fat. He stuck his thumbs into his belt, and glared at her in the swaying light; a meek and harmless creature, dowdy and friendless, and with a terrible cough. "Come in," he said, falling back. "Give me your baggage to port. Come in, you poor old woman, come in."

Kowalski, she learned, was only a version of his name. The real one had fewer vowels and more of the lesser-used consonants in proximity. He had learned English from the World Service, picked up on his illegal receiving set; latterly, from the instructions on packets of frozen food.

For some years Mr. K. had been a shift worker at the sausage-and-cooked-meats factory. His shift was permanent nights; he preferred it that way. He had a grey skin, for he never saw the day-light, and sad nocturnal pupils to his eyes. His moustache was ragged and bristly, and he wore trousers of some thick coarse fabric like railway workers used to wear, held up with a thick leather belt; he wore an undershirt without a collar, and over this in extremely cold weather a sagging pullover of an indeterminate grey-green-blue shade. His figure was gross, his steps were slow, he mumbled as he walked, and shifted his little eyes this way and that. He dreamed of dugouts and barbed wire, of the rat-tat-tat of the machine gun and of corpses that came to light with the April thaw; of partisans, of decimated villages, of pine forests where wolves and wild boar ran. He did not know whether the dreams were his, or those of novelists, or of the long-slaughtered school-teachers who had taught him to sing folk songs and turn somersaults on a polished floor.

At Fulmers Moor the patients had minded pigs. The pigs stared out across the furrowed ground at the traffic going by to the city. Mothers would point them out to their children: look, darling, pigs. At the back of the field stood the men, loose-mouthed, their boots encrusted with clay and muck, the feed buckets swinging from their great red hands. When the children pointed to them, excitedly, their mothers pulled them away from the car windows.

When Muriel saw Mr. K. he reminded her powerfully of these men. And perhaps he has tenants, she thought. She noticed how he tapped the walls, rattled the doorknobs as he perambulated about the four floors of his house; how he peered into dark corners, how he kept a knobkerrie within reach when he sat down to his bread and marmalade at the kitchen table. Home from home, she thought.

Inside Mr. K.'s kitchen, time had stood still. Modern conveniences were few or none. There was an old porcelain laundry sink in the corner, with a cold tap. There was a kitchen range, and most of Mr. K.'s leisure hours were spent in tending it, tipping in coal and riddling it with the rake and pulling out the dampers. It was exhausting work, and filmed his forehead with sweat, but it did not seem to have any effect on the temperature.

"You want work?" Mr. K. enquired gruffly. "Poor old woman, you too sick to work."

He was in his way a kindly man. "Sit down," he invited her. "Brew of tea for you."

When the tea was poured out and the sugar bowl passed, Mr. K. reached across the table. He snatched his lodger's mug from between her hands, and deposited his own before her; sat back to watch the effect, his eyes scouring her face. She picked it up and tasted it. "More sugar," she said, helping herself. Mr. K. seemed satisfied. He blew on his own tea and took a sip, and dabbed at his moustache.

"Go to hospital," he advised. "Old folks' hospital. She's crying out for staff."

His lodger shook her head. "They'll never take me on. A poor old woman like me."

"Temporary they take you on," Mr. K. said. "Temporary, subject to union. You try. You see. You get a nice job, my dear old lady. Bring the bedpans, wash the floors, for those of greater age."

"I'm used to hospitals," she said, "I could give it a try. Course, I could go charring as well. If I saw a nice ad for a private house. You'd have to write me a letter to apply, I'm not ever so good at writing. Course," added Poor Mrs. Wilmot, "I could put my own signature."

Later that week Mr. K. stopped her on the stairs.

"I heard a voice," he said accusingly.

She stopped, caught her breath, coughed a little. "My poor side," she said, rubbing her ribs. "What voice was this then?"

"Female voice. You get visitors?"

"I'm all alone in the world. Course," she suggested, "it could be her from the top floor."

"Miss Anne-Marie? That's a quiet female! Goes out for her giro, comes in, no trouble, no cooking smells."

"Well, you ought to ask her, that Miss Anaemia. I expect she's got a high-pitched boyfriend."

Mr. K. passed a hand over his eyes. "I don't sleep for worry. A parcel of my clothes have appeared, mysteriously laundered."

He saw her watching him. "Left dirty," he explained, "come out clean."

"That's no cause for consternation. I wish we all could say as much."

"But Wilmot, I have heard movements in the cellar. Perhaps they have caught up with me."

"Oh yes? Who's that then?"

"You have a day to spare?"

"Needs so long, does it?"

"If I say, the gentlemen from Montenegro? If I say, the boys from Bialystok?"

"There's worse than that, where I come from."

"Where is this?" A shadow of fresh apprehension crossed his face. "Yorkshire?"

"Oh, come off it," Mrs. Wilmot said. "You're all right now. This is a free country, haven't you heard?"

"But I carry my countries around with me," said Mr. K., "here, inside." He smote his pullover. "I will never be free. I am an exile by profession, Mrs. Wilmot. I am a badly wanted man."

"And you've been hearing voices, have you?"

"Noises, and human speech." He hugged himself, one stout forearm locked over the other. "A voice cried out in the pantry: Let us pray."

The winter passed. One day, Poor Mrs. Wilmot—who only worked an evening shift—went into town for a day's shopping. She went into Boots the Chemist to get a bottle for her cough; shuffling away from the pharmacy counter, she saw the most amazing sight.

There on a display stand, packed in little Perspex boxes, were what appeared to be row upon row of human eyelashes. Fascinated, Muriel moved closer. She gazed down, no expression on Mrs. Wilmot's face. Dismemberment, she thought. Bones in the canal, those detachable teeth the real Mrs. Wilmot had. The teeth that other people had, at the hospital. Evelyn's body, sliced up after death. And distributed? She bent over the display stand and peered at it. Would she know Evelyn's eyelashes if she saw them? Some were black and spiky, others were feathery and fair; all were for sale.

At once she saw the solution to her problem. Alone in her room she had been practising Edna; but Edna needed a shape. It was easy to assume the abject form of Poor Mrs. Wilmot, but the imitation of Edna's vitality seemed to deplete her own inner resources to the point of near-extinction. She could not risk a situation where Edna and Poor Mrs. Wilmot wiped out Muriel entirely; who would mediate between their demands, and organise their different clothing? But if she could be Edna, yet not Edna; Edna's soul in an invented body, a body made up of other moving parts? A body for self-assembly, an easy-build knock-down effort? Eyelashes; and something for the head, auburn or blonde, to go over Muriel's hair. She straightened up and looked around her at the glowing counters of cosmetics. She pictured Mother; Mother reassembling herself, trotting her spectral bones round the department stores until she found those bits of her that had been dispersed. "Can I help you?" an assistant enquired.

"Of course you can," she said. "I'll have the whole shop."

"What?" Crisp started up from the bed. She hadn't realised she'd spoken out loud. In fact, she'd forgotten he was there; it seemed hours since her remembering began. With a great yawn, Crisp swung his legs to the floor. He looked at her intently. "Do you ever think about the future, Muriel?"

"Of course I do," she said angrily. "I'm not an animal."

"I don't think about it."

"But there's possibilities, Crisp. You don't have to be a reverend. You can be a safe-breaker, a shopkeeper, a tailor's dummy. You can be a monumental mason."

"Perhaps. Arson's not much to keep you going."

"You could be a singing telegram. You want to get yourself organised." She paused. "I won't always need to be three people.

It's only till I give them their comeuppance . . . all those people that were in my life. Mr. Colin Sidney and Mrs. Sylvia Sidney, and Miss Florence Sidney, and Miss Isabel Field. I used to think about them when I was taking the cigarette packets apart . . . when I was on Ripping. I keep myself busy, but I always feel, you know, as if there's something I need . . . and they might have it."

Crisp let the newspapers slide to the floor. "I'll have another snooze," he said. Barelegged and bedraggled, Muriel went out for what was left of her free afternoon.

CHAPTER 3

The label of the collecting box was peeling off a bit. Muriel smoothed it with a damp forefinger. No one ever read it. Trapped in their doorways by her accusatory stare, they delved into their pockets and purses and paid up. Stopped on the street, they produced a coin and moved away as fast as they could. One man, caught on his front step, tried to argue with her. "I believe in the primacy of individual effort," he said. Muriel brought up her boot—it was wet that day—and caught him painfully on the kneecap.

She didn't need the money. It was the social side of it she valued. Lauderdale Road was a good area. People gave generously; there was guilt behind those festoon blinds.

What if I did Buckingham Avenue, she wondered idly. What if I went up the path of number 2 and rang the doorbell; what if Mother answered the door?

Think when old Mrs. Sidney came up the path, Master Colin's mum. Think when she came for her seance, with her crocodile shoes and her bag over her wrist. By the time she went out again something had gone permanently wrong inside her head. Death wasn't what she'd thought; she was put in a home before the year was out.

When she was bored with collecting Muriel retraced her steps towards the town centre. She passed the public library, where she often called in to steal books. She didn't go inside, but stopped in the lobby, arrested, as she had been before, by the advertisement for the Colorado Beetle. She didn't study the text, but gazed entranced at the creature; a gaudy beast, and, as portrayed, about the size of a small kitten. She was not surprised they were thought a public menace.

Then back to the shopping mall; there were some keys she had to get cut, Sylvia's house, Mr. K.'s house. She made a point of getting hold of keys, because you never knew when they might be useful. She paid for the keys out of her purse, not out of her collecting box, but she put it on the counter, and when the man had served her he slipped a 5p piece into it. Never let it be said that she was greedy, that she kept it all to herself. If in the mall she saw a wheelchair, parked by the litter bins and next to the municipal flowerbeds, she would often toss its occupant a small coin, with a cheery "There you go, you poor cripple," as she passed by.

Now she left the precinct behind. It was teatime; the sun was declining, the air was mild. Out towards the land of the link road she tramped in her sandals; the houses ran out on her, the pavements grew pitted, torn posters flapped from the broken walls. SORRY NO COACHES said an ancient sign in the window of the Rifle Volunteer. Across the wasteland the shop could be picked out easily; no other building had a roof for a quarter of a mile. Doggedly she struck out across country, picking up her feet over the fallen plaster and the tangle of low-growing weeds. She stopped to examine an iron grate and a pile of broken bottles. A breeze got up, and brown paper blew against her legs.

There were notices outside: GOLD AND SILVER ARTICLES WANTED, HOUSE CLEARENCES BEST PRICES PAYED. She pushed the door, heard the bell ping. From the darkness at the back of the shop came the clarion call of a bugle, and at the next moment, a squat and powerful figure leaped into view, brandishing a sabre.

"Cut it out, Sholto," Muriel said.

Sholto dropped his guard and sucked his bottom lip. He replaced the bugle on a high shelf. As he emerged from the dimness his manner became obsequious. He was blue-chinned, seedy and wild-eyed, and as he shuffled forward, sword in hand, it would have been no surprise to hear him claim that now was the winter of his discontent. Instead he smiled at Muriel, displaying his dreadful teeth, and asked her, "What can I suit you with today?"

"A cage," Muriel said.

Sholto ignored her. It was his pride that he sought out the secret whims of his clients. "Assorted brass knobs, 50p each. Door handles assorted, £2 a pair. What about a brass fingerplate?" He slapped one down on the counter. Muriel looked at it without interest. "And here—" he reached up to a shelf and produced an outstretched brass hand—"we have some brass fingers to go with it."

Muriel was looking around, poking into the piles of musty books and old clothes. It reminded her of the conservatory at Buckingham Avenue; long summer afternoons stirring through her late father's newspaper collection, Mother toddling through the hall, muttering her spells against spirit intrusion. Oo-oo-oo, Muriel would cry, and tap the cracked windowpanes, and flap her newspapers. Happy days! where Sylvia's kitchen extension stood now.

Sholto rubbed his chin. "Or what you could do with," he said, "is a phrenologist's head." He produced one, pushing it across the counter. "Look, Muriel."

Muriel stared down at the head, and traced with her finger the black lines which divided the skull.

"What are these lines, Sholto?"

"Those show the faculties. Look. Faculty of Imitation. Faculty of Calculation. Time and Tune and Wit."

"Is that how people work? I've often wondered. Does one person have them all?"

Sholto's grimy fingers probed the head, turning it up to squint at its base. "It's only a bit cracked," he said. "I could make you a special price."

She thought of her wig stand, the blank white slope of its skull. This was progress. One day these faculties would knit together, and she would go out into the world complete. Personality, more thorough than a plastic surgeon, would remould her formless face. "Look," Sholto said. "Faculty of Progenitiveness. Faculty of Amativeness."

"Oh, copulation," Muriel said. "If I had £7.95, I might buy that for my employer, Mr. Sidney."

"You could have easy terms," Sholto suggested. Muriel shook her head. "What about a bunch of keys then? £1.50, pick any bunch."

"What do they unlock?"

"How should I know?"

"What's the use of them?"

"They're not use. They're ornament."

"I have keys." Muriel's eyes roamed about the shop. "You sure you haven't got a cage, Sholto?"

"If I run across one, I'll give you first refusal."

"I'll have some assorted knobs then," Muriel said sulkily. She began to rummage through the box that Sholto pushed towards her. "What did you think to the trip?"

"Rip-roaring. What makes Crisp do it, though? Don't give me this about the C of E. He's only copying Effie, the time she set that cleaner on fire. He never was happy with his own brand of insanity. No sooner would you say you were Picasso than he'd claim to be Salvador Dali. Remember that time Philip said he was a helicopter? Crisp said, 'I'm Leobloodynardo,' and started drawing on the walls."

"He was never a person of deep originality."

"Oh, I see, been at the library books, have we?"

"I can talk, if I want to."

"You're getting very friendly with Crisp."

"He's all right."

"I hear wedding bells," Sholto said. He clicked his fingers. "Ding-dong."

"That's castanets."

"All right, don't get shirty. Going back up the Punjab, are you? Want a bag for your knobs?"

It was five-thirty when Muriel arrived back at Eugene Terrace; the tail end of the hot afternoon. Inside the Mukerjees' Emporium, a drowsy girl with a pitted bluish face sat by the till on a high stool. She glanced up without interest as Muriel passed the window; her shoulders moved fractionally, and her eyelids drooped again.

Crisp had left. There was a note on the table: GONE TO EVENSONG. And I brought doughnuts for our tea, Muriel thought crossly. She dumped the paper bag on a chair and walked around the room for a while, looking in Crisp's drawers and under his mattress; there was nothing of interest. The room was close and stuffy; outside it smelled like thunder. At least, that was what the people at the doughnut shop said; she could not smell it. Over the Punjab, the sky had turned a leaden colour; pigeons huddled together on the guttering, heads sunk low into their feathers like vultures in cartoons.

Muriel shed her clothes again. With the weight of the day upon her, it wasn't difficult to become Poor Mrs. Wilmot. Her shoulders slumped, her knees bent, her toes turned in; she sprayed her hair with dry shampoo, and flattened it to her head gritty and streaked with grey, and secured it with two large hairgrips. As she did this, the years crept up and weighed her down; her joints locked, her mouth grew pinched, her hands began to shake. She put on Mrs. Wilmot's elastic stockings and leaned over with a rheumaticky quiver for her bedroom slippers. What was the real Wilmot doing, she wondered. Probably having a cup of tea or something. Experimentally, she opened her mouth in a silent laugh.

Finally she put on Mrs. Wilmot's coat, which she needed in all weathers, feeling the cold as she did; it was a coat Sholto had found in a dustbin, no shape at all and the colour of the fluff that collects under beds. She went downstairs. A plump little boy of about twelve years old minded the till. The family were so numerous that, despite the shop's long hours, she had never seen the same Mukerjee twice. His eyes behind his thick spectacles were glued to his Darth Vader comic; Wilmot passed, and he didn't look up.

When she returned to Mr. K.'s house she was surprised to find him up and about. "I thought you'd be having your sleep," she said, as she shuffled dispiritedly into the kitchen. "Course, you know what's best for you."

Mr. K. was taping up the kitchen window. "In case of poison gas," he explained. As he stretched up his garments parted company, exposing the greyish roll of fat above his hips.

"Pardon me," his lodger said, "course, you know best, but couldn't it come through the letter box?"

"A welcome thought," Mr. K. said. "I shall tape it instanter. Would you graciously put on tea kettle?"

Mrs. Wilmot made the tea while Mr. K. went out into the hall to secure his letter box. When it was brewed she poured out for them, and they sat companionably at the kitchen table.

"Woman watching house again today," Mr. K. said. "Drove by, stopped, got out, waited ten minutes, passed on. Miss Anaemia said it is Snoopers, from the department."

She nodded, and drank her tea.

"Who is this Snoopers?" He did not expect an answer. There were no answers to the questions which plagued him. He sucked his tea through a sugar lump, and eyed his roll of adhesive tape.

"Any law against keeping pets?" his lodger asked suddenly.

"What?" said Mr. K. "Cats, dogs, horses?"

"Beetles."

"The famous British sense of humour," Mr. K. said sadly.

"It's no joke. I've seen them advertised." She picked up her shopping bag and made off towards the kitchen door with it, her large feet padding softly in their pink bedroom slippers. "I'm going to get a cage," she muttered. "Great big striped ones as fat as melons."

Muriel climbed the stairs to the first landing. It grew colder as she ascended, and the smell of decay was pronounced. The ancient paper, with its design of cabbage roses, was peeling from the walls. "Hello there, Mrs. Wilmot," someone whispered. It was Miss Anaemia, creeping down from her third-floor attic. She emerged into the faint light from the long window, filtered through years of dust; a fragile young woman, little more than a child, with a child's flat body, minimal features, and a skin so translucent that it was easy to imagine that you saw the circulation of the thin blood beneath it. Her red hair was plastered damply to her head, and her whole body seemed to jump and quiver in a state of perpetual fright.

"I hear you've got problems, course I don't want to pry," said Poor Mrs. Wilmot.

"Shh. Not so loud."

"I thought you were at the Polytechnic. Course, I don't know, I've no education."

"I was." Tears welled up in the girl's large eyes. "They made a new timetable. They've got split sites. They moved my lectures. I couldn't find them. So I stopped going."

"Couldn't you ask them?"

"I did, but nobody seemed to know who I was."

"Well, there you are then. Cellar vee, isn't it? Che sera, sera. And what do you do with yourself now?"

"I'm a claimant. I make up different names. Primrose Hill's one I go under. Penny Black." She whispered to herself. "Black Maria, Bad Penny. Faint Hope. Square Peg."

"Is it frightening?"

"It's terrifying," Miss Anaemia said. "It makes your palms sweat." For a second, before she descended the dark staircase, she laid the palm of her hand, ice-cold and clammy, against Muriel's cheek.

CHAPTER 4

"Anybody home?" No answer. That didn't mean, of course, that the house was empty. Sylvia went into the kitchen, poured herself a glass of Perrier water, and took it upstairs. Alistair's door was still shut. She felt sticky and grimy from the plastic chairs in the committee room, the car's vinyl upholstery, the dust that hung in the air. Other people's tobacco smoke had got into her lungs.

She peeled off her clothes, shrugged her towelling robe on, and made for the bathroom. She thought she heard a rustle behind Alistair's door. "Are you in there?" she said. "Alistair, if you don't come out soon I'm going to kick this door in." There was no reply. She didn't mean it, of course; it was just the small change of domestic violence. She locked herself in the bathroom, took a brisk shower, then scrubbed her face with a soapy substance full of little bits of grit. Exfoliation, she said to herself. How she wished she could really shed her skin, and shed the past with it, dispose of that embarrassing image in the photographs of ten years ago. She had heard of people trying to "purge themselves of their past." The images employed seemed to become more nasty and drastic the more you thought about it. Exorcism . . . the exfoliation procedure had left her face blotchy and scored with little red lines. She stared at herself in the bathroom mirror. All right, do it, she thought. Find that other old photograph and throw it out. Why today? Well, why not? As murderers often find after years of wishful thinking, the action of a second can free you from the weight of a decade.

She went into the bedroom and opened Colin's top drawer. A tangle of underwear, and socks he never wore, rolled into balls, fraying round the tops. A colour film, some small change, some bottles of aftershave; most of it bought by Florence, gentle hints from the year when Colin had decided to grow a beard. It hadn't lasted long, the beard. Nothing lasted long with Colin; the enthusiasms he took up at evening classes, his project for growing vegetables, his ardour for joining the Social Democratic Party—which had fizzled out, come to think of it, when he couldn't find a stamp to send off his application form. Only his neckties evoked constancy. What was this greasy grey string, left over from the last time ties were narrow? Here was a yellow knitted one, and here was a great flowery orange thing, a relic of the sixties. Dear God. Kipper ties, they called them.

She heard the front door bang.

"Mum? Mum, it's me, Claire, I'm home."

"All right, Claire," she called. "I'll be with you in a minute."

"Mum, can I get waffles out of the freezer?"

"Get what you like. I won't be long."

With a sudden urgency, she began to rummage through the drawer. Here at the back was the five-year diary that she had once given Colin for Christmas. It was not locked; its key was still taped to it, in a tiny polythene envelope. Colin had never filled the diary in. He considered, he told her, that he had no life worth recording, and to be sure that he was right, she had checked every few months and found the pages blank. He could have filled it in, she thought, after I took such trouble to get it for him. Being a history teacher you'd think he'd like to keep a record. She felt she would like to make sense of the past; of those white years, 1975, 1976, '77, '78, '79. Where had they gone? She had a mental picture of an autumn evening, the year they had moved to Buckingham Avenue; Colin sulking in the garden, refusing to come in though it was getting cold and dark. He hated the sight of me, she thought, he would have left me for two pins; it was only after Claire was born that he calmed down. Presumably his affair was over by then. Something was missing afterwards, as if a large part of his vitality had been drained away. At times she caught him watching her. He looked like someone staring out of a famine poster; preternaturally wise, still, and lacking in a future that was of interest to anybody.

Here it was: a crumpled snapshot under his oldest socks. Its presence there was a tacit admission. He must know that she went through his drawers at intervals; after twenty years he was familiar with her methods of keeping one step ahead. He was not one of those self-contained men who can keep their love affairs a secret. He was one of those pathetic, guilty men, whose deepest need is to be found out.

She sat down on the edge of the bed, switched on the bedside light, and held the photograph under it. She had done all this before, at intervals separated by months when the knowledge that he still kept the picture would nibble away at her complacency, like a woodworm in furniture. Staring and staring didn't give you any more information. She was young and slim, the girlfriend; woollen hat and scarf, boots, hands thrust into the pockets of a rather anonymous jacket. She leaned against the offside wing of the family Fiat, the one they had got rid of in 1976. Dark hair, shadowy eyes; the effortful smile was like Colin's own. There was a dim backdrop of leafless trees.

Perhaps she was a teacher. Who else did he meet? Sylvia sucked her lip, brooding. A second later she leaped from the bed in alarm. Her heart pounded; a jangling scream split the air. She tore out of the room, yelled down at her daughter below. "Claire, for God's sake stop that cooker timer!"

"What?"

"Push the knob in, make it stop, it's driving me spare."

The noise stopped. "I didn't set it off," Claire called up indignantly.

"Who did then?"

"Alistair."

"Don't be daft, he's in his bedroom."

Slowly she made her way back, clutching the photograph. Time's up, she thought sourly. Life's solid all through, done to a turn, a little bit longer and we'll smell burning. She took a deep breath, trying to control the thumping behind her ribs.

"Mum, are you coming?"

Claire was whining from the foot of the stairs. "In a second." She picked up the photograph she had discarded earlier, the one of herself from the family album. She held up the two for comparison. Her hands shook a little. No wonder he preferred the young girl; for a time, anyway. Date for date they matched. Winter 1974; summer, 1975. I'd know her anywhere, she thought; I'd know her right away. She ripped the photographs through and slipped them into the pocket of her jeans, meaning to drop them in the kitchen bin when no one was looking.

CONFESSIONS etc. (2)

". . . that very strange people do congregate. They find each other out and form ghettos. The inadequate personality, the incipient schizophrenic, they feel under threat. Their identity is precarious and human relationships threaten to overwhelm them. But even when a person is totally alienated the need for minimal human contact is still there. So tramps live under bridges, and derelicts in common lodging houses."

Isabel put down her pen. She wasn't making headway. Whenever she tried to express herself, jargon got in the way. Years ago, she had been to an evening class to improve her writing skills. It didn't seem to have improved them. It had been pointless.

And yet, not quite. It was at the writing class that she'd met her Married Man. Everybody has one; you have to meet them somewhere. Colin hadn't taken the course very seriously. He'd sat there, looking about him, smirking at people's efforts. They'd gone to the pub after the class and he'd asked her to run away with him. She'd thought he was joking. At first.

Her mind wandered as she tried to put events in order. Her *Confessions* kept straying off the point. I'll make an outline, she thought, and work from that.

"AXON: The records are lost/inconsistent/have gaps in them. So many different workers have been on the case. By the time it got to me it was nearly hopeless.

THEN: for months at a time I couldn't get into the house.

WHEN I DID Mrs. Axon locked me in a bedroom.

WHILE I WAS IN THE BEDROOM——"

She hesitated, then wrote: "MRS. AXON DIED."

"I could have done better.

"But I made a mess of it.

"Why?

"Because I was frightened.

"Why?

"The fact is I couldn't keep my personal life straight. There was this awful problem of Colin, I didn't know what to do about him, he was so emotional, he seemed to need me so much, but I didn't have anything left over from my work to give to anybody. Everything was a problem, job/Colin/home."

I can't send it to the newspapers like this, she thought crossly, I'll have to tidy it up, there are times I wish I'd never, but no, don't say that; what a relief it will be when it's done.

"At that time my father had just retired. (He was in banking, like my husband, and that's why I went into it when I left social work, I thought it was safe.) He was always in his room, doing his hobbies, or so I thought. In fact he was doing much worse. He used to sneak off and pick up women, old women, awful women, the kind of woman who sleeps rough. It was all he could get, I suppose. He wasn't very prepossessing himself. He said he was lonely.

"He used to meet them in the launderette or at the park, or in the bus station café. He used to buy them cups of tea. They'd be grateful. They didn't mind doing it out of doors, even in cold weather. He used to come home with clay on the knees of his trousers. I didn't know what to do.

"He started bringing them home, and I was frantic in case the neighbours found out. For me, in my position . . . He could have caught something, a disease. He could be getting them pregnant, they weren't all old. There I was, telling other people how to run their lives. I used to hide his glasses. He could hardly see without them; but I think he used to get out, all the same.

"And then the day came when I did get into the Axon house. There was something funny about the way Muriel looked, and the way her mother talked; as if they were carrying on some elaborate piece of acting, and as if I couldn't see what was right under my nose. Her mother said Muriel had been out of the house. 'On the razzle' was the expression she used.

"I went away and the picture of Muriel remained in my mind, sitting, lumpen, her face downcast, in her peculiar blue smock made out of some kind of furnishing fabric. At first it didn't occur to me that she might be pregnant. I only saw her, in my mind, ambling through the park, or drinking tea out of a paper cup down at the bus station. It occurred to me, as I ran down the Axons' front path; and now, all these years later, the thought wakes me up in the middle of the night.

"I didn't report my suspicion. I didn't do anything. I cleared off and left the Axons to their own devices. I didn't go back to the house until I absolutely had to, and by that time Muriel (if she'd really been pregnant) had already given birth. What happened to the baby? Was it a boy or a girl? I think I read somewhere that babies' corpses often mummify, and turn up years later, uncannily preserved."

She stopped writing. It didn't seem very coherent. There was so much that only made sense in the light of her state of mind at the time, and no doubt she had been over-imaginative. That was a fault of hers.

She took a clean sheet of paper and wrote on it,

"I think my husband is having an affair. I don't know who she is and I hope I don't find out. I like deceiving myself. It is comfortable. It is the House Speciality."

Perhaps I should have a drink, she thought. My style leaves

something to be desired and perhaps after a drink it would improve. Perhaps a drink would help her to see the connection between things, the connections she sensed and sought. There was no gin, so she had whisky. She wasn't fussy these days. Alcohol takes you to the heart; you see the True Nature of Events.

There was a feeling of circular motion. It was not entirely the effect of the Scotch on an empty stomach. Here she was, back in town. Here she was, the Wronged Wife; she'd once been the Other Woman. It is a progression people make, but she didn't see that. Her situation seemed special, sinister, ensnaring. Funny that it's only after ten years things seem to fit together.

What I need, Colin thought, is a large gin and tonic.

"Anybody home?" No answer. He dropped his jacket—he had not worn it all day—on the chair in the hall, and went into the living room. "Why doesn't anybody let a bit of air in around here?" He swung open the french windows that looked over the garden. Ought to spray for blackfly this weekend, he thought. He turned to the wall units and opened a cupboard gingerly; he could not trust the door to stay in place, having constructed the units himself last summer with the help of screwdriver provided and simple instructions in Japanese. He held the gin bottle up for inspection; it was a quarter full, so he poured himself a measure into a tumbler which came to hand and, picking it up, set off for the kitchen to look for ice and tonic. There would be lemons, for sure; there were always lemons around Sylvia. She cooked them and squeezed them and ate them and rubbed them on her elbows, like the Esquimaux using up every part of the beast. He found a drop of tonic in a bottle at the back of the fridge. It looked flat. He shook it and watched it fizz, then opened the freezer. There was something like raspberry jam all over the ice cubes. He sighed, slid out the tray, and took it to the sink. He twisted it and nothing happened, so he hammered it against the stainless steel for a while, looking out of the kitchen window; he twisted it again, and the ice cubes flew out and fell into the sink with a clatter. He picked up a couple, pursuing them as they shot away from his fingers, and ran them under the tap to try to get the jam off; before long the ice and water were indistinguishable, and both were running through his fingers.

"Hello, Dad," said Claire, coming in. "What are you washing the ice cubes for?"

"Because somebody, I don't say who, has been smearing jam all over the place."

"It must have been Alistair."

"It's funny that he put it round your mouth too, isn't it?"

"Is this your drink?" Claire put her forefinger into his tumbler and licked it. "Yuk, that's horrible."

"Watch out, you'll have jam in it."

"I tell you what, Dad, I could make you some tea."

"This will do me nicely, Claire. If you'll take your fingers out of it, I'll have it without the ice."

"You could have tea as well. I've got my forms for Brownies."

"Perhaps later, pet. Where is Alistair, is he still upstairs?"

"No, I saw him with Austin. They're in the churchyard."

"Oh yes, what are they doing? Exhuming somebody?"

"What's that?"

"Digging up bodies. Really, Claire, we'll have to do something about your vocabulary."

"No, stupid, they weren't digging up bodies. They were singing. They've got some beer."

"Really, at this time of day?"

"They've not got a bottle opener, so they're knocking the tops off on the gravestones. They wouldn't let me do it."

"I wonder what the vicar would have to say."

"About what?" Sylvia asked, trundling in with the laundry basket. She stared at him. "Drinking?"

"Yes. Why not? Would you like to join me?"

"Why are you saying that?" She stopped dead, eyeing him. "As if we were in a TV play. As if I were some other woman."

"I don't know what you mean. I only asked—"

"There must be at least three hundred calories in that. Is it Slimline Tonic or not?"

"It's flat anyway," Colin said. Its momentary sparkle had subsided by the time he emptied it into his glass. "I can make up for it if I go carefully over the weekend."

"Very likely; when Florence comes round with shortbread on Sunday afternoon and gets into a state if you don't eat it."

"Well, perhaps I could just have one piece, and hope she'll take it in good part. Would you pass me a knife for my lemon, please? Besides, you know, if you want the honest truth—"

"If I want the honest truth, I suppose I'll go begging."

"Sylvia, what is this?"

"Nothing."

"I'm not really interested in losing any more weight."

"You'll regret it," she sang. She moved across the kitchen towards him, trying to lighten her tone.

"Mum," said Claire, "you shouldn't carry a knife with the pointy side like that, it's dangerous."

"It's called a blade, Claire," Sylvia said calmly. "You'll regret it when you go off to the squash club, and collapse and die."

"You're not allowed to die at my squash club," Colin said. He took the knife and stuck it in his lemon. "It's like the Palace of Westminster, no one is allowed to expire within the precincts. They'd run you outside and leave you on the pavement."

"It's hardly a thing to joke about, in front of Claire."

"Claire might laugh." Colin stood with the slice of lemon poised on the blade of his knife. "I know you won't. Humour's not your strong point, is it?"

"When did you start hating me?" Sylvia asked. "I'd like to know. Can you remember what year it was? When did you start hating me, and when, if ever, did you stop?"

Colin turned away, letting his slice of lemon fall on the counter top. He could not imagine what had prompted this. The photograph of his former mistress lay snugly under his wife's pelvic bone, the bleak little face staring at the lining of her pocket. A bluebottle alighted on his glass and walked slowly and purposefully round the rim.

The hospital where Mrs. Wilmot worked was named not for St. Luke, the physician, but for the tax collector, St. Matthew. Its main building, within the memory of many of its patients—memories most acute for their early lives—had been the union workhouse. It still looked like a workhouse, grey and draughty, with its high ceilings and stained walls. In the part of the building which was now taken over by offices, you could still see the old wooden benches, built with a ridge in their backs so that the paupers would not lounge about and get too comfortable. Its general air was so depressing, its inmates so futureless, and its corridors so drab that even though the area unemployment rate was 16 per cent, the hospital could not keep its staff. They could not live, they found, with the prospect of what was in store for them.

The wards here did not have interesting names, just letters. The best patients were in C Ward; the worst were in A. Perhaps this psychological ploy was meant for the staff, for the patients were beyond encouragement.

The Staff Nurse called out to Poor Mrs. Wilmot as she trailed in: "Hello there, love. Would you mind mopping up after Mrs. Anderson? She's had an accident."

"Course, I don't have to." She took her coat off and laid it over a chair. "Course, I'm entitled to a nurse to do that. Course, I don't mind."

"Oh, you are a brick, Mrs. Wilmot," Staff said. "I don't know where we'd be without you."

The ward smelled; not of its incontinent patients, but of what was almost worse, disinfectant, air freshener, talcum powder, drug-induced sleep. And now of food; the dinner trolley rolled in, purées and mashes under their metal covers.

Staff took up a bowl, and perched on the edge of a bed.

"Try this potato, love," she urged, forking it appetisingly.

Her patient rolled her head away and puckered her mouth.

Mrs. Anderson lay huddled in the next bed, no movement except for her breathing, in out, in out. Why did she bother, Staff wondered. She never spoke or moved. Neither did Mrs. Sidney, in the bed beyond; nothing at all, except from time to time a peevish flicker of her sunken eyes. The ladies of A Ward were so old, so sick, so far away; they clung to the very fringes of human existence, to the outer edge of whatever could be taken for sentient and separate life. Their shrunken bodies hardly disturbed the sheets, their tiny skulls on the pillows were no bigger than grapefruits. Yet Mrs. Sidney was not so old, really; one in twenty people over sixty-five suffered from senile dementia, and she had been lying in this bed when she should have been a spry old pensioner going off to the shops with a bus pass and a basket on wheels. She'd been on A Ward (Female) for eight years; Staff had been on it for eight weeks. She didn't know how much longer she'd last. Even C Ward was better, where sixty old ladies sat round the day room, fastened into their highchairs, and chattered at each other, occasionally wept, and sometimes threw things. The A Wards, conveniently, were closer to the mortuary; few left by any other route. But I'll leave, Staff thought; I'll get myself to a coronary care unit, where I'll meet a stressed executive: and soon I'll be a bride. She dreamed of it, when she dozed on night duty; instead of a train she wore a stiff white sheet, with the monogram of the Area Health Authority in red on a tape by the hem.

"Don't feed Mrs. Sidney," she said, looking up. "I want to keep her tidy. She's expecting visitors tonight."

She gave up on Mrs. Anderson's neighbour and dropped the plastic spoon into the bowl. She went to the end of Mrs. Sidney's bed and stood looking at her. It was plain that she was expecting nothing; except death. After some time had passed, Mrs. Sidney acknowledged her with one serpentine blink. "You know you're going to be moved, don't you, Mrs. Sidney? Are you listening? You do know what's going on?"

Expect a mummy to answer you, Staff thought. Expect Tutankhamun to boogie into the sluice. The old lady stared through her as if her solid bulk were gauze. "Want me to comb her hair?" Mrs. Wilmot said. "Course, perhaps you want the student to do it?"

"I wouldn't bother," Staff said. "She's got so little of it left, and wouldn't it be just our luck if today's the day it falls out entirely? You know what relatives are. Still, they're very good. Second time in eight weeks. They were phoned up about her move. Not that she knows them. Pointless really."

"Pointless," Mrs. Wilmot agreed. "Course, walls have ears, don't they? So she might be able to tell what you say."

"I do sometimes wonder," Staff said. "I do sometimes wonder what goes through her head, staring and blinking, blinking and staring all day long. You wonder what goes through any of their heads."

"Course, you'd think they'd cure them."

"Oh, there's no cure." She'd tell anybody; anybody who came on her ward. "There's no cure for the march of time. I wonder what her son will say, about moving her. They'll be here any minute, I expect."

"Well, I'll just look in on the gentlemen," Mrs. Wilmot said. "Seeing as I'm here, seeing as I'm done for now." She dragged off across the corridor at her usual abject pace, her eyes downcast. "Spread a cheery word," she said.

Coming upstairs—they were the only visitors around—Colin said to Sylvia, "Could you just give me some idea of what this is about? I come home, pour myself a drink, and you start in on me."

"Nothing," Sylvia said, balefully.

"There must be something. I mean, there must be something that set you off."

A silent car ride lay behind them. He combed through the day's words and events to find something that could have offended Sylvia, and yet he was conscious that she was not so much offended as sad and puzzled, floundering in a morass of unwelcome thoughts. He knew the signs; he could diagnose them in other people. "Perhaps it's the prospect of visiting my mother," he said. "Is it? I'd have come alone."

Sylvia didn't answer. She had never let him come alone. When they reached the ward, she said, as she always did, "The smell." He said, as always, "I expect you get used to it."

She felt self-conscious, in her outdoor clothes, and in her shoes which made such a noise. Walking down the ward beside Colin was like walking down the aisle; heads turned, to pin you with a judgemental stare, and suddenly you were large and clumsy and you felt your face going red. Here they were at the altar, this shrouded stonelike object. They stopped at the foot of the bed.

"Hello, Mum," Colin said in a loud voice. There was a sudden little movement from the patients all along the ward, as if they were joined by an electric wire from bed to bed. It subsided; they were still, mute. Mrs. Sidney had not joined the demonstration. Would she blink or would she not, was the question.

Sylvia sighed. "I'll get us two chairs," she said. She crossed the ward. She felt that the deaf watched her, that the blind heard her pass; she was an intrusion, a big woman blown in from the outside, her body glowing with its self-conceits. The Staff Nurse came up. It was the one with the overshot jaw, the red-faced woman who'd been here last time.

"How are we?"

"Fine, fine."

"You know doctor wants to move her?"

"Hardly seems any point."

"The thing is, off B Ward, they sometimes go home."

Sylvia's eyebrows shot up.

"Oh, not in this condition. But if she showed signs, you know . . . the fact is, they want to close this place down, and any-body they can get out, they will get out; because although we're having a new geriatric unit at the General, we're not going to have enough beds."

"But look at her. She's not showing signs, is she?"

"No, well, but the doctor must think she is. Course, I'm not saying it could happen. I mean, if she shaped up a bit, started to feed herself, she could go on C Ward. Sit in the day room and watch the telly. It'd be more of a life for her. Know what I mean?"

"But that's ludicrous," Sylvia said. "There's as much chance of her sitting up and watching telly as there is of you winning Miss World."

"Well, you never know," the Staff Nurse said rather huffily. "We have to try and hold out some hope, you know. Otherwise we'd all do ourselves in, wouldn't we? Shall I take those flowers?"

She strode off, stiff-armed, holding the bunch well away from her apron. Sylvia dragged the chairs over to Colin. He was leaning over his mother now, his expression intent. "You know," he said, "you know, really, I think she might be a bit better. I think there was just a flicker of something, I think I caught it in her eyes as I bent over her."

"Oh, Colin." She dumped the chair. "You've been saying that for years."

"I expect you're right." He sat down heavily. "But you're the one who always brings her flowers."

"It would look so mean if we didn't. What would they think?"

They conversed in whispers. It would be just like every other visit; they would sit for twenty minutes, a length of time which seemed respectable, and then they would put their chairs back by the wall and walk away, Sylvia first, Colin two paces behind her. At the swing doors they would pause and look back, and find it difficult to distinguish the little hump of bedding that was Mrs. Sidney from all the others in the long silent row.

"Do you think she'll know if they move her?" Sylvia asked.

"I can't see how. I mean, she doesn't seem to notice her surroundings, does she?"

"She used to be in that bed. Over in the corner."

"Yes. Then she moved two beds up, didn't she? That was in 1979."

"Of course, I don't suppose she had a change of bed really. I expect it's the same bed, and they just wheel them."

"Yes, I suppose so."

They fell silent.

"It would be a big change," Colin said, after a while. "Moving down the corridor. Think, I mean, if you'd been on the same spot since 1979. Moving down the corridor would be like me getting a job in Port Stanley."

"Why Port Stanley?"

"I don't know—I mean anywhere foreign and a long way off, that would be a big upheaval. Why are you so obtuse? I always have to explain myself."

"Then why are you so obscure?" Sylvia whispered. "You say things without rhyme or reason. Please don't start a row in public. You embarrass me."

"It's hardly public." He turned and looked around the ward.

"Don't stare at them. They're not all cabbages. Some of them have feelings left."

"Sorry." Colin readjusted his gaze, returning it to his knees. Another silence fell. Sylvia looked at her watch.

"Go in a minute, shall we?"

"Okay." Colin eased back his chair on its rubber feet. Another visit was coming to its close. "I expect she'll—" He broke off. "Sylvia?" he said. "She moved."

"What?" Alarmed, Sylvia stood up. "Where? Where did she move?"

"Her hand, I thought . . . just a twitch." He had jumped up too and now leaned eagerly over his mother. "Hello, Mum, can you hear me? Are you there?"

"Of course she's there," Sylvia said. "What a daft question. Where do you think she is? Hong Kong?"

"Why Hong Kong?" Colin straightened up. The old lady was not even blinking. Her no-colour eyes, which had once been hazel, stared straight at the opposite wall. Her skin had turned to leather, though she had never been the outdoor type; her mouth was only a crack, wide over long-empty gums. Colin thought he could see, buried in the crinkled folds of her neck, a pulse beating; there, just over the top button of her nightdress.

"Well, I should hope so," said Sylvia, when he pointed this out. "She must have a pulse, mustn't she?"

"I think she's excited. I think perhaps she's heard what we've said about moving, and she's excited."

"I'm afraid that's wishful thinking. What is it to get excited about?"

"Perhaps we ought to tell the nurse." They stood over her for another minute, watching her. "I daresay you're right," Colin said at last. "I must have imagined it."

"Come on." Sylvia touched his elbow. "Don't upset yourself."

He felt almost heartened, at this tender gesture from her. Possibly she did care about his feelings; possibly he was something more to her than a household object, at her disposal. Oh, the relentless optimism of the man! He squeezed her hand. "Why don't we stop off on the way home? Have a drink, just unwind a bit? It *is* the end of term."

"I don't want to be out when Suzanne gets home, she'll wonder where we are. I don't know what she's coming for, I didn't expect her till the weekend. She sounded funny on the phone."

"Oh, she'll fend for herself," Colin said, "there's food in the fridge. It's probably boyfriend trouble."

"Could be."

"You know how it is, first year away from home. She has to learn to stand on her own two feet. I remember when I first went off to university—"

"Shut up!"

"What?"

"Shut up," Sylvia said. "Stand still. Watch her." She leaned forward, her eyes fixed on the figure in the bed, her tongue between her teeth; as if she were defusing a bomb. "She did move," she said quietly. "You were right."

"Well, thank you," Colin said. At once his indignation evaporated; sobered and awestruck, he stared at the old lady. Slowly, fractionally, the walnut head was moving; drooping on the chest.

They held their breaths. For a long moment Mrs. Sidney

rested, looking up slyly from under her eyelids. You were told I was showing signs, her expression seemed to say. A stiff broken-winged flutter brought her arms to her sides. Knobbled, stick-thin; the wasted muscles remembered leverage. Fraction by fraction she rose upright in the bed.

"Here, Mrs. Wilmot!" the nurse called. "Come and look at this!" She waddled off down the ward in the direction of the men's block. "Come here, Mrs. Wilmot!"

Sylvia gripped Colin's hand. Minutes passed by the ward clock. There were times when she seemed to stick, but there were times when, comparatively, she seemed to hurtle. Finally the sheet fell away. Nothing but a nightgown of yellow winceyette held in the old lady's bones, but her face had become animated, lips twitching, eyes opened wide.

"She's going to speak," Colin said excitedly. He dropped Sylvia's hand and leaned over his mother. Mrs. Sidney's expression was congested with effort, her jaws moving as if years of chit-chat were banking up in her throat. "Again?" Colin said. "Again, Mum, try again."

"What did she say?" Sylvia demanded.

"I don't know." Colin steadied himself with a hand on the bed. "Something about a house. Bleak House? Buck House? Can't be, can it?"

"There's no sense in that, Colin."

"You want sense as well? Come on, Mum, speak up, try again."

Here was Nurse, bustling back, the old ward orderly padding behind her. "Can you credit it?" Nurse said. "And I didn't believe Dr. Furness when he said she was coming to. Mind you, praise where praise is due, Mrs. Wilmot here has spent hours with your mum, just talking to her, like, just tidying out her locker and making her feel she's wanted. It's the personal touch, that's what it is."

Mrs. Sidney turned her head. "She's doing great," the nurse said. "Here's your son, Mrs. Sidney," she bawled. "Here's your son and daughter-in-law. Here's Mrs. Wilmot. You know Mrs. Wilmot, don't you?"

In the depth of cloudy irises, something moved; a chance, a stray, a fugitive thought. Her mouth trembled. Gaze kindled. Slow, dilute tears rolled out of her eye. "Colin?" Quivering lips moved around his name.

"Oh, Mum, speak again," Colin said. His voice cracked with emotion.

"She recognises you," the nurse said.

"And me," said the old lady called Wilmot. "She recognises me, don't you, lovey?"

Mrs. Sidney's head twisted towards the new voice. She stared. Something darkened behind her eyes, quite suddenly, as if a blind had been pulled down. "She's gone again," the nurse said, disappointed. "Stay where you are, though. You never know."

They stood, frozen, waiting for her to move again. Presently she did so; not speaking, but raising her right hand in a rigid, almost regal, wave.

Over on B Block (Male) Mr. Philip Field sat in a side ward, planning his funeral. He was hesitating, for the tenth time, between "The Lord's My Shepherd" and "Love Divine, All Loves Excelling." Was not the latter more often sung at weddings? He couldn't recall the tune. He'd had a stroke—or so they said—and there was much he couldn't recall. If only his daughter were here, she might be able to help him out. They could have a singsong. It would be like old times. His wife, who had deserted him years ago, had played the piano.

Isabel might come more, now that she'd moved back to town. But he doubted it. She was sick herself, she said; instead she'd send that wimpish husband of hers. Isabel was a champion at prevarication, at excuses; at giving you what you didn't want, long after you'd forgotten you'd asked. What good was Ryan? He was a banker, but he didn't want to talk about banking practice. He said it was all different now. He just sat there fidgeting, cracking his silly jokes. The only money he was interested in was the money his wife's father was going to leave him.

They disapproved of him, that was it. He was a man who in his time had gone in for a bit of honest fun. With the wife gone, it was a case of having to; he'd had urges. What do you go for nowadays, he asked Ryan, sniggering. Key parties? He wanted the details. Ryan looked po-faced; as if he were turning someone down for a loan.

But he watched his son-in-law watching the young nurses. Ryan was a hypocrite, he decided.

Some days he thought he'd be leaving this godforsaken place; some days he knew he wouldn't. Bits of his body—a hand, a leg— seemed to have developed a will of their own. Scraps of memory, detached from their moorings in the far past, floated up to occupy the forefront of his brain. This seemed a bad sign. He was determined to leave his affairs in order; that included the disposition of his remains. After all, he knew Isabel. She couldn't seem to function these days without a drink inside her; and after she'd had a drink, she would forget what she was doing and lose the undertaker's number.

Accordingly, he had sent to a selection of funeral directors for their prospectus and terms. He had half-hoped a representative would call. In the United States, they would have called. They knew the meaning of service. Not that he had truck with foreign methods, in general; but he remembered how, in Paris once as a young man, he'd been impressed by the high seriousness of the undertaking business, by the Pompes Funèbres on every street, their windows draped with black velvet and stuck over with specimen Mass cards and plans of family vaults. Ah, Paris . . . He lay back against his pillow. It was clear that Isabel would not be coming in tonight. He closed his eyes; all in a moment, his fancies passed from the lugubrious to the lubricious. Furtively, he touched himself under the sheet. Nothing doing. But give it time. He'd have something to show the little student nurse, a lovely surprise for her when she came to tuck in his sheets.

Everything was going along nicely when the door opened. He flicked open one eye to appraise his visitor. It was an old woman, an orderly, a downcast and shrunken personage; hardly meat for his fantasies. He gave her no encouragement, merely closed his eyes again, and went on with what he was doing. But she continued to come in, intruding her woebegone form around the door; she stood over the bed, looking down with her lacklustre eyes, and forced him to take notice of her.

"You're interrupting me," he told her. "I want to be left alone. If you're looking for my tray, the male nurse took it."

She didn't seem to have heard him. She walked to the foot of the bed and picked up his charts.

"Hands off," he shouted. "That's confidential. Doctors only."

"I thought it was you, Mr. Field."

As he looked at her, a change seemed to come over her. Her bony shoulders straightened. She grew by an inch or two, and her melancholic manner fell away. The years fell away too; it was 1974, she was a girl alone, on a go in the park, and a lonely old gentleman was hanging around by the swings. Muriel grinned at him.

"Hello, old cock," she said.

CHAPTER 5

When Sylvia opened her handbag, you never knew what might come out of it. It might be a tract; it might be a revolver.

This morning it was a little pink card. She pushed it across the table to Suzanne. "That's the number of the clinic," she said. "Ring them up right away for a quote. If you don't want to go locally, I'll drive you back up to Manchester; Hermione's given me the name of her man on John Street."

"It's Saturday," Suzanne said.

"There'll be somebody there, don't fret."

"Anybody would think you were forewarned."

"Sometimes my community work comes in useful."

"Hang on a minute, Sylvia. This is your own flesh and blood."

"I prefer not to think about the flesh and blood aspect. It hardly is, at this stage."

"But it's a potential life. She has to think it out. It's a matter of conscience."

"Oh, bugger her conscience," Sylvia said. "What about her career?"

Suzanne surveyed her mother from red-rimmed eyes. She did not look pregnant. She was a thin, listless girl, though pretty enough in a commonplace sort of way.

"What a brutal woman you've become," she said. "I'm surprised I exist. I'm surprised you had any children."

"Our generation didn't have your opportunities," Sylvia said.

"If I wanted an abortion I could have fixed it up myself through the Student Health Service. That's what it's there for. I don't need your money to go to John Street."

Another family impasse. Colin's mind leaped, as it did so reliably, to a face-saving distraction. "You've mentioned it to Hermione?"

"Yes, I told Francis on the phone."

"Oh, the vicar," Suzanne said. "If you were a grandmother, you might not act so stupid."

"Now look, Suzanne—"

"It's obvious the way things are going. You just don't want to know, Dad. Other men . . . at her age."

"I think you ought to be concerned about your own situation; not about the way your mother and I run our lives."

"If Mum takes up with the vicar it will be in the papers. It will be a topic of general interest."

"You silly baggage," Sylvia said. "Are you going to pick up that phone, or must I do it for you?"

Suzanne picked up her glass of orange juice instead, and looked at her parents over the rim. "Cheers," she said. She swung to her feet, using the tabletop for support, as if her condition were much more advanced. She turned in the doorway to say something. Her brother came through it, knocking her aside. "Hiya, Wart." She gave him a cool glance, passed beyond retaliation. She had other things on her mind.

Alistair strode into the room, flung open the cupboards, and began to sneer at their contents. "Never any decent food," he complained.

"What did you want?"

"Sausages. Austin gets sausages."

"I hardly think so. In a vegetarian household."

"He has his own sausages. He's autonomous."

"Then go round," Colin said. "Perhaps he'll give you some."

"What's up this morning?" Alistair enquired. "You were having one of them funny silences, when I came in."

"A pregnant pause," Colin said. Sylvia made a sound of disgust. "It just popped out," he said abjectly.

Alistair poured half a pint of milk on his cornflakes, lambasted them with the back of his spoon, then dredged up a quantity of the compacted mass and thrust it into his mouth. "Just ignore me, just go on," he said. "Not getting divorced, are you?"

His parents exchanged a glance. "Should we have expected it, at some stage?" Colin said musingly.

"Not these days. Not this."

Alistair was gazing glumly at his melamine dish. Suddenly he lifted it and banged it down on the table. "Why do we always have these? Why don't we have no decent china?"

"Listen, sunshine," Sylvia snapped, "if you want gracious living, go and get it somewhere else."

"If you did get divorced I wouldn't live with you. Not either of you. I'd get a flat. I'd be a homeless young person. I'd be entitled."

"Well, as soon as you set up house for yourself," Colin said, "you can have thin pork links served on Crown Derby. Will that make you happy?"

Alistair got up, muttered, and kicked his chair. He was muttering as he walked out of the room, and hauling up his sleeve, no doubt preparatory to injecting himself with some addictive substance.

"I wonder why we bother," said Colin.

"I wasn't aware that you did bother. You've always been more concerned with the welfare of other people's children than your own."

"Oh, teachers' children are always worse than others. Their parents know from experience that there's nothing to be done with young people, and when they get home, they're not even being paid to try."

Suzanne said, "I'll talk to you. I won't talk to Mum. I don't want to be treated like a counselling session down the Bishop Tutu Centre. She's too good at making up other people's minds for them."

"She only wants what's best for you."

"I bet Hitler used to say that."

"She can't understand your saying you don't want an abortion. Myself, I wonder . . . I mean, it's difficult to see how an intelligent girl like you becomes pregnant by accident."

Colin's tone was moderate, discursive. He had always said that young people should have the largest possible measure of moral freedom. He had said it in the sixties, and had gone on saying it through the seventies; the sentiment was now in its third decade. He found it a little difficult, at times, to distinguish his own children's faces from those of the hundreds of juveniles who passed through his office in the course of the academic year, and he sometimes wondered if he would readily put a name to them if he met them on the street. Perhaps it was just as well. It was the first thing that Sylvia had learned on her social sciences course; the individual is always an exception, and the individual never matters.

"Has it not occurred to you," Suzanne said, "that I might want the baby?"

"Do you mean you got pregnant on purpose?"

"Not exactly."

"Not exactly, eh?" Like her mother, Colin thought. Contraception had never been an exact science with Sylvia. Perm any six pills out of twenty-one. None of the children had been planned, but not quite unplanned, either.

"I don't want to push you on the point," he said, "but as you have chosen to come home and involve us, I think you might take us into your confidence about the father. Is it somebody on your course?"

"No."

"Well, are you—fond of him?"

"He's married," Suzanne said. "A married man."

"How could you?" Colin said. He took a moment to digest it. "At your age, and with all those bright young men to choose from?" Suzanne shrugged. "I don't know what to say, Suzanne, I don't understand you." He sighed. "You haven't been the same since you came back from that peace camp."

Sylvia—who said "life must go on"—had gone out to do the weekend shopping. Colin thought it an astonishing proposition, considering her views, but he was glad to see her out of the house, and Claire with her. Karen was upstairs doing her homework; Alistair had not for some years been in the habit of accounting for his movements. For a weekend, the house was very quiet. The long stretch of the summer holidays lay ahead. It was another fine day, and the sun poured into the living room, hot and dazzling through the french windows. Suzanne sat in an armchair, her legs curled under her, her expression remote. No doubt she was thinking straight through the summer to the months when she would be quite changed by her decision, when the consequences of her choice would come home to her.

"If I have the child," she said, "he might marry me."

"Marry you?"

"He's always wanted a child. They've been married for years but they've never had one."

"Do you mean that you're trying to break up this man's marriage?"

"If that's how you want to put it." She stretched and yawned. She felt torpid, too lazy and warm to answer questions. She had been through it already in her head. She would have the baby for him, and he would marry her. In her life so far, she had never wanted anything very much; but what she had wanted, she'd usually got. There seemed no reason why this should alter.

"Have you discussed it with him?"

She leaned her head against the back of the chair. "Not as such."

"Not as such? You mean you've discussed it under the guise of something else?"

"That's what people do, isn't it?" She closed her eyes for a moment. "They discuss things, find out what each other's attitudes are. That's how they get to know each other. They talk generalities, don't they?"

"So that it may look to the outside world like a silly girl trying to break up a marriage, but it is really more like one of Plato's symposia?"

"I don't know anything about that," she said, yawning. Perhaps she really did not. There is an entrance fee to the museum of our culture, and for this generation no one had paid it. "Do you want my advice?" Colin asked.

"No."

"Why did you come home then?"

Suzanne reached out to get a cushion from the sofa, and shook it gently to make it comfortable. "I've given up my room at the hall of residence, and I need a permanent address so that I can claim benefit. Ask Florence. She'll tell you."

"I see." Colin's tone was grim; he meant to sound like a man who was mastering his temper only with effort. In fact, there seemed a leaden familiarity about the situation; as if he were an old man, with many many daughters. He looked at his watch. Sylvia would be back soon, and she would expect him to have some answers.

"Am I keeping you from your badminton?" his daughter enquired.

"Squash," he said bleakly. "No, that's all right. So that's what you see for yourself, is it, living at home and claiming benefit?"

"You would hardly want me to live on you. Look, it's temporary, Dad. It won't put you out. Karen can move into Claire's room, and I'll have my own room back. I need some privacy. As soon as we make our arrangements, I'll be off."

"Who? You and your man-friend?"

"Could you just draw the curtain a bit, Dad? The sun's in my eyes."

"Suzanne, do you have any evidence that this man you are involved with wants to set up house with you? When you tell him you're expecting his child, he may be horrified."

"I don't see why he should be. It's a perfectly natural thing."

"But has he told you, in words of one syllable, that he means to leave his wife?"

Suzanne closed her eyes again. "Oh, he means to."

"Do you think you could make the effort to keep awake? Your whole future is in the balance here."

"I don't know why I'm so sleepy. It must be my condition."

"Did you want to get pregnant? Are you one of those women who have to prove they can?"

"Everyone has to prove they can. All my friends have been pregnant."

They infuriated him, the little nest-making pats she gave to the cushion, settling it against the side of her head. "Haven't you any ambition?"

"What sort of ambition?"

"A career."

"There are no careers. There aren't even any jobs. Didn't you know there are three million people out of work?"

"You don't have to be one of them. Not if you graduate."

"It only postpones it. What do people do with degrees in geography? There aren't any cosy teaching jobs to take up the second-rate people, not these days."

"Cosy?" Colin thought of his probationary year; a time of his life when he had seriously considered hanging himself. "Why did you bother to go to university, if you thought like this?"

"I can just see your face if I'd told you I wanted to be a hairdresser."

Colin was aghast. "Did you?"

"Not a hairdresser especially. There are times when you're just as thick as Mum."

"Literal-minded," Colin said. "Not really thick."

He was touched, when he thought about it, by the way she still called them "Mum" and "Dad." Not that he expected her, like Alistair, to hail them as "Old Cow" or "Paunchy"; rather that in the somnambulistic self-sufficiency she had acquired, he expected her to label them Occupants of Parental Home; to find them some grey unemotive category that she could use on official forms. She was still such a child, after all, with her flat chest and her bitten nails.

"Suzanne, sit up like a good girl and listen to me. I'm going to tell you something I've never told anyone before."

"Oh, I wouldn't do that." She stifled another yawn. "When people tell you that sort of thing, they usually regret it. And then they hold it against you."

"That may be so, but I feel bound to, because I so much don't want you to make a mess of your life."

"And when people say that, they mean they're about to plunge in and muck up all your plans. Look, I know what I'm doing. I'm an adult."

"I don't think those two things follow."

"Go on then. Tell me your story. 'When I was about your age . . .' " She uncurled herself and rubbed her calves. "I'm getting cramp. I ought to go and lie on the bed."

"You can go up on the roof and perch on the ridge tiles," Colin said, "but for God's sake listen to what I'm going to tell you. About ten years ago—"

"What's the use to me of something that happened then?"

"The whole world doesn't centre around you, Suzanne. As it happened, mine didn't in those days. I was very much in love with a young woman whom I'd met at an evening class. I was contemplating leaving your mother in order to live with her." Colin rose from his chair and walked over to the fireplace; which had recently been rebuilt, and gas-logs installed. It had cost him an effort to speak; he could not turn his face to his daughter and show her that his mouth was trembling, and that his eyes had filled with tears. It would shake her faith in him, in his rectitude and solidity; if indeed she had any, after his confession. Simply to speak of it brought the pain back to him; how clogged and salty the throat, how heavy the weight behind the ribs. He had felt like this for months after his break-up with Isabel. It was the time of his life that, in modern terminology, he recognised as the nuclear winter; the many months of cold and dark.

"At an evening class?" Suzanne said. Her smooth sleepy voice was derisive. "What in?"

"It was called Writing for Pleasure and Profit," he replied. He could not imagine why it was only this aspect of the business that engaged her.

"So which did you get? Pleasure, or Profit, or some of both?"

"Neither really. We soon left. It wasn't for us."

"So that it may look like a silly man breaking up a marriage, but it is really more like adult education?" Suzanne examined her fingernails. "I can't imagine you going off with somebody. What was she like?"

"That doesn't matter. I didn't go off with her, can't you see that's the point I'm trying to make? I wanted to, I meant to, but in the end I couldn't, because of the responsibilities I already had. I made her promises; in fact, the first time we met . . . it was a time when, looking back now, I feel that more or less I was out of my mind."

"So you got back in your mind and forgot all about her?"

"Oh no. It's not as easy as that."

"Didn't you know what you wanted?"

"I wanted a new life. But in the end, you see, I preferred the life I had. My nerve failed. It's often that way."

"For you, perhaps. I expect it was just money really."

"I wish," he said, "you would not speak so disrespectfully of money."

"But how could you have supported another wife, and all of us?"

"Oh, you see the difficulty! Men do so seldom leave their wives."

"It happens every day."

"It happens not so often as you think."

"But my case is quite different."

"So you say. But you don't know what might happen, you don't know what might pull him back to her. It was Claire that pulled me back. Your mother got pregnant. You might think that if I could contemplate leaving a woman with three young children, then I could leave her with four; but as soon as she told me, I thought of the baby, the innocent baby who couldn't possibly be blamed for any of it. And then it seemed a horrible thing—" Colin stopped. He saw that he was doing himself no good.

"So it was the baby that decided it." She smiled. His confession, which had been so difficult to make, had not disturbed her at all. It had not helped her; she was beyond help, simply impervious.

"I suppose what it shows," he said, pricked into a final effort, "is how unpredictable human emotions are. I thought that my marriage was over. But here I am."

"Yes, here you are. But people want children: you can predict that. He's always wanted children, and Isabel has never been able to have any."

"Who?" Colin said.

"That's the name of his wife. Isabel."

He felt a superstitious shudder. It was as if she had taken the name straight out of his brain.

"This woman, who is she? What's her maiden name?"

"How should I know?"

How dreadful, he thought, what a ghastly coincidence that they should have the same name; his Isabel, and this unknown woman so soon to be tricked and left by the spry, the young, the fertile. "Poor woman," he said.

"Poor nothing. She's a prize neurotic. She's made his life a misery."

"There's no married man," he said angrily, "who has an affair, who doesn't tell the girl that his wife makes his life a misery. I did it, about your mother."

"Well, that's true, isn't it? She does."

"That's beside the point. Oh, I don't know." Colin ran his hand through his hair. "Perhaps I was wrong to say that human emotions are unpredictable. Predictable is just what they are, from where I stand. If there's one thing you can rely on, Suzanne, it's the perfidy and cowardice of married men. And if there's one thing you can't rely on, it's contraceptives."

"Oh, we didn't use contraceptives," Suzanne said. "It's unnatural and unnecessary. I read a book about it. People should go back to simpler methods. Like withdrawal."

Colin could not believe what he had heard. "Who is this imbecile?" he demanded. "Who is he, this moron you've got entangled with? What's his name? What does he do for a living?"

"His name's Jim Ryan," she said, stony-faced. "You probably haven't met him yet. He's your new assistant bank manager."

When Miss Anaemia came downstairs, she found Mr. Kowalski kneeling on the floor in the hall, his ear pressed to the knob of the kitchen door. "New doorknobs," she said brightly. "Get them on the market, did you? Or are they another mystery?"

Mr. Kowalski got to his feet with a groan. "Man rings the telephone," he told her. "I answer, says 'I am the Resurrection and the Life.' Is a code."

"Could be," the girl said. "Or a wrong number. Anyway, I was telling you, this woman came. She accused me of having relations with a man."

"Dirty minds," Mr. K. said. He touched her elbow in a commiserating way. Her helplessness moved him. "Poor girl. I think I have seen you long ago. In Warsaw."

"I've never been east of Thanet Island."

"I spoke metaphorically," Mr. K. said.

"It must have been my double. I've got a double, you know. I must have, because someone stopped me in the street once and said, 'How's your Auntie Frieda?' It was embarrassing. Anyway, this woman, she wanted to inspect the bedsheets. I told her she could if she liked. On the way out she pretended she'd forgotten which was the door. She walked in the cupboard."

"Planting a microphone," Mr. K. suggested.

"No, looking for his coat. This bloke. If I'd got twenty blokes, they couldn't touch my benefit. But if I've got one, they say he's supporting me."

Mr. Kowalski did not know what she was talking about, and this was not the only cause of his distress and alarm. He took the girl's arm. "In Bratislava we had a funeral," he said. "This seemed to work, but lately, everything takes a turn for the worse. This Snoopers. Phone calls. Voices of strange women. Like Auntie Frieda in the street. They get in here and change my doorknobs. I lock a door, they unlock it. This house is going to the bad."

"Perhaps we all ought to move out. Get a change of address."

"But where? If you are falsely dead in Bratislava, what avails leaving Napier Street? Besides, my dear, there is the dough, the bread, the vouchers. Those are expressions," he said, "I keep a book of them. What would happen to regular employment at sausage factory?"

"Oh, you needn't go away as far as that. A job's a job." She felt a restless pity for him; as much as you could for a nutter.

"This is all I do," he said. "I might as well be dead all these years. This is all I do, go to a factory for preserving meat." He shambled across the room, aimless, like some large farmyard animal avoiding its pen. Tears glinted in his bloodshot eyes; probably they'd been there all along, only she hadn't noticed them. She never thought much about anybody else; claiming benefit was a full-time occupation. Her mind was getting narrowed down somehow; certain phrases like "means" and "rebate" seemed to have taken on an over-riding significance, layers and layers of portent, which only peeled away for a split second, just as she was waking or falling asleep. When she saw a queue, she had an urge to join it. A hundred forms she must have filled in, two hundred; all this information spinning away from her, out of her head and off into space. The process was extracting something from her, filing away at her essence; she was no more than the virgin white space between two black lines, no more than a blur behind a sheet of toughened glass. "Toodle-oo," she said to Mr. K. and went out to pick up her dry cleaning. She was always having things cleaned nowadays; her own and other people's. She liked the dockets they gave you, with their mysterious serial numbers and list of exemptions closely printed; she liked the hot, depleted, bustling air, and the staff (flaking skins, pinpricked fingers) who were liable for nothing at all.

Muriel was feeling lonely. The Colorado Beetle hadn't turned up after all, and her life was certainly lacking in something or other. Companionship, that was it. At a loose end this Saturday, she wiled away her time filling in a coupon for a man for Lizzie Blank. She ticked the boxes describing herself as clothes-conscious and creative, and as her interests opted for good food and psychology. She put down her height as six foot two, because she didn't want to be messed about by any dwarves.

Evening came. On Saturday evening she went out on the town. She was a rich woman. She could afford whatever she wanted, a club with a variety act and the pub and fish and chips afterwards. It was Lizzie who had the outing. Poor Mrs. Wilmot would not have liked it.

Mr. K. had barricaded himself into the kitchen. He huddled over the stove, thinking of his long career in that part of Europe that now lay beyond the Berlin Wall. Sometimes he would take out his old atlas, open it at page 33, and trace the borders with his finger. They did not mean much; all borders seemed uncertain. He shuddered at the sound of the great boots on the stairs. "Poor Mrs. Wilmot would never tread so." Later, when the house had fallen quiet, he crept out and looked around him; looked up the stairs, and out of the small round window by the front door. Presently he knelt down, steadying himself with a hand on the wall. For a moment he was tempted to pray: Hail Holy Queen, Mother of Mercy, hail, our Life, our Sweetness and our Hope. Instead he leaned forward and cursed into the kitchen door-knob, in his fluent but ungrammatical Russian.

"Life is Sacred," said Florence Sidney, heaving herself into the back seat of the Toyota. "If I've said it once, Colin, I've said it fifty times, it would have been more considerate to us all to have bought a vehicle with four doors."

Shut up, you're in, aren't you? Colin thought mutinously. Aloud he said, "The Rolls is away being gold-plated. You know the problem."

"There's no need for sarcasm," his sister said. "Where's Suzanne, anyway? She could have come with us to see her grandmother."

"She's got enough on her plate at the moment," Sylvia said.

"I think you're very wrong to encourage her into an abortion."

"It looks as though you may get your way anyhow," Colin said. "She isn't listening to us. Look, let's give it a rest, shall we? We've enough to do at the hospital."

Saturday afternoon visiting was two-thirty till four-thirty. It seemed strange not to take the familiar path to A Ward (Female). Colin was no admirer of change for its own sake, and was disconcerted by the turn his mother had taken.

The Ward Sister met them at the door. "I'm so pleased you've come," she said. "We've made out who she is."

"What do you mean, who she is?"

"Well, she's taken on quite a new lease of life. You must remember, Mrs. Sidney, I'm one of the old timers, I remember your mother when she came in."

"She's not my mother," Sylvia said. "She's their mother."

"It comes to the same," Sister said carelessly. " 'I'm nothing,' she used to say. 'I'm empty, I'm nobody at all.' And then a few weeks after that she just gave up speaking, didn't she?"

All that was quite true. When they had come out of duty to sit by her silent bed, she had never shown any sign of noticing their presence at all. She must move, when they were not on the ward; but not much, the staff said, they moved her. What you mainly needed for geriatric nursing was a strong back.

"And so," said Sister, "since you left the other day she's chatted on nineteen to the dozen. We've not been able to shut her up. We had to give her a little pill to keep her quiet for a bit."

"But it's all a mystery to me," Florence said. "Whatever's woken her up again, after all this time? What did you mean, you've made out who she is? Who is she?"

"Princess May of Teck," the nurse said. "You know, Queen Mary, as she was before she was married. It took some doing to make it out. It was Dr. Furness that hit on it when he was doing the ward round, course he's had an education."

"But is it usual to think that you're a member of the royal family? I mean—"

The nurse gave Florence a sideways look. Every variety of madness was quite usual here, as was every degree of decline and dilapidation. "Dr. Furness said it was a benign delusion. It's not unusual, as these things go. There was a poor old lass came in with hypothermia, last winter it would have been, that thought she was her present Majesty. Used to knock her drip bottle about, thinking she was launching a cruise liner. The thing is, we were so short of beds we had to put her on A Ward, temporary. We think perhaps that's what gave your mum the idea, she did use to give her some funny looks."

"She gave people funny looks? That's more than we ever got."

"Perhaps she was beginning to come round then, do you see? Only perhaps it was a bit cold for her, and she went back in till spring."

"What happened to her? The other old lady?"

"She passed on."

, "But she left a legacy," Colin said. Delusions were handed on now like tables and chairs; shabby furniture from vacated brains.

On B Ward (Female), two long rows of ancient ladies faced each other, propped up by pillows; solid slabs of pillows, which bolstered their brittle bones. There was an air about them of tenacious and bottled vivacity, like the faces of those tribeswomen, bowed and wrinkled, who are surprisingly revealed to be only thirty years old. Their skeletal fingers, jigging on the bedcovers, seemed to be playing with strings of beads. Sometimes, a line of spittle running from their mouths, they would call out to each other in the querulous voices of the deaf; when a nurse passed they would hail her, and point with an imperious downward finger to troubling bits of their anatomy hidden under the sheets. As Colin and his wife and sister walked down the ward, their beaky heads swivelled, like a row of birds on a telegraph wire; their little voices piped in exclamation, and the sleeves of their bedjackets fluttered. They were all showing signs of upset; it was nearly time for the tranquilliser trolley.

"Hello, Mum," Colin said. His heart sank. He noted her tight lips and her ramrod spine, and he knew she was back. Propriety had always been her obsession; she looked him over, and looked at Sylvia and Florence, and spoke in a dry and peremptory tone: "Ladies, where are your gloves?"

Florence took a step back, colliding with the nurse.

"Steady up," the nurse said.

"I can't do it," Florence said. "I know what the end of this will be. You'll want to send her home. I can't take care of her, not any more. I gave up my career at the DHSS for her, and I've only just got myself under way again, after all these years. I won't do it, you'll have to keep her."

Sylvia put her hand on Florence's arm. "Okay, duck, don't get ahead of yourself."

"Anybody would think you weren't glad to see her better," Sister observed. "We'll probably pop her on C Ward for a bit, see how she goes. Though we'll have to get her on the go a bit, they need to be mobile. We don't know what the future holds, do we?"

Mrs. Sidney's face was quite altered: altered almost beyond recognition. In her younger days she had been fond, Colin recalled, of royal reminiscences, of the memoirs of escaped nannies and underfootmen. I shall have to watch my own reading matter, he thought; check myself over for signs of what I might become. He regarded her, aghast. Florence produced a tissue from her coat pocket and shed a tear. Sylvia frowned.

"Never mind gloves for now," Sister said to her patient. "Aren't you going to have a bit of an Audience?"

"Do you mean to say you go along with her?" Sylvia demanded. "You encourage her?"

"Put yourself in our place," Sister said. "Any response from her is welcome to us. What do we care who she thinks she is? If we can say to her, turn on your side, Your Highness, while I put this cream on your bottom, that's a sight better than heaving her over, a dead weight. And when we bring the cocoa round, and she thinks she's at the Lord Mayor's Banquet, she gets it down her, doesn't she? She's eating like a champion, she's twice the woman she was."

"It's such a shock." Florence pressed the tissue to her lips. "I can't take it in, can you, Colin?"

Colin turned and walked away, down the ward to the window. He peered out into the enclosed court below. It was a dingy back area, a tangle of pipes running across the scarred red brick, slits of windows with frosted glass open an inch to the sultry air. If there were a fire, he thought, how would they get them all out? A chalked sign on a wall said MORTUARY. Colin's gaze followed the direction of the arrow. A hospital cat stalked across the cobbles, leaped into a pile of boxes, and disappeared from view.

In the side ward off B Block (Male) Mr. Philip Field had decided to upset his daughter Isabel. He lay in bed, his eyes half closed, his hands folded across his belly. His daughter sat rigidly on a hard hospital chair at some distance from the bed, her face downcast.

"I think I might have a psalm," he said. "Yes, I think I'll go for 'The Lord's My Shepherd' after all."

"You aren't going to die," Isabel said.

"You know what Dr. Furness said. I could go at any time."

"How do you know that?"

"I listened in."

Isabel turned her face away altogether and gazed at the door, as if hoping for but not expecting relief. "Eavesdroppers never hear anything good," she said. "Nor do they deserve to."

Mr. Field tugged at the blanket fractiously. "I might have 'For Those In Peril On The Sea,' " he suggested.

"Whatever for?"

"For other people. There's no need to be selfish at your funeral."

"It seems a bit late to turn over a new leaf."

Isabel's voice, like her features, was colourless and remote. Her reproaches carried no weight. "I could have 'Abide With Me,' " her father said. "Like the Cup Final. 'Where is death's sting, Where, grave, thy victoree?' I'm thinking," he added, "of changing my will."

"Oh yes?" It had the effect of making his daughter look at him, though still without much interest. "And who are you planning to leave it to? You've only got me. You were never fond of dogs and cats, so I don't suppose you were thinking of the RSPCA."

"Ah, that's an assumption you make, that there's only you. There were more women than your mother in my life."

He smirked.

"Yes," Isabel said, "but I don't want to hear about that." She smiled tightly. "Put it behind us, shall we?"

"Funny you should say that."

"I don't see what's funny."

"You never know when people are going to come back into your life."

She stood up. "Will you stop?" Her face flushed, and she clasped her hands together, almost as if she were afraid she might hit him. "I told you, I'm not interested, I don't want to hear."

Mr. Field looked pleased now. He'd wanted reaction, and he'd got it. "Keep your hair on," he said. "They can hear you down the corridor."

"I didn't come here to listen to you rehashing your sordid past. Haven't you got beyond that?"

"Don't you remember, Isabel, when you used to lock me in and hide my glasses?"

"You got out all the same."

"You bet I did."

"It makes me ashamed."

"So it ought. Putting upon a lonely old man. Cruel."

"It makes me ashamed to belong to you."

"I'd like to think I have other children somewhere. Ones that aren't so particular."

"If you have, where are they?"

"I told you not to shout."

The door opened and a student nurse stuck her head around it, topped by her pert paper cap.

"Everything okay, Mrs. Ryan?"

Isabel turned to face her, shakily. "Why is he in a side ward?"

she demanded. "Wouldn't he be better on the main ward, where he'd have the company of the other patients?"

The little nurse averted her eyes, and looked cross. "Perhaps you'd care to take that up with Sister, Mrs. Ryan."

"Well," Florence Sidney said. She repeated it, shaking her head. Her brother took her arm and guided her across the car park. Sylvia trotted ahead of them; she was more resilient than they. Colin's expression was gloomy. Only a week ago, he had been a comparatively happy man. The holidays were approaching; if they did not promise a rest, there would at least be a break in routine. He was looking forward to some long early morning runs, and perhaps a game of squash at lunchtime, and then to having the house to himself in the afternoons while Sylvia was out and about on her various missions; to having his time free for some brooding, for some quiet introspection. This is really what I am, he thought: a quiet man in pursuit of a coronary.

But now everything was upset. He couldn't care for this reanimation in his mother. It could only be a complicating factor, the necessity to pander to the royal whim. And Suzanne: the decision was hers, but the consequences would come home to the family. Of course the man would not marry her, and she would have to live at Buckingham Avenue with the baby. He could not leave her to cope by herself in some bedsitting room or some damp 1950s walk-up that the council might let her have. There would be a further strain on the household budget; though he was a professional man, securely employed and more affluent than most, the Sidneys lived in that particularly common and edgy sort of poverty where daily life is comfortable only if nothing is set aside for contingencies. Besides, he could not imagine Sylvia with a grandchild in the house. She was energetic enough to cope with a small child while Suzanne went off to finish her course, but if she smelled of nappies and baby cream she would lose the admiration of the vicar, and then she would vent her spite on him. It was all a terrible mess.

But worse than all this was the conviction, running all afternoon at the back of his mind, that Isabel Field was about to re-enter his life. It was hardly reasonable to suppose that his Isabel was the one Suzanne spoke of, or was it? He did not feel very sure what was reasonable. Blind chance, he knew, could catch you a painful blow with her white stick.

The last time he had seen Isabel it had been a windy day, spring 1975, lunchtime, outside the coroner's court. Standing in the municipal car park, chilled from waiting, they had exchanged a few words less about themselves and their lack of a future than about the upsetting events which had brought them to the inquest, and which had occurred so recently in Evelyn Axon's hall. (It was his own hall now, of course, but he thought of it as a different house.) Though the verdict had been natural causes, a miasma of unease hung over the business; these had been Isabel's clients, and she had failed to foresee or prevent whatever had led up to the old woman's death. There had been bruises on the corpse, weals, fingermarks. It was more than likely that she had been beaten by her daughter—half mad or half-witted—that reclusive slab of a woman, hunched into the shadows, whose features Colin could never recall. Whatever the truth of it—and it hardly mattered now that the old woman was dead—Isabel's distaste for the affair had made her resign. "I'm out of it now," she had said.

And she had told him—he remembered the occasion perfectly, as if it were yesterday—that she intended to go in for banking; it was in the family. "It will be less complicated," she had said.

For months after their break-up, he had been in the habit of taking the car out in the evenings and driving to the quiet street where Isabel shared a bungalow with her retired father. Once he had even parked opposite, waiting where he used to wait to collect her on their few and nervous nights out. But the blank façade of the house had told him nothing he did not already know.

Once or twice a year since then, he had made a point of driving down that street. He never saw her. No doubt she was long gone. A FOR SALE sign had been planted in the front garden. She had married, moved away; her father (he supposed) was dead. She had gone south, emigrated, spun off into outer space.

Then they had moved to Buckingham Avenue themselves, to the dilapidated house that had come so cheap. All his weekends were devoted to DIY. On weekday evenings he would stumble about in the twilit garden, a stone inside his chest. It was like being consigned to purgatory, and still expected to go on schoolmastering.

But his heart was harder now. The sclerotic process had taken him over entirely and made him no longer the man he was, but a much more friable, brittle organism, with a shortened lifespan for any emotion. He had no feelings, since then; none that lasted, or meant anything.

Sylvia's voice broke in on his thoughts. "Give me your keys, Colin. I'll drive. You look shaken up."

". . . Actions which," said Sister, "in a younger and ambulant pervert would no doubt lead to criminal proceedings. Only just before the weekend he was found with his hand up the skirt of one of the cleaners, an elderly and respectable person called Mrs. Wilmot."

"I feel ashamed," Isabel said.

"Don't blame yourself, Mrs. Ryan," Sister said, in a tone which suggested that of course she should do so.

"He's in what they call his second childhood. Maybe I should have brought him up better."

"The vices do become compounded," the nurse said complacently. "The eccentricities, the little tics. It's in the babe in arms, Mrs. Ryan, and at the end of a life, that we see the true character revealed. Can I offer you a cup of tea?"

"No thanks. But in view of this behaviour of his, wouldn't it be better to have him on an open ward where you can see what he's up to? Surely you're increasing the problem by keeping him in a private room?"

"Why, bless you, Mrs. Ryan, your father has no compunction about what he does in public."

"He disgusts me," Isabel said. "He'd be better dead. I wish he were."

A token reproof came and went on Sister's face. Isabel's voice was frayed; it quivered. Leaning forward to replace the file, Sister caught a whiff of the alcohol on her breath. Only seven o'clock in the evening, and not the first time, either. A young woman like that, with a husband and every advantage. She had room, to talk about disgust.

When they got home, Colin went straight upstairs. He could not get Isabel out of his mind. Sylvia was in the kitchen making some coffee, and Florence was with her, lamenting the future and the lives they would lead if the hospital decided to pursue its intention of discharging its long-term patients into the care of their relatives. Poor Florence: mass unemployment had saved her career, and now another item of state policy was threatening to undo her. It wouldn't happen, Sylvia was saying; the old lass was too far gone, they could not discharge her while she thought she was May of Teck, and given a week or two she would no doubt lapse into her usual vegetable state.

Colin met Suzanne, hanging about aimlessly at the top of the stairs. "There's no point skulking around," he told her. "Don't you want to know what's happened with your grandma? I suppose you take no interest."

Suzanne's eyes were swollen and puffy, and her lips were raw, as if someone had hit her. "What now?" Colin asked.

"I phoned him. Jim."

"And what did Jim say?"

Fresh tears began instantly to trickle down her cheeks and off the end of her nose. She put out the tip of her tongue and tasted one, as if sampling the quality of her grievance. "I can guess," Colin said. "Why don't you have a lie-down? I'll see you later."

He went into his bedroom and closed the door. He sat down on the bed, catching the faint rise and fall of the women's voices below, waiting for a moment in case his daughter burst in after him. When he heard her bedroom door close, he stood up and went over to his chest of drawers. He slid open the small drawer, top left, and groped about, searching for his photograph. After a moment he pulled the drawer out fully and began to turn over his possessions, slowly at first and then with an increasing sense of urgency. Still nothing. He bent and peered into the back of the drawer, then slid it out completely and upended it onto the bed. Systematically he worked through his worn socks and unworn ties. There was an old address book, long superseded, its leaves curling at the edges, full of the large looped handwriting of his earlier self. He took it by the spine and held it up, shaking it to see if the photograph would fall out, but the only result was a yellow scrap of paper. He picked it up: PRIZE DRAW, CHRISTMAS FAYRE 1963, ST. DAVID'S SCHOOL, ARLINGTON ROAD. 1st Prize, Bottle of Whisky, 2nd Prize, Bottle of Sherry, 3rd Prize, Box of Chocolates. His heart beating faster, he began to fling his possessions into little piles on the duvet cover, and when this disclosed nothing he began to toss them into the wastepaper basket, the packs of shoelaces and the small predecimal coins and the bottles of after-shave, all unspent, all unopened, all the detritus of a half-used life. Soon the wastepaper basket was over-flowing, and there was almost nothing left on the bed. What there was left, he threw back into the drawer, picked it up, and replaced it. No sooner had he closed it than he opened it and searched it again, but the lining paper now showed its white spaces, there was no possibility . . . he tore the paper out, patted his hand over the wood. Nothing, still nothing. It had gone then. He scooped up the scraps of lining paper from his feet and compacted them into a ball. He was about to toss it into the rubbish, but instead, clinging to a last hope, he overturned the wastepaper basket onto the floor. The cap of one of the aftershave bottles came off and rolled under the wardrobe. Sitting on the end of the bed, bent double, he sifted through the rubbish at his feet. Nothing again. So it was not there. Gone. So Sylvia had taken it. He felt little need or inclination to raise his head from between his knees. Why not just stay like that? At least for some hours.

He had no idea, of course, when she might possibly have removed the photograph. He had not been in the habit of checking that it was there. He thought it was a fragment of Isabel, salvaged and indestructible, but it was not indestructible at all. He had not been in the habit of taking it out to look at it; he had been in the habit of knowing it was there.

He had been a fool then; he knew that Sylvia might come upon it. It was more likely than not. But somewhere inside, perhaps he hoped that Sylvia would be redeemed, that finding the photograph and dimly comprehending its meaning, she would no more remove it than one would remove flowers from an enemy's grave. Survival was the only victory; surely she would see that.

But this was unrealistic. Whoever thought there was anything dim about Sylvia's comprehension? Had she burned it, he wondered, or torn it up? Or had she done neither, but laid it aside for her private consideration? And what would she do to him now?

Slowly he sat upright, letting his hands lie loosely on his knees, gazing at himself in the dressing-table mirror. He formulated a phrase or two: the last thread of my aspirations has been cut. He felt self-conscious, rocking this startling grief, while the Old Spice soaked into the carpet. It's all right for you to laugh, he said angrily to the face in the mirror, but it matters to me, it matters a lot. He knew he was not formed for tragedy. Everything he had done and thought had been contained within the streets, the gardens, the motorway loop of this sad English town. But why did he need a wider sphere of action? The town was in itself a universe, a universe in a closed box. There was no escape, no point of arrival, and no point of departure. Every action, however banal, opened into a shrapnel blast of possibilities; each possibility tail-ended or nose-dived into every other, so that there was no thought, no wish, and no perception that did not in the end come home to its begetter. He slid forward onto his knees, meaning to investigate the stain that was growing at his feet. Of course, I could pray, he thought.

It's me, Colin Sidney; it must be, oh, ten years, God, since we were last in touch, but what's that against the aeons? I asked an awful lot, a decade ago, but now all I want's a bit of peace; isn't Peace your specialty? There was no answer, just a faint chatter and rustle, the sound of pigeons coming home to roost. He took out his handkerchief and began to dab at the broadloom.

CHAPTER 6

Breakfast time again. Sylvia slapped some diet margarine onto a minute square of toast and slowly spread it out. "Do you know what I read? I read that women of my generation had four children because that's how many the Queen had. Subconsciously, you see, we looked up to her as a role model. What do you think of that?"

"I've never heard such a load of tripe," Colin said.

His wife sat ruminating for a moment; for it was Point 9 of her 12-Point Diet Plan to eat at a leisurely pace and make each mouthful last. "But it might be true, mightn't it? I mean, a couple of years ago what would Suzanne have done? Straight off for a termination. But now . . . fertility's the in thing."

"I see what you're driving at. You don't find Princess Di nipping off to the abortion clinic, do you? You don't find her popping out for a quick vacuum extraction."

"Exactly."

"There could be something in it." Strange, Colin thought, how the preoccupations of the sane reflect those of the insane. And vice versa, of course.

❖

At the second phone call Jim had softened his line a little. He had stopped offering Suzanne the money to terminate her pregnancy, and told her to do what she bloody well liked. Suzanne did not repeat his exact words to her parents, or his sentiments, even inexactly. She was convinced that once Jim had got over the immediate shock, he would rally round and have a serious talk with his mad wife about an imminent separation.

On Tuesday morning, when Muriel arrived to clean at Buckingham Avenue, she stepped inside and found the atmosphere instantly familiar. The curtains were not drawn back properly, and the place was half in darkness. Upstairs, a long shadow slid across the landing. She heard a door slam shut. Sylvia sat at the kitchen table, slumped over a cooling cup of coffee. "Help yourself," she said. "The kettle's just boiled. The milk's sour, though."

"You're drinking milk, Mrs. Sidney?"

"Why not?" her employer said. "What does it matter? We're all getting old. I'm not going to keep my figure, I'm just fooling myself." Sylvia looked away. Her mouth was set in a thin hard line. "My daughter's pregnant." She propped her elbow on the table and sucked despondently at a thumb nail. "Lizzie, you haven't got a fag on you, have you?"

"Oh no, Mrs. Sidney, I never touch them."

"Don't you?" Sylvia's voice was dull. "I thought you had all the vices, duck."

"Which one is it, Karen?"

"Christ no, she's only thirteen."

"They say you can never tell these days."

"It's true, you can't. Better get to the shops, I suppose. Need anything?"

"No, but thank you all the same for asking. What a good woman you are, Mrs. Sidney! It's a privilege to wash down your fitments."

Sylvia smiled weakly. How odd the woman was. "But how

126

could you be any other," Lizzie asked. "Now that you see so much of the Reverend Teller? Oh, and by the way . . ."

Sylvia looked displeased now. "Yes?"

The daily was fishing in the pocket of her apron. "I saw Mr. Sidney, God bless him, he was rooting through the dustbin. Is this what he was after?" She held out her palm. On it were the two halves of a photograph. "Picture of Mrs. Jim Ryan," Lizzie said.

"What?" Sylvia stared down at it, horrified. "Picture of who?"

"It's a lady called Mrs. Ryan." I've seen her at the hospital, she was going to add, but bit it back in time. Her night job was another life, wasn't it?

Sylvia's fingers trembled. She took the photograph from Lizzie. She tried to fit the halves together; the girl's face, dreadfully bisected, stared back at her. There was a knowing look in each eye.

"It can't be. You've got the name wrong."

"Oh no, madam, I'm acquainted with this lady, I couldn't make a mistake."

"You're quite sure? You're quite positive, are you, who this is?"

"On my mother's life."

"There's no need to go to that extreme," Sylvia snapped. Her mind groped, very slowly, around the possibilities. "I want to know if you're quite certain."

"I told you. The old girlfriend, is she? Well, love makes the world go round, Mrs. Sidney. There's only one reason the gentlemen keep pictures."

"Shut up," Sylvia said. "That has nothing to do with you."

"Mr. Sidney seemed upset. Frantic, he was, throwing the rubbish about, got all yoghurt pots over his feet. I knew he was after it, but—" she gave Sylvia a broad wink—"us girls have got to stick together."

I'd like to sack you on the spot, Sylvia thought; except that if we're going to have a baby on our hands, I daren't. "Now listen," she said. "You don't mention this to anyone, right? Not to Mr. Sidney. Not to Suzanne. Understand?"

"Clear as day."

"So watch it."

At least she doesn't know the whole story, Sylvia thought. She's put a name to the face, but she doesn't know about the complications. And I won't tell Colin I know; not yet, anyhow. "Go and do the bathroom," she said. She looked down at the photograph again. It seemed to swim before her eyes. A sudden pain lanced through her right eye, her nose, her jaw. She was going to have a crashing migraine, any minute now.

Going up the stairs with her sponge and her bottle of nonscratch scouring cream, Muriel felt an intense gratification. There was no need to connive with destiny; the family were managing nicely for themselves. The air was choked with tension and spite, and on the landing all the doors were closed; it was just like Mother's day. The children were locked in their rooms, sniffing glue and crying. From behind the doors came the soft sounds of breathing. It was nothing now but a matter of time. There would be strange pains in the dark bedrooms, despair in the breakfast room where Mother's kitchen used to be. Food getting cold, food getting bad; soon the lightbulbs would go, and no one would bother to replace them. The bills would go unpaid, and dirty milk bottles would stand in a row on the sink. Sylvia's hips would grow to 44 inches, as was their nature, and she would waddle and roll about the house, and hide when the doorbell rang. Just as Colin's athletic joints would swell and crack with rheumatism, so autumn moisture would crack and swell the plaster and brick of the new kitchen extension. He would take to drink, perhaps lose his position. Sanctimonious Flo would be found out in some lewdness, and Suzanne's untended child would wail from the back garden, bleating for the peace of the clouded water from which it came. The evergreens would grow, blocking out the light at the back of the house; foul necessities would incubate in the dark. Soon cracks would appear in the walls, and a green-black mould would grow along the cracks and spread its spores through the kitchen cupboards, through the wardrobes and the bedlinen.

Given time, the roof of the extension would fall in. Where the lean-to had stood, the house would be open to the sky. Rubbish would fester uncollected, and the rat would be back. The girls, ostracised by society, would fall prey to crippling diseases. Alistair would be taken away to prison. No member of the household would fail to see their lives and motives laid bare. Their trivial domestic upsets would turn soon to confusion, abandonment, and rage. Acts of violence would occur; there would be bodies. Could they prevent it? She didn't think so. There was Resurrection, in various foul forms; but what came after? Now Muriel's rules were in operation, and the Sidneys were entirely in eclipse.

When Suzanne came downstairs at last, driven by hunger, Lizzie Blank said: "Don't take on so. It happened to me once."

"Did it?" Suzanne looked at her; she was interested. "I bet you've led quite a life."

"Oh yes," said Lizzie Blank. "A devastated charmer like me."

"And what did you do?"

"I got rid of it."

"That can't have been so easy, when you were young."

"No, but I had my mother to advise me. She knew all about that sort of thing."

"Did you have a good relationship with your mother?"

"In ways."

"I wish I had a good relationship with my mother. She's trying to push me into an abortion, you know, but Jim and I want this baby. Didn't you ever regret it, Lizzie?"

Lizzie thought for a moment. "I suppose I did. Not at the time. But nowadays I miss it. I reckon we'd have been two of a kind. And I need company."

"That's so honest of you, Lizzie. You're . . . such an honest person."

"I'd have liked to give it an inheritance. A lovely house like this."

"Do you think this house is lovely? I hate it. It stifles me."

"You'll be out of it soon enough."

"I'm going to get a flat or something, just till I get things sorted out with Jim."

"Jim your intended, is he?"

"Oh yes. But he's got to go through the divorce, you know. These things take time to sort out."

"So you could be on your own till the baby's born?"

"I hope not. I'm going to find a place, and he can move in with me as soon as he makes Isabel see sense. I mean, there's no point in dragging out a failing marriage, is there?"

"None at all. Mind, his wife will stop in the house, you'll need furniture, all that. Door furniture and fire irons I can get for you cheap, I have a friend. But I expect you'll need a cooker, you won't be able to afford to go out to restaurants."

"No." Suzanne looked bemused. "I expect I'll need a cooker."

"I've got money put away, you know. I can always let you have a loan."

"Oh, that's so sweet of you, Lizzie. But I hope I won't need it."

"Well, I like to oblige my friends. You'll have to look in the paper for a place to rent. I got mine out of a window at the newsagent's. But it wasn't easy."

"I know. There's not a lot of accommodation about. It's the same in Manchester, until I got my place in Hall I had to sleep on somebody's floor. But you can't do that with a baby."

"You could always stop with me a bit, until you sort yourself out."

"Oh, Lizzie." Suzanne burst into tears. "I'm sorry, I can't help it. To think that you should be so kind, when you're almost a stranger and don't know me at all, and my family who've known me all my life should be so horrible." Impulsively she threw her arms around the daily woman and kissed her violently rouged cheek.

"The offer's there," Muriel said.

The last days of the summer term were worse this year than Colin remembered. There was the usual rush and muddle, the disorderly behaviour on the corridors; and then there was his mood. For three days running he lost his temper before Assembly; the days went downhill from there. He was churlish in the staff room, and was seen kicking the stencil machine. He lost an entire stack of reports—Form 3C's—and they were turned up at last by one of the cleaners, who would surely reminisce about it for a year or more. He stayed late, signing them, tidying his desk, then lurked about in the staff lavatories, butting his head at a square of ill-lit mirror, trying to spot grey hairs. He couldn't wait for the term to be over; though what ease, what leisure awaited him at home, better not to speculate. Better not to think too far ahead. He was conscious of an almost physical revulsion, a shrinking away, whenever he tried to imagine how his tangled circumstances might be unknotted. Even when school was let out and his pupils were set free to run amok down the High Street, he paced the empty corridors warily—echoes, white tiles—as if expecting an ambush.

Sylvia flew about the house, bossing the daily woman, nagging the children; she jangled her car keys and sprinted down the path. He tried to corner her, scrutinise her expression, lead her into conversational byways which would perhaps reveal what she made of the situation. Nine years ago she had been obtuse. Now social intercourse had sharpened her wits. Weekly at the Bishop Tutu Centre she listened to tales of human improvidence, criminality, and perversion. Nothing shocked her, she said. Let her only enquire too far into current events, and she might have to swallow her boast.

"Colin," said Sylvia.

"Yes?"

"You ought to go and see this man Jim Ryan, and find out what's going on." She turned away, so that he couldn't see her face.

Colin swallowed. "Where, at his home?"

"No, not at his home, Colin. At the bank."

"Oh, but the fuss . . . at his place of work . . ."

"Is there going to be a fuss?"

"Well . . . that depends on his attitude."

"Perhaps you'd rather I go?"

"No," he said hurriedly, "no, Sylvia, I wouldn't want that. I'll deal with it. I promise you. We need to give Suzanne a little more time to come to terms with the reality of the situation. Then if she still insists that this man is going to set up house with her, I'll do whatever's needed—only please, Sylvia, let me do it in my own way."

"You're sweating, Colin."

"The topic makes me uncomfortable."

"Yes, I suppose it would." He searched her face. "Perhaps I could ask Francis to talk to her," she said.

"You can hardly ask a clergyman to talk her into an abortion."

"Oh, Francis has some very modern attitudes. He's full of common sense, you'd be surprised."

Here we go, the same sickening conversational merry-go-round. Why doesn't she take off with Francis, if that's what she wants? I won't stop her. And Suzanne should have Jim. And I should have Isabel. Even if it is some other Isabel; I should marry her for a penance, and for the sake of her name.

I think I'm going mad, Colin thought. And not a bad idea at that. Have the summer in a padded cell somewhere, and come home when it's all over.

Francis—the Reverend Teller—came round just after midday. Claire was in the kitchen, making one of her cups of tea for Brownie Tea-Making Fortnight. Colin and Sylvia were preserving, between them, a strained silence. Colin noticed how his wife's face brightened at the sight of Francis passing the kitchen window. She looked alert and keen, like someone ready to tackle a major social issue.

"Cup of tea?" Claire said.

"Why thank you, Claire, that's kind. I'd rather have coffee, if it's no trouble."

"I don't do coffee. Only tea."

Sylvia got up. "Hello, Francis. I'll get it. Claire, come from under my feet."

"Don't put yourself out," said Francis in his relaxed way, which somehow implied that he was used to people putting themselves out but would waive his rights on this occasion. He was a solid man of forty-five, with blunt features and short cropped hair; despite his pacifist outlook, he was given to khaki clothing of military provenance, to ribbed sweaters with elbow patches, to epaulettes and complex trousers with pleated pockets buttoned on the thigh. When he laughed he showed pointed teeth which were unmistakably carnivorous. His whole person, Colin thought, exuded contradictions which were just too deep for hypocrisy and just too common for clinical schizophrenia.

"Hermione's got us on the old camomile tea," he said. "Gets it at the health-food shop. Must say I get a bit tired of it. Cup of Nescafé, strong, black, that's the way I like it. Got any sweeteners?"

"How about sugar?"

"Oh, of course we have," Sylvia said. "Colin, do you have to embarrass me?"

The phone rang in the living room. Karen answered it.

"Mum, it's for you, it's Meals on Wheels."

"All right, I'm coming."

"Try this," Claire demanded, blocking her path and proffering a teacup. "Excellent, very good, or good?"

"I'm going to the phone, Claire. Give it to your father." Side-stepping her daughter, she gave Francis a sidelong glance as she left the room.

"Francis, you're an intelligent man," said Colin.

"Yes?" said Francis guardedly.

"I have to ask you something. No, not now, Claire, put it down. Do you believe in coincidence?"

"Coincidence?" The vicar took his pipe out and sucked it. "Funny you should ask me that."

Colin understood that the vicar had made a joke. A forced tremulous smile was his response. "No, but really?"

"I say, this is jolly good," said the vicar, tasting Claire's tea. "Of course I believe in it. Otherwise, when you were out on the street, you'd never see the same chap twice, would you?"

"Yes, well, that's coincidence at its most basic level—"

"Oh, very basic," the vicar agreed. "I say, what do I do now, fill in this mark sheet?"

"But I think I mean coincidence as a force, as an organising principle if you like, as an alternative set of laws to the ones we usually go by."

"Oh, Jung," said the vicar. "Where's a pencil? I see, so I put this little tick in here . . . Synchronicity, eh? The old acausal connecting principle. Arthur Koestler, old J. W. Dunne. *An Experiment with Time.*"

"Yes, I know all that. But what do you think of it?"

"Murky waters," said the vicar. He took his pipe out of his mouth and indicated with it; Hermione did not allow him tobacco. "Look here, let's pinpoint this, Colin. What exactly is it that you're asking me?"

"I don't know. Please, Claire, no more tea. My life seems to be falling apart, or rather—well, reorganising itself on some new principle entirely."

"For instance?"

"Oh, you know how it is. You have hopes, they're disappointed. You put the past behind you, find a modus vivendi. Suddenly it's under threat. The past seems to be the present. I look at the faces about me, some familiar, some not so familiar, and I imagine I can see echoes—shadows, I suppose you'd say—of other faces. The air seems to be full of allusions. I look at people and I imagine them to be thinking all sorts of things. I don't know whether it's reasonable or not."

"I wish you could give me a more concrete example."

"Cup number 27," said Claire. "The milk's smelling a bit funny again, never mind."

"Well, all this about my mother . . . it's as if she's come back from the dead. It's so unnatural to see somebody sit up like that and speak for the first time in years . . . it's deeply sinister, it's predictive, that's what I feel."

"Predictive of what?"

"I don't know. I wish I did know, if I knew I could prepare us for it. Our lives have been quite calm, all considered, for the past ten years, as calm as they can ever be when there's a young family growing up. . . . But now there's something hanging over us."

The vicar smiled; comfortable little pads, like hassocks, appeared beneath his chilly eyes. "Oh, come now, Colin. A touch melodramatic, if you don't mind my saying so."

"Things happen . . . they seem to have meaning, but they don't. A while ago I was mowing the front lawn. It was a lovely day. I was enjoying myself. Suddenly there was a set of teeth staring up at me."

"Teeth," the vicar said. "Human teeth, Colin?"

"Yes, human teeth. Claire, I can't drink this. The milk's off."

Claire burst into tears. "You're supposed to put down for the tea, not the milk. How can I get to fifty cups if nobody will drink it?"

The vicar said, "I'm afraid it sounds like a classic case of . . . something unpleasant."

"I'm glad you agree," Colin said.

"So have you thought of, you know, seeing someone? A chap?"

Suzanne phoned up Jim's house. Her heart fluttered wildly when she heard the ringing tone. There was a dull pain in the pit of her stomach, her throat was closed and aching. She wrapped her hand so tightly round the receiver that the nails turned white. All day she had been steeling herself to make the call. Again and again she had pictured it, rehearsed it in her mind. To make it easier for herself she had invented some superstitions and pegged them around her fear. I shall let it ring twenty times, and if after twenty times she does not answer I will be reprieved, and I can put the phone down with a clearer mind because it will be a signal that ringing her was not the right thing to do.

Between ring twelve and ring thirteen, the baby has grown a little, added a few cells to the person it will be. She sees herself relaxing her grip, replacing the receiver, walking away and out of the room to climb the stairs and lie on her bed. She closes her eyes. At the nineteenth ring, the phone is answered.

"Hello?"

Her voice sticks in her throat; comes out as a shrill little gasp. "Is that Isabel Ryan?"

"Yes, who's that?"

"Don't you know who I am?"

"I'm afraid not. Who are you?"

"It's Suzanne Sidney."

There was a long pause. She had expected it. She waited. There was no answer, but she had not heard the receiver replaced. Perhaps she had laid it quietly on a table and gone away. She could not imagine Jim's house. He had never described it. She did not know where the phone was, in the living room or in the hall; or perhaps Mrs. Ryan was lying on her bed, talking over an extension, and the receiver now suffocated in Jim's pillow. But somehow she sensed that Mrs. Ryan was still there; breathing, breathing quietly, gathering her wits. When the silence had gone on for a long time she said, "Do you know who I am?"

"Yes." The woman's voice sounded very far away. "Yes, I remember, I know who you are."

Suzanne waited. Then she said, "I think we ought to meet."

"You want us to meet? Why?"

"I should have thought it was obvious. We have things to talk about."

"I can't imagine what things. Suzanne, how old are you now?"

"I'm eighteen. Don't you know?"

"I couldn't remember. I'm not sure that I ever knew your age exactly."

"What *do* you know about me?"

"Not much."

"Aren't you curious?"

"Suzanne, is something wrong?"

"I'm pregnant."

"I see, and are you . . . distressed about that?"

Mrs. Ryan's voice had a strangely detached, professional note;

as if the whole thing had nothing to do with her. What a cold woman she must be, Suzanne thought. Everything Jim has said is true.

"No, I'm not distressed." She licked her dry lips, tasting their salt. "I'm rather proud, actually. I just need to talk the situation out with you."

"Well . . . that's all right, I suppose." She sounded puzzled. "Have you talked to other people about this? Your father?"

"Oh, he thinks I should have an abortion. Nobody seems to understand."

"You certainly should have proper counselling before you make your decision."

"I want to meet you. Alone, or all three of us, it doesn't matter. I think we ought to talk this out."

"Suzanne—no, calm down now—I can't think what to say, this has come upon me out of the blue. You see, how can I advise you? I don't know you at all. I suppose he's told you that I was a social worker . . . but really I can't imagine what he's told you."

"He's told me a lot. Everything that matters."

"But there's nothing left between us. It's been over for years."

"That's exactly what he said."

"Oh, so you think that an uninvolved person could help to sort out your problem?"

"You're hardly uninvolved."

"Look, have you tried the British Pregnancy Advisory Service? Their number must be in the book—"

"How can you be so callous? That would be very convenient for you, wouldn't it, if I got rid of it? You don't know how it feels, because you've never had any children."

There was a silence. She sensed that Isabel was deeply shocked by her remark. Perhaps she had gone too far; though it was no more than the truth. After a long time, the woman spoke.

"Suzanne, listen carefully. Much as I regret the situation in which you find yourself, I don't see how I can help you. What you do doesn't matter to me, one way or the other. And even what your father thinks, that can't matter now. I have troubles of my own." She hesitated; a long hesitation. "Perhaps in some way I'm missing the point?"

"I think you're missing it by a mile." Fright made Suzanne aggressive. "You do know who I am, don't you? You do know about our relationship?"

"We're not related," Isabel said. "What on earth do you mean?"

"Oh, very clever," Suzanne said. Her voice was shrill with exasperation. "He did tell me about you, how crazy you were, how you didn't give a damn for anybody but yourself."

"He said that?"

"And more. He said he sometimes wished he'd never set eyes on you."

Another pause. "Yes, I see. Well, I don't really need to know this. Not at this juncture. Goodbye."

Click. She had rung off. The bitch, Suzanne thought; the monster. Jim had not told her then. He had not told her there was going to be a baby. Unless she did know, and was trying to ride it out. There was something very strange about the woman's attitude altogether. Perhaps she was just one of those people who never face up to anything until they have to. Immediately she picked up the phone again and rang Jim at the bank. She asked to be put through to the assistant manager. He answered at once.

"Suzanne? I thought we agreed you weren't to call me at work?"

"Yes. We did."

"I told you: let me call you."

"But you never do, Jim."

"No. Well . . ."

"I rang up your house just now."

"That was silly."

"Why silly?"

"I gave you that number for . . . emergencies."

"Emergencies." Suzanne digested the word. "I spoke to Isabel," she said.

Jim swore softly. There was silence for a moment. The line crackled.

"Your wife . . . I'm not sure if she's very stupid or very clever. She didn't seem to know about the baby."

"She does now, I take it."

"Of course."

"Suzanne, get off the line. The switchboard will be listening in."

"All you care about are appearances."

"Appearances are all I've got," Jim said. "I'm ringing off now. I'll be in touch."

Suzanne put down the phone. She trailed upstairs.

Isabel lay on the bed, her head turned sideways on the pillow, watching the telephone as if it were alive. She felt sick; she didn't know if it were the phone call, or what she had drunk that morning. It's not often you get a call like that.

So that's what Colin thinks of me. Why did he talk about me at all then? What combination of circumstances made him confide in that hysterical teenager? And how did she get my number?

Her mind moved slowly, very slowly, in smaller and smaller circles. One day I ought to call Colin, and ask him how the past is catching up. Compared to her, he had nothing on his conscience. Errors personal, errors professional . . . memory with violence. Like a series of snapshots, or outline drawings, flip them through at speed and watch them move . . . Daddy slinking home from the park, Muriel Axon with her idiot head lolling above her strange blue smock. She suspected, and didn't let herself suspect; she had made connections, and tried to break them. She had punished herself; but of course that would never be enough.

She wasn't joking when she said she had troubles of her own. She smoothed her hand down over her body. It was all most unusual. There was nothing inside her but her liver, getting harder and harder. It was a horrible death, people said; but then it was a horrible life, wasn't it? She ought to be able to feel it, a tender mass expanding just below the margin of her ribs. Everybody knows what happens to people who harbour guilt; they get malignant diseases, and die. Not just little Suzanne who was pregnant. She had carried the weight around for ten years. Now it was becoming visible, that was the difference.

On Friday Suzanne went down to the Housing Aid Centre. She took some magazines to wile away her time, and a box of tissues, because she knew that she would keep crying every few minutes. She could no longer do anything about this; it was as if a tap had been turned on inside her head.

Yesterday she had told her mother that she saw no point in going back to university in the autumn. That had precipitated another row. She expected her father to see the sense of what she was saying because at least he knew something about education, and he could have confirmed how difficult it would be for her to go on studying. But her father seemed afraid of her mother nowadays. He didn't want to offend her. Mum had said that she needn't think she was going to mope about the house getting more and more pregnant, waiting for this man who was probably never coming. Claire had made her a cup of tea, and she had knocked it over in temper and fright. The atmosphere in the house was poisonous. As she ran upstairs again she had seen Lizzie Blank watching her; the look of speculation on the woman's face had been quickly replaced by an expression of sympathy and concern, and immediately she bent down, scrabbling under the hallstand with her dustpan and brush. The vacuum cleaner had packed up, the tumble dryer had broken, and the iron was overheating; perhaps there was something wrong with the wiring? Wiring? her father said: I haven't had the estimates for redecorating the kitchen yet, do you think I'm made of money? She began to cry again, at the look Lizzie Blank gave her, at this evidence of compassion from a total stranger.

At the Housing Aid Centre she sat for two hours in a waiting room surrounded by mothers with children. The women were pallid and harassed; each one of them was hung about by three or four plastic carrier bags. Although it was the height of summer, they wore great cardigans. She could not take her eyes off these cardigans; sagging and shapeless, hanging almost to their knees, or shrunken and felted and standing stiffly away from the narrow bodies inside them. Some of them wore jeans, others wore summer frocks with gaping plimsolls on their feet. Their hair hung in rat's tails, they had spots around their mouths, some of them sported tattoos. They made her feel an uneasy guilt, as if she had somehow been transported to the Third World. Some were heavily pregnant, some had babes in arms; they all had a couple of toddlers, running about the room, sucking from bottles or trainer cups, crumbling biscuits in their sticky hands. Every few minutes the one called William fell over, bashing his head on the corner of the table which stood in the centre of the room. Their mothers watched them with lacklustre eyes, unable or unwilling to check them. They climbed over the women's legs, snivelling and bawling; one of them took Suzanne's *Spare Rib* and tore it apart like a circus strongman. Suzanne didn't protest. She felt it was no use to her anyway. "Give over with that, Tanya," the child's mother said, "give it back to the lady," but she didn't move from her position, slumped forward on the metal stacking chair, her legs splayed in front of her and her eyes on the floor. No one spoke to Suzanne. She felt conspicuous. She should have padded herself with a cushion or something. The Centre's workers scampered about with paper cups of coffee, light-footed and glowing in their seersucker flying suits and their rainbow-coloured trainers.

"So just let me get a note of this," her worker said at last. "Lavatories two, bath, shower. Kitchen, lounge, breakfast room, utility, bedrooms four, okay?"

"But I can't live there. That's my parents' house."

"Well, it does seem to be the most viable option, I'm afraid."

"I'll take anything you have to offer."

"But we couldn't offer anything, you see, on the basis of what you've told us. Not unless they throw you out. And it's no good colluding on that, we'd have to have proof, and unless you were actually out on the street with the baby, there wouldn't be anything we could do."

"I suppose I should have given Manchester as my address. I

only had a room in a hall of residence, and I haven't even got that now, so you'd have had to find somewhere for me."

"In that case we'd have sent you back to Manchester. We'd give you your fare."

"It's impossible, isn't it?"

The girl shrugged minutely.

"I mean, those women out there, some have got two babies, and they all seem to be pregnant again. Why do they have so many children?"

"Because for children," the girl said patiently, "you get Points."

Charge Nurse Toynbee was just going off as Poor Mrs. Wilmot reported for duty. "Cheerybye," she said, snuffling. "Have a lovely weekend, won't you?"

"What about you, Mrs. Wilmot? On the razzle?"

"Shouldn't be surprised," she said, wheezing and sniffing, laughing her soundless laugh. "Course with me knees I don't go dancing, but I enjoy meself all the same." She went off down the corridor for her metal bucket and her mop.

Standing in the recess by the patients' bathrooms, near B Ward (Male), she watched Mr. Field's visitors leaving. His daughter looked paler than ever, shocked and wary. Her clothes were disordered; she was wearing a strange red anorak, smeared with oil, that could have belonged to her husband. She strode down the corridor; her husband scurried after her, his expression abject. He too was pale; his eyes seemed unfocused, as if he had been drinking. But it was only just after seven. Mrs. Ryan swept open the firedoors and passed through. Her face was set; she was a woman who had been disabused of one monstrosity, only to be presented with another. In the corridor beyond she started to run. Her shoes squealed on the corridor floor. Her husband swore, and broke into a trot. At the other side of the firedoors he stopped. He turned, and looked back through the smeary plastic panel. He hesitated, then began to walk back uncertainly to where the cleaner was standing, a bucket and a bottle of Pine-O-Shine in her hand. "Who are you?" he said.

"Me?" the despondent greyish face looked up at him. "I'm Mrs. Wilmot. I do cleaning."

"Do you know my wife?"

"Your wife? Oh no, Your Worship."

"What?" said Mr. Ryan.

"I said, oh no, Your Worship."

"She thought you were watching us. She said there was something familiar about you."

"Familiar?" The old woman looked scared and aggrieved. "I wouldn't be familiar."

"She thought she'd seen you before."

"Yes, course, sir, because I clean here."

"Yes, of course you do. She's got herself worked up, as usual. My apologies."

Mrs. Wilmot blinked; a single rheumy tear began a slow path down her left cheek towards her chin. "Oh, look now, I didn't mean to upset you. I wasn't accusing you of anything."

"You was." Mrs. Wilmot's voice quavered. "Theft, cheating, familiarity. Spying on you. I'll tell the charge nurse. There's tribunals. I'm entitled."

"Look, no one's accused you of theft, don't be silly." Looking uneasy, Mr. Ryan dug into his pocket and shuffled some small change into the cleaner's palm. "Why don't you . . . get yourself a cup of tea, or something?"

"Stout's what I have," said Mrs. Wilmot. "Sweet sherry."

"Yes, I see. Please don't upset yourself. Look . . . here you are."

Mrs. Wilmot bit off a tearful wail. "Brandy Alexandras." Mr. Ryan fled along the corridor after his wife.

"That dirty old Field's son-in-law accused poor Mrs. Wilmot of spying on his wife," said the Night Sister. "He accused her of stealing from his wife's handbag. And being drunk on the ward."

"Honestly," said the student. "She's only just got over her Sexual Harassment at Work. Poor Mrs. Wilmot, imagine. She ought to sue him."

"Bloody relatives," said Sister, "coming in here once a month and throwing their weight about. Salt of the earth, Poor Mrs. Wilmot. That blasted Field is a menace to womankind, if he pegged out tonight, I wouldn't touch him, I tell you: I'd leave him for the day shift."

"You do that anyway," the student said, earning a dirty look. "Mrs. Wilmot," she called out, "are you going to help us with the Horlicks?"

Mr. Field, his breathing stertorous, was propped up on a bank of pillows. "Another upset," he said. "Stupid girl, my daughter, always whinging on about something or other, never listens." He coughed hoarsely. "She's had another row with that wimp she married, sounds as if he's been getting a bit on the side. I was telling her what I wanted on my headstone, but she wasn't taking it in."

"Here's your Horlicks. Looking forward to dying, are you?"

"If I don't make arrangements, nobody will. I was thinking about a verse for the paper." He leaned over to open the drawer of his bedside locker. The *Reporter* shook a little in his hand. "Here's one I like:

> We shed a tear although we know
> Our dad is now at rest;
> God wanted him for an angel and
> He only takes the best."

"You don't really think you're going to die," Muriel said. She stood at the end of the bed, her colourless eyes fixed on his face. "You think you're going to hang around for months, putting your hand up nurses' skirts. You'd do it to your own daughter if she'd let you."

144

"It's not right," the old man said. "I should have grandchildren to put in a verse for me. My daughter hates me. She wished me in hell. That's not right, is it?"

"I could come and see your grave," Muriel said. "Me and my little mite." She approached the old man, peering down at him myopically. "I've got an idea about that. Just the bones of a scheme."

"Or this one," said Mr. Field, ignoring her.

> *"He went with ne'er a backward glance,*
> *And ne'er a complaining sigh:*
> *He knows he will see his dear ones again*
> *In the heavenly bye-and-bye."*

"I'm a changeling," Muriel said. "Did you know that, when you did it with me in the park? I'm not a human thing."

"Whatever's that?" said Mr. Field, coughing. "What's a changeling when it's at home?"

"It's a substitute. It's what gets left when the human's taken away. It's a dull-brained thing, always squawking and feeding. It's ungrateful. It's a disappointment to its mother."

"How you talk," Mr. Field said, showing his gums. "How about a kiss and cuddle?"

"Don't you laugh. A changeling's nothing to laugh at if you found one in your house. My mother didn't have the wit to drown me. If you throw them in some water you sometimes get your own baby back, but she didn't do that and so she had to put up with me. A changeling's a filthy thing. It's got no imagination."

"Well," Mr. Field said, "it must be an uncommon condition."

"It's not uncommon. You see them on the street. You have to know what to look for, that's all."

"Not much you can do about it, then?"

"A changeling's a cruel thing. It likes its own company. It likes its own kind. I thought if I had my little changeling back, we'd suit very well."

"Oh yes?"

"So I thought," said Muriel, sitting down on the bed, breathing hard, "if I could get a loan of a baby, just an ordinary one, I could try the trick in reverse. Throw in the changeling and get a human; throw in the human, and get a changeling."

"You're touched," Mr. Field said. "I've never heard of this before. It's horrible."

"A changeling can't talk."

"But you can talk. You're talking now."

"I learned it from other people. Everything I know, I learned from other people. I want to give my child a better life. Well, it's natural."

"Your child's dead," Mr. Field said in alarm. "That's what you told me."

"I don't know if changelings do die. Anyway, there's resurrection. Leave that to me to worry about."

"Where are you going to get a baby? You're tapped. You ought to be locked up. I've never heard anything so morbid. Get off my bed. I'll ring for the nurse."

"Nurse won't come. Nurse never comes."

"Look here," Mr. Field said, "you wouldn't do me a mischief, would you?" Suddenly he had turned cold; his eyes were glazing, he trembled a little, and dribbled from the corner of his mouth.

"Save me the trouble," Muriel said indifferently. "Your nose is turning blue, old cock. I think your heart's giving out. What does it feel like?" She waited. The room filled with his laboured breathing. "I'll do you a verse," Muriel said. "Our daddy's life is ended, No use to wail and blub, Let's toss him in his coffin, And all go down the pub." Leaning forward, she knitted her fingers into the front of the old man's pyjama jacket. "If God has called our daddy, We'd better come to terms, By squatting at his graveside, And cheering on the worms."

Mr. Field gaped up at her, his mouth opening slowly. No sound came out. Muriel flung back the bedcovers and with one movement haled him out of bed and onto the floor. He landed with a dull thud, and lay looking up at her, his legs kicking feebly.

For a few moments longer his mouth continued to open and shut. Muriel sank her thick neck into her shoulders, assumed a mournful expression, sniffed once, and walked out of the room, closing the door quietly. When the Night Sister did her rounds, Mr. Field was cooling rapidly: the surgical scissors she had armed herself with were not necessary. She summoned the student to help her heave him back onto the bed, and then left him as she had promised, to be laid out by the early morning shift.

Mr. Kowalski, too frightened now to keep to any observable routine, had given up his evening shift at the factory. He spent much of his day sitting fearfully by the stove, compiling his book of idioms. At night he took a turn round the block, keeping his eyes peeled. He was lonely, he said, and hungry for love. These sad nocturnal promenades were his only diversion. Mornings, he dozed off.

A letter came, pushed under the door. There was a rude message from the postman, saying would they please unseal the letter box, having regard to his bad back, who did they think he was, Olga Korbut? Muriel picked it up. It was addressed to one of her, to Lizzie Blank. Good thing Mr. K. didn't see it. He'd have thought it was a letter bomb, or something. She sneaked it off upstairs.

After work that night she went off to Crisp's to get into her Lizzie costume and meet her new beau. If she was a bit late, he wouldn't have to bother about that; she would explain that she worked evenings and had been kept later than usual. She was fresh and spry for dancing, ten-pin bowling, whatever he had in mind; it wasn't as if her work tired her. But would they hit it off? That was the question. Under her wig, under her make-up, she could guarantee that no one would know her from a human being.

But as it worked out, she was very disappointed by the young man from the dating agency. At the pub where he had arranged to meet her, he towered above the other customers; his height was all of six foot seven inches, and his long thin face was as morose as Poor Mrs. Wilmot's. People made remarks as they ordered their round. Muriel thought they should have gone to the Rifle Volunteer, where she was known and known to be dangerous.

"Clyde's my monicker," the giant said. "What I always say is, Clyde's my name, confectionery's my game." He laughed gratingly, but when he looked her over his face fell. "You're not six foot two," he said. "I've been done."

"So?" Her voice was flat. "You want to make something of it?"

You could tell that Clyde was not used to threats. Distressed, he sat over his pale ale, cracking his knuckles in a thoughtful way. "No, I've thought it over, you'll do," he said at last. "I'm not that bothered about the height. What I really wanted was a bird with big knockers but they don't give you a space for that on the form. Here, I've brought you something." He thrust two enormous fingers into his breast pocket, and produced a shrivelled rosebud, its leaves curling and its head almost severed from the stem. "Single red rose," he said. "It's romantic. My last girl was always hinting for me to buy her one. They think you're mean in the shop. They expect you to have a bunch."

"Who was your last girl?" Lizzie asked. "Somebody from a circus?"

"Now don't take on," Clyde said. "Here, they're calling last orders, and I've hardly wet my whistle. Your round."

In the scramble for last orders, several customers tripped over Clyde's legs. He cursed them horribly. "I may as well tell you now," Lizzie said, "you won't do for me. I like manners."

"I've a good job," Clyde insisted. "Fancy cakes to customers' requirements. I'm highly thought of. Every year I do a butter sculpture for the Rotarians' dinner dance." Lizzie shook her head. "Well, we're not packing it in yet. I've paid out hard-earned money for this introduction. I can see you're just my type. I could really take a fancy to you."

Lizzie was adamant. Clyde's morosity deepened. "Have a heart," he said. "You're the first bird I've really had a chance with. It's not good for me to be rejected, it gives me complexes. I'll follow you," he warned. "I'll track you down. I'm very loyal. You'll never shake me off."

"If you follow me, I'll call a policeman."

"I bet you would," Clyde said. "I bet some of them policemen are customers, eh? If you're not a pro, why do you dress like one, eh? Women like you shouldn't apply to agencies. You could be liable for it, you put down your wrongful employ. You put you was medical, bet you've never been near a hospital in your life. Except down the clap clinic."

"That's where you're wrong," Lizzie Blank said with dignity. "I'm leaving. You can drink my drink if you like."

"Oh, come back," Clyde said. "Come back. I really like you, you know."

But Lizzie swung the door back in his face, and stepped out alone into the street.

It was Sunday teatime. Florence brought her shortbread round; and her thoughts.

"Girls manage," she said. "Girls today are independent. There's no stigma any more."

"Nobody said there was stigma," Sylvia said levelly. "Nobody mentioned it. But we've got to think about her future."

"What about the baby?" Florence cried excitedly. "Isn't that entitled to a future too? It may not be very convenient for you, Sylvia, it may not fit into your plans, but it's a question of the sanctity of life."

"If you say that phrase once more," Sylvia said, "I'll pick up this shortbread and force it piece by piece down your throat until you choke."

"There's no need for that," Florence said composedly. "I'm entitled to speak my mind. And it's no good telling me that I don't know Life, Sylvia. We at the DHSS know all about hardship. From behind our counter we see human existence in the raw. You can't tell me anything."

"I can never understand it," Colin said. "You people who are against abortion and euthanasia are always against artificial insemination and surrogate mothers as well. I don't know what your position is. Do you want more people in the world, or don't you?"

"I think you're being just a teeny bit frivolous, Colin," Florence said. "I've nothing at all against artificial insemination. For cows. The point I'm trying to make is that even if this young man doesn't want to marry Suzanne—and she can hardly expect him to up and leave his poor wife—then there's no reason why she shouldn't have the baby and bring it up herself. Lots of people do it. They always have."

"I wish you'd stop discussing me," Suzanne said. "It's my choice and I've made it. Leave me alone. I want to be on my own."

"Do you?" Sylvia said. "I've got news for you. You will be, love—whether you want it or not."

Colin went into the living room. He threw himself into a chair and switched on the TV. His daughter followed him. "Do you know what Jim says now?" she demanded.

"No, but I can see that you're going to tell me."

"He says he's got to stay with Isabel because she's on the point of a nervous breakdown. Her father's just died and she's gone all to pieces about it. She says she wished him dead so she's to blame."

"Her father?" Colin sat up. "What was he called?"

"How do I know? Dad, whenever I ask you for any help all you do is ask the most irrelevant questions. This woman Isabel, I could tell she was mad when I talked to her on the phone."

"You talked to her on the phone? What did you do that for?"

"I thought we might meet and talk things over."

"Did you tell her your name?"

"What do you mean? Of course I did."

"What did she say?"

"Look, don't get all excited, Dad, I know you think it was the wrong thing to do, but put yourself in my shoes. I told you, she sounded crazy. She didn't seem to know what I was talking about."

"Perhaps Jim hadn't told her about you."

"I thought that . . . but if he hadn't, how would she have known my name at all? It was as if she knew me—do you know what I mean?—in another context entirely."

Colin fell back into his chair and stared at the TV. It was an early evening variety show. To the accompaniment of facetious patter, a magician held up a burning spike and passed it slowly through the forearm of his studio volunteer. The audience applauded. The magician withdrew the brand, and held it flickering aloft. The volunteer's face wore a set, worried smile. There was an expectant hush; a roll of drums; and then the magician, with great deliberation, whipped the flame through the air and poked it cleanly through his victim's chest.

CHAPTER 7

Now the summer was over. Suzanne moped about the house, making no plans. Her father understood her failure of will. "When the baby's born," she said, "Jim will think differently about it."

Every night she scanned the FLAT LETS column in the evening paper. The properties were taken by the time she got to the phone. She talked about going back to Manchester to her friends, to join a squat in Victoria Park, but she did nothing about it. Pregnancy made her lethargic. Such energy as she could summon she spent on keeping out of her mother's way. "You should have got rid of it before it was too late," Sylvia said. "Upsetting us all like this. Breaking up our family life."

Outside the house, Sylvia was busier than ever. She had joined a body called ECCE, invented and chaired by the vicar—Environmental Concern Creates Employment—and she spent a lot of time with Francis, attending meetings and lobbying at the town hall. ECCE wanted a grant to get to work on some of the derelict land left in the wake of the motorway link. It wanted to take a few teenagers out of the dole queue, perhaps "offer hope," as it put it, to some of the older, long-term unemployed. Urban renewal was its object. Colin could not applaud it, not entirely. Come friendly bombs and fall on the entire North West and Midlands was more his idea. He could not remember a time—except after his break-up with Isabel—when his mood had been so black.

The vicar, he noticed, talked constantly about sewers. We were living, he said, on the legacy of the Victorians. Britain's sewers had reached crisis point; a whole army of the unskilled could be put to work, renewing the system. To anyone who would listen he painted a vividly horrible picture of the disruption and decay which the pavements hid from view. Hermione had become a vegan. Colin felt sorry for him at times. His standards of comfort must be low, if he found comfort in Sylvia.

It was understandable that Sylvia should wish to spend as much time as possible outside the house. Each member of the family seemed to have marked out his own territory. Alistair, seldom at home himself, kept his bedroom locked whether he was in it or not. No one cared to imagine what lay behind the door. It had not been cleaned in months. Suzanne stayed in the bedroom from which she had evicted Karen; moon-faced and lank-haired, perpetually tearful, she crept downstairs when she heard her mother going out, and lumbered up again when she heard Sylvia's key in the front door. Karen had colonised the living room. A studious child, she did her homework with a green felt-tipped pen, sitting at the big table. Presently she was found to have carved her initials in this table, and to have commenced a more ambitious work, "ALISTAIR IS A W—." She was mutinous about the interruption to her labours. Colin might have let her finish, if it would not have meant the expense of a new table. He did not know that the young were interested in carving any more. It seemed a charming survival from a more innocent age.

The kitchen was occupied by Lizzie Blank, the monstrous domestic; without her labours, the house would cease to be a going concern. She was joined there by Claire, who was doing her cookery badge; her boiled eggs were often the only hot food prepared in the course of a day, but after the consumption of a few dozen they tended to pall. Sylvia, if she wanted peace and privacy, was driven to the marital bedroom, repository of her blighted hopes.

Is it possible, Colin asked himself, that I once really loved Sylvia? Did my heart beat faster at her approach? And not just with fear? Since the debacle ten years ago, Colin had come to believe that romantic love is an artefact, an invention of the eighteenth century. In a proper world, waning passion for breast and thigh would have been replaced by a solid affection for broad acres, an admiration for the odd copse and millstream. Given a proper respect for the social order, he would never have looked twice at Sylvia; it was hard to imagine her bringing him anything except some bad debts and a consumptive cow. In a proper world, their marriage would never have happened; he blames the century for his plight, the Rousseauist affectations of his forebears.

Meanwhile the two back rings on the cooker had given out entirely. The electric kettle had fused, and they had to boil up water in a milk pan. The toaster burned everything that was put into it, then catapulted it around the room, and the washing machine, unless operated on the Delicates cycle, pumped water all over the floor.

That pernicious fallacy was flourishing again in Colin's life: that given Isabel, it would all be different. He knew it was a fallacy, and it caused him pain; he tried to uproot it from his life, to stamp it out. But he scanned all crowds, department stores on a Saturday, the people at the railway station that he passed every night as he drove home from school. The image in his mind was the image of the woman in the photograph, and what frightened him most was the knowledge that he might pass her in the street, stand behind her at the checkout in the supermarket, and not even notice her, so fast and so much did women change, making over their bodies and their emotions like deceitful insects from one year to the next. Isabel was an aberration; but must he not have his aberrations? He looked into the faces of women drivers who pulled up next to him at traffic lights.

The academic year had now begun. The bill came in for redecorating the kitchen. Sylvia thought that, after all, they ought to buy a new dining table; she could not undertake the purchase and laundering of tablecloths, because she and Lizzie Blank would soon be fully occupied. Mrs. Sidney was coming home. Twice a week now they went to St. Matthew's to see her, and the hospital was talking about a discharge date.

Throughout the summer, the old lady had remained unshakable in her royal delusions; but these had not hindered her physical progress. She was moved to C Ward; she had her own chair in the day room, and made her neighbours miserable by grilling them on protocol and criticising their dress.

"Look here," said Colin, when Sylvia sent him to buttonhole the consultant. "You can't seriously expect us to manage her at home. One of the nurses told me that it was quite usual to believe that you were a member of the royal family. That can't be right?"

"How painfully," said the physician, "has she imposed order on the chaos of her internal world! All time has stopped for her. Reality is many-sided. If she remains incontinent, of course there are these special pads you can get."

"But for God's sake," Colin said, "we're not nurses, we won't know how to deal with her. What will she think has happened, where will she think she is? She's used to hospital life."

"Ah," said the doctor, "there we have it. We believe the rigidity of institutional life has provided a too forceful model for her inner reality. She has become occupied with rules, procedures, precedents, and routines. The institution has become, in fact, an external psychosis. Besides that," he said impatiently, "if she shouts at you we can give her a pill."

"I've never heard such rubbish," Sylvia said when he got home. She was sitting in the kitchen with Francis; Francis, with evident enjoyment, was eating a boiled egg. "It's a con trick, all this about discharging people into the community. They're doing it to save money."

"Quite true," Francis said, dabbing at his upper lip with a piece of kitchen roll. "Community care properly carried through is a most expensive option. Done shabbily, it's cheap. The social workers, God bless them, have been urging it for years. Now they've fallen right into the budgeters' trap."

"I've never heard you ask God to bless anyone before," Colin said.

"Francis is right."

"I know he is. That doesn't help us though."

"Daddy," Claire said, "you should see the way Lizzie eats eggs, it's really disgusting. She cuts a piece off the end, then she sucks it out—like this—"

"And Florence won't give up her job to look after her," Sylvia said. "She loves it, turning people down for heating allowances, that sort of thing."

"Oh, now why should she give up her job?" Colin said. "Be fair. She did her share of caretaking before Mother went into St. Matthew's. If Mother comes home, we'll have to split her between us."

"You mean, me and Florence will have to split her. You'll be sheltering behind your job. I'll be running up and down stairs with disgusting buckets and bandages—"

"You make it sound like Scutari."

"—and you'll be sitting in your nice tidy office ruling lines and sticking little coloured pins in wall charts."

"Perhaps Colin can help out at weekends," Francis suggested. "And can't you get an attendance allowance?"

"I'll have to ask Florence about that," Colin said. "She'll know the daily rate for a lady-in-waiting."

"I wish I had a job," Sylvia said. "I wish I could go out to work and escape the things that are going on in this family. I should have done that years ago, got a full-time job and made myself independent and let you lot get on with it. At least before I was married I had an income to call my own, but since then I've been a slave to my family."

"I always thought you married straight from the schoolroom," the vicar said. "What was your work?"

The question caught Sylvia unprepared. "I was in charcuterie," she replied hastily.

"Can you get Lizzie to work some extra hours?" Colin asked. "We'll afford it somehow."

"She has a night job. Hermione wanted her, but she said no."

"Well, ask her again. Perhaps her circumstances have changed."

"I could up her hourly rate a bit."

"No, I don't think you could. Unless bankruptcy takes your fancy."

"We can't expect her to work for love. When the baby comes we'll be wading around up to the knees in excrement."

"We will be anyway," the vicar said, "if something isn't done about Britain's sewers. Do you know that in Greater Manchester there've been fifty major collapses in ten years? They measure them by how many double-decker buses you could drive through."

"What an extraordinary concept," Colin said whimsically. "I wonder if the passengers are given any warning?"

October came. Suzanne was in her fifth month; the miners' dispute with the National Coal Board was in its eighth. Sylvia laid candles in, despising the government's assurances that there would be no power cuts. That would be the limit, she said, spending New Year's Day in the dark. Suzanne stopped telephoning Jim Ryan, and gave herself over to waiting. "I'm glad I'm pregnant," she said. "It's something to do."

Not far away, in Wilmslow, an Iron Age corpse was found in a bog. "Here, let me see it," Alistair said excitedly, tearing the newspaper from his father's hands. " 'The whole body survived because of the absence of—' what's this?"

"Oxygen," Karen said, reading over his shoulder. "Didn't you do no chemistry? 'Because of the absence of oxygen in the water-logged bog.' "

"Here, give it to me, it's mine," Alistair said, shrugging his sister off and hunching over the newspaper. " 'May have been a ritual sacrifice.' We could do with something like that for us rites."

"What rites?" Colin enquired.

"That we have at us den. Austin runs them, sometimes we have guest ministers. It's like evensong, but bloodier. Listen to this, Kari. '. . . bashed him twice on the head with a narrow-bladed axe, and slashed his jugular vein to obtain his blood.' "

"I hope this isn't giving you ideas," Sylvia said disapprovingly.

"This is how he was found. 'Face twisted and squashed into one shoulder, forehead deeply puckered, teeth clenched tightly together . . .' " Alistair laughed raucously. "Sounds just like you, Dad."

Colin took the paper from his son. He ran his eyes over the description of the bog man, and noted that the historian Tacitus had opined that the barbarians drowned in bogs those who had committed "heinous crimes, such as adultery." He felt indignant; the poor man might just have been mugged. There was a knock at the kitchen door. Lizzie Blank was arriving for work, taking off her leopard-skin jacket. "Can I have that paper when you've finished with it?" she asked. Colin sucked his underlip speculatively. "He is expected to go on show to the public," he read, "freeze-dried, at the British Museum, in about two years' time."

These days Muriel found that she was seeing less and less of her old friends. She still called at Crisp's to change her personality, but very often he was out, and there was no longer a note on the table to say where he was attending service. The nights began to draw in, and Sholto's shop was burgled, cleaned out over two successive nights by people who came in through the skylight. The shop was to be closed down anyway; he had lost his job, and was sleeping rough. They were drifting apart; she doubted that there would be any day trips next summer.

Clyde, from the dating agency, had been as good as his word. He'd told her he'd track her down. It was foolish of her, she now realised, to have let Lizzie Blank use Poor Mrs. Wilmot's address. He was neglecting his butter sculpture in favour of hanging around in the street. He scanned the upper windows of Mr. K.'s house, and paced around the block with his great hands swinging.

You had to credit him with determination, and initiative too. He knocked at the door one day, with a baker's tray and some cock-and-bull story, and gave Mr. K. a wheatmeal loaf.

Mr. K. shut the door on him before his story was over. The features seemed to have shrunk in his coarse bristling face, as if his eyes wanted to turn and look into the skull. He held the loaf at arm's length, and carried it into the hall; there was a small table in the hall, and there he placed it. With one hand he massaged his ribs, around the heart.

When Miss Anaemia came home she stopped off to poke its crust with her starved finger. "Your bread's come," she called. She went into the kitchen. "What are you doing cleaning a gun?" she asked. Then she burst into tears. "They've stopped my giro," she said. "They've accused me of cohabiting with a giant."

"Wait," cried Mr. K. He put down the gun. "It is the same giant who delivered the loaf, there could not be two such. I took him for some pal of Snoopers." He wrung his rag between his hands. "I have asked Poor Mrs. Wilmot to cast light on the matter, but she cannot. She says that she does not know the giant, and the giant does not know her." He sat down shakily in a kitchen chair, holding his head. "I am ill, my dear young lady, with the suspense. I have a message in the hall, menacing me about my letter box, signed by Olga Korbut. That is why I am cleaning my Luger. As for the bread, it is no doubt poisoned. Please to leave it where it is, and if in need take some of this Hovis."

"Thanks very much," Miss Anaemia said. She scrubbed away her tears with the back of her hand and picked a slice or two out of the wrappings. "Cheers," she said. Her emotions were short-lived; it was just as well, of course. It didn't do to get excited about the future, or too attached to any project; you never knew when some change in the benefit rules would turn your life upside down. It was companionable, here at Napier Street, but they were talking about chopping rent allowances and making young people move on. In the world outside people called her Anne-Marie, and asked her to account for yourself; have you seen a psychiatrist? they said. If she left here she'd have to go home to Burton-on-Trent and live with her mum and dad, who never spoke to each other, and who made it clear that she was a big disappointment, and asked why she hadn't gone to work for Marks & Spencer. They only take quite wholesome people; Mum and Dad didn't seem to realise that.

On the night of old Mrs. Sidney's discharge, Poor Mrs. Wilmot gave in her notice. She would be sadly missed, the nurses told her, by staff and patients alike. A willing, stooped, humble body, with her heart in the right place; the cleaners were being privatised, and they would not look upon her like again.

She went down Eugene Terrace, to Crisp's house. He and Sholto were eating sausage rolls together. "If you want a revenge for Effie," she said, "you can get on with it now."

Crisp said the hospital had killed Effie, that she'd got pneumonia and they'd let her die; seeing that she was old, and mad, and not worth the antibiotics. In fact she had been far gone when the ambulance brought her in, frozen and raving. But they had to amuse themselves. Crisp was trying to get into trouble by hanging around with juveniles. As for Sholto, he said he was sick to death of the soup at the night shelter. They were both scheming to be sent back to Fulmers Moor. It didn't matter to her, because her scheme was one she had to carry out alone; she didn't need their help, or anybody's.

Mother had not materialised; but often, as she polished the scratched dining table at Buckingham Avenue, Muriel thought she felt her hanging in the air. She wanted her and didn't want her, that was the trouble. She couldn't explain that to Crisp and Sholto. She said goodbye to them and went downstairs. It was ten o'clock when she got out into the street, and the Mukerjees were closing up the shop. A plump Asian gentleman was drawing away from the kerb in his big car. He drove slowly behind Lizzie Blank as she minced along to the corner. He put down his electric window, leaned out, and made her an offer. She stopped dead, staring at him. As if he had not made his meaning clear, he held up a fat paper packet and jingled it. "Ten pounds in five pees, all yours," he told her. He smiled encouragingly, showing a gold tooth. They were heading for the wasteland; there were no street lights now.

Just his white cuffs gleamed in the darkness, and his gold ring and his gold tooth. "Name your price," he told her. Her heart began to thud. She felt a desperate strangling rage rise up inside her. When the box breaks, the baby will fall, out comes Little Muriel, teeth bones and all. She raised her fists at the man in the car, and a great hoarse bellow rose out of her chest and echoed back down the dark caverns of the Punjab. Sweat starting out on his face, the man put his foot on the accelerator and roared away into the night.

When the ambulance drew up outside Florence's house, all the family except Alistair were waiting in the front garden. Colin's face was drawn with apprehension, but his wife and sister looked like women who knew exactly what to expect. The two little girls, who had been briefed about their grandmother's misapprehensions, were giggling and practising their curtseys; Claire had insisted on wearing her Brownie uniform. Suzanne lurked in the shadow of the porch, with a blanket round her shoulders. As the winter came on she looked more and more demoralised and disreputable. There were whole days when she didn't speak a word to anybody, and didn't set foot outside the house.

The back doors of the ambulance opened, and the ambulance men lifted Mrs. Sidney and her wheelchair and set them carefully on the ground. One of them waved in the direction of the family. They swivelled the chair in the road, edged it onto the pavement, and pushed it to the front gate. Mrs. Sidney was swaddled in a gay scarlet blanket: only the top of her head showed. "Here we go," the attendants cried, running her up the path. "She can walk, you know, but she says it's not etiquette. Are we glad to see you lot! Took one old lass home last week, the whole family had done a moonlight. Like the *Mary Celeste*. Took the police a week to find them. Said they'd gone up to Aberdeen looking for work on the North Sea oil."

As they brought the wheelchair to a halt, Mrs. Sidney's skeletal hand emerged from her wrappings. She pulled the blanket aside from her face and peered out. "Where's your father?"

she enquired of Colin in her rasping voice. Colin looked at Sylvia for aid.

"Tell her," Sylvia said. "Tell her he's dead. Don't pander to her."

Colin cleared his throat. "He's passed on, Mother. Don't you remember? It was, oh, ten or eleven years back."

"Don't be ridiculous," Mrs. Sidney said. "I expect he's off shooting at Sandringham. Who is that woman in a certain condition, standing in the porch?"

"Well, can we give you a hand?" the ambulance men enquired. "Where do you want her? Upstairs, downstairs, in my lady's chamber?" Suzanne stood back to let them pass. They winked at her on the way out. "Give us a call if you start up sudden, love. Twenty-four-hour service, that's us, no job too large or small."

"What nice men," Claire said. "I wonder if they'd like a boiled egg?"

"All yours!" they cried, as they sped off down the path.

Mr. Ryan—Jim—was a spare eager man in his early thirties. He had a sandy moustache and brown dog-like eyes.

"Sit down, Mr. Sidney," he said. He paused, unhopefully. "I don't suppose it's about the account, is it?"

Colin pulled a chair up to the desk. "My wife thought that perhaps we ought to talk, but I don't know . . . perhaps somewhere else would have been preferable?"

"It hardly matters," Ryan said. "As long as you keep your voice down."

"I haven't come to make a scene."

"No . . . well, that's all right then." Mr. Ryan shrunk a little in his swivel chair. His eyes wandered over Colin and away to the framed print of a fishing village which hung on the far wall. The quay seemed strangely deserted; little boats bobbed on blue-black waves. "Only it wouldn't help if I lost my job."

"Is that likely?"

"She's a customer."

"Of course."

"And we have our professional ethics."

"Like doctors and dentists? I didn't know that. I mean, if a woman comes in to open a deposit account, you don't ask her to take her clothes off, do you? Not in the normal case; though I can see there are exceptions."

"You'd be surprised what happens, Mr. Sidney." Mr. Ryan's dark eyes flickered; he picked up a paper clip from his tray and began to unbend it. "You really see life from behind this desk. When the customers get divorced, they come into your office and fight."

"I had no idea."

"Oh yes. They get very personal." He met Colin's eye briefly. "That's not what I came into banking for, I don't enjoy it at all. They come in to divide their account, and then next thing you know, they're arguing about fellatio and who's going to have the hamster."

Colin took out a packet of cigarettes. "Smoke?"

Ryan shook his head gloomily, as if at this moment any silly habit would have been a relief. "It's no joke," he said. "I don't like it. It upsets me."

"You don't like emotions." Colin lit his cigarette. "Leave it to the women, eh?"

"Why not?" said Ryan, sneering a little. "They have the expertise, don't they, or so they say? They keep shifting the ground, you can't keep up. To them, big rows are like, what do you call it, fashion accessories—they have a new set every season."

"Have you got an ashtray?" Colin said. I won't be drawn, he thought, I'll keep my cool. He looked up. "I can't help observing, Mr. Ryan, that you are a man of what . . . thirty-three, thirty-four?"

"Whereas Suzanne is eighteen. You think I took advantage of her."

"I haven't heard that expression in years," Colin said. "But still, in this case . . . I can't imagine where you met."

"We met at the university," Ryan said. "We have these annual

163

promotions, you know, you must have seen the adverts. We call it our Someday Package. Someday You'll Make a Million, that's the slogan. The people who dream up these things are living in the past. They still think there are jobs for graduates."

"Yes?"

"And there was your daughter, coming in for her free plastic clipboard with the logo, and her free packet of felt-tipped pens. Myself, I thought the felt-tips were a mistake, a bit juvenile, but your daughter said, on the contrary, you know, she being a student of geography, they'd be useful to her—and that's how we got into conversation."

"And then?"

Ryan ran a hand through his hair. "Then I asked her to meet me for a drink . . . you know how it goes. You know the rest. It's not interesting, is it?"

"Well, only in one respect."

"And what's that?"

"I hoped you could enlighten me as to why you let her get pregnant!"

"I didn't 'let her.' What do you mean? You'd think—I know she's only eighteen, you've pointed that out, but you'd think she'd have the sense to swallow a pill."

"She told you she was on the pill?"

Mr. Ryan stared at him, mute; then each capillary flushed and blossomed, turning him pink from his hairline to the white collar of his striped shirt.

"It's a fad," Colin said calmly. "They don't like the pill. I thought you'd come to an agreement about it. Natural methods."

"What?" Ryan said. "What are you talking about?"

"Sorry. I'd have broken it more gently . . . not that it matters now. Academic interest, as people say."

"It's of more than academic interest to me! What was I supposed to do?"

"Withdraw, I think. It's natural population control. Peasants do it. In Italy. There's a book about it."

"Well, I must have missed that." He was scarlet now with shock and indignation. "I'll have to join the Book of the Month Club, won't I, before I pick a girl up again, I'll have to go by W. H. Smith and check out what bloody insanities she might have in store for me. Is that right?"

"Or go for a woman of thirty," Colin said. "They'd be on the pill, wouldn't mind poisoning themselves for a fine upstanding man like you. Oh, really, Ryan, get hold of yourself, calm down, if you've any brain there won't be a next time. Does your wife know?"

"Does she know? Your daughter told her on the phone. When I got home she was waiting. I knew right away there was something up. She said, 'I've had a most disturbing phone call from a girl called Suzanne.' That was it. I had to tell her everything."

Plod on, Colin thought; the old pedestrian tone.

"I think Suzanne expects you to leave your wife and set up with her."

"Leave my wife?"

"I'm afraid she took your relationship too seriously."

Ryan covered his face with his hands. "I've been conned all along then, haven't I?" he said wearily. "This wasn't my understanding of it. Not my understanding at all. It was just . . . a fling. One of those things that you do."

"A fling?" Colin said. "Come on, mate. This is 1984. Victorian Values."

"Nothing Victorian about the way your daughter ran after me—"

"No, but there is this about it," Colin said patiently, "that you pay for what you do. It isn't the scot-free seventies, you can't expect to go littering the countryside with your by-blows and expect the state to pick up the tab. You've got to feel the guilt, Mr. Ryan, you've got to put your hand in your pocket. You'd really better think of limiting your activities. Or you might get one of these special diseases."

There was a short silence. Ryan slumped in his chair. "I offered to pay for the abortion."

"She doesn't want one. Anyway, it's too late for that."

"Girls today . . . I can't take it in." With his fingertips Ryan worked the skin above his eyebrows. "She must understand . . . you must make her understand . . . I can't leave my wife. It's simply not one of the options. Isabel's not well."

"Not well?" Colin said sharply. Ryan sat up, at his tone.

"Her nerves. At least I think it's her nerves. There's something amiss. To be honest—may I be honest with you?"

"Feel free."

"I suppose I thought, with Suzanne, that she would take my mind off things. I'm a very troubled man, Mr. Sidney. So would you be, if you had Isabel to deal with."

"Would I?"

"You see, Isabel was twenty-six when I met her, and unmarried. No one had taken her on. I thought I was her first lover, though later I learned different. She was wary of me, very wary, do you know what I mean? She put men off, men in general. It took me months to get anywhere near her. The day we were married I don't think I knew her at all."

Ryan picked up a sheet of paper from his desk and began to fold and pleat it between his fingers. "And do you know her now?" Colin asked.

"Oh, now . . . She drinks. Gin mostly. Or whisky. Quite a lot. She has rages, the most horrible emotional storms. If you knew her you'd understand why I looked elsewhere, but at the same time, as a practical matter, if I left her what would she do? I can't just dump her, can I? She can't take care of herself."

"Look," Colin said desperately. "You don't have to tell me any of this."

"Oh, but it's a relief, get it off my chest. Her father died just recently in hospital, and that's made things worse, because they were always at outs, you know, and she's got some idea that she wished him dead. It seems that before he died he told her he'd got . . . well, I don't know, some sort of responsibility, an illegitimate child I think, some woman he met in a park. Now she goes on and on about it. She talks about her life, the life she's had."

"We all have a life."

"But you have to put the past behind you, don't you?"

"If it will let you."

"That's what she says. She says time's circular, she can feel it snapping at her ankles."

"She has a point."

"There was this other man, before we met." He had made an aeroplane; he held it up, admiring it distractedly. "In the last few months she's talked about him all the time. She says she thinks he understood her, as much as anyone has ever understood her. But he let her down. Of course, with her being as she is, I don't know if he ever existed. She might have made him up to torment me."

Made him up? "No, I don't think so," Colin said. "She wouldn't do that, would she?"

"She can go back to him if she can find him." Ryan sniffed. "Let him have an innings."

"Perhaps he wouldn't want her now."

"Not if he knew her, he wouldn't want her. Not if he knew how she was now."

"Not anyway. It's a long time ago. We have to try, you know—" he spoke gently, realising it—"to put ourselves together in the circumstances in which we find ourselves."

"But she doesn't, do you see? Isabel gets drunk on her past, she goes crazy on it. She used to be a social worker, I suppose she saw some terrible sights. Sometimes she talks about this old woman who locked her in a room, and about these invisible things that came out and touched her legs. She says she thought she was going to die."

Colin felt afraid; a tight ball of shame and regret pushed up into his diaphragm, shortening his breath. He stood up, pushing his chair away clumsily, and walked across to the far wall. He inspected the seascape. "Perhaps she needs help. You know. A doctor. That kind of help."

"Help? She needs an exorcism. Oh, she can put on a good front. All the social work skills. They know how to detect neurotics, you see, and alcoholics, and so they know how to pretend they aren't. She keeps herself on a very tight rein. You wouldn't know, to meet her, that she's had breakdowns."

"Breakdowns?"

"Two, three. I'm not sure really. They all shade into one another."

"I had no idea."

"No, why should you have? I didn't tell Suzanne, except just the usual, you know, the complaints one makes. Suzanne seemed to understand me, at the time—" He shook his head. "I wouldn't have thought that she'd have such weird ideas, but you can never tell, can you?"

Colin examined the picture, looked at the cracks in the frame. How could Isabel have settled for Jim Ryan? But all marriages are mysteries. What had Suzanne seen in him? Weakness; something of her father perhaps. Strength was being like Sylvia; making your opinions felt. Ryan was still flushed, his thin straw hair stuck up in tufts where he had raked his fingers through it when he talked about Isabel. He was a mass of little tics, of amoral reflexes, of tiny mental knee-jerks that kept him out of guilt and anguish and justified himself to himself.

"Do you always say people are mad if they threaten to inconvenience you?" Colin turned away from the wall. But his heart was not in it. Suzanne was abandoned; Isabel was sick. Sylvia was at home, waiting to know what he had made of the situation.

"Well, it is an extraordinary idea, you have to admit," Ryan said. "Looking to Italian peasants for advice on birth control. It's nearly as daft as some of Isabel's ideas. I sometimes think, you know, all these people, walking the streets, pretending to be sane—they ought to go out at random and pick up a few people, and examine them to see what delusions they've got."

"Perhaps it's this town," Colin said. "I think they put something in the water."

A further quarter-hour passed in exchange of pleasantries. Colin smoked his last cigarette. He crumpled up the packet and dropped it into the wastepaper basket. Ryan said, "I don't know why I'm telling you all this about my wife, it's personal stuff." He would regret it tomorrow; he was beginning to regret it now. He floated his paper aeroplane across the desk. It flew up, bombed sharply downwards, and landed at Colin's feet.

"Right then," Colin said. "There's nothing to add, is there? I'll be on my way."

Ryan leaped up to see him out, as if he were a client. His hand, extended, hung in the air. Colin stopped at the door. He turned. "I am the man your wife says let her down. I knew her ten years ago. We had an affair."

Ryan stared at him for a moment; but he had run the gamut of his talents for self-expression. He merely resumed his seat quietly, as if he were in church. His brown eyes had an opaque glaze. "Do you want to discuss it?" he asked.

"No," Colin said. "I never want to discuss it as long as I live." Half out of the door he paused, and spoke over his shoulder. "I'm moving my account."

Head in his hands, Ryan groaned.

He saw her as soon as he closed the door; with the precision of nightmare, moving from a blurred backdrop and into view; defined, in her strange anorak with the racing-team flashes, against the mill of senior shop assistants rattling their cash bags, and the housewives rummaging for biros in the depths of their bags. Once he would have been surprised, but now he was not surprised any longer. Figure thickened a little, features blurred; dark eyes alight in her usual pallor, the complexion he remembered.

Can you set a term to passion? Two years? Five? Ten? For a moment he was going to call out to her, but then he didn't, and as he didn't, he noticed the irretrievable moment, splitting off and slipping away. From the fraction of a second which this failure occupied, his life changed; unnoticeably, irreparably, in silence. It was just like York Minster; no one had actually seen the lightning strike. Long before he had recovered his wits, long before he had time to gauge the extent of his loss, the queue for the quick-service till had parted, and swallowed her up.

When Colin got home his wife said, "Go next door for the Royal Variety Performance. She's been waiting for you."

In a daze, he went back down the front path. He hardly noticed his surroundings; the plants in the stone urns were withered and brown, unable to withstand the onward march of the autumn weather. It was strange that Sylvia had not taken them out; perhaps they had died overnight. He let himself out through his own front gate and went round the corner to Florence's. Really, with all the coming and going between the two houses, it would be better if he made a hole in the hedge. How lucky it was, come to think of it, that Florence had not moved to a smaller place, as friends had often urged her. Trite, mundane, his little thoughts ran on; he knew them acutely, every tiny quibble, but he felt remote, as if he were viewing them down a telescope. Tick, tick, tick. Sylvia and Isabel. Like the Pit and the Pendulum.

Florence met him in the hall. "This digital clock's gone mad," she said. "It's already tomorrow by it. I didn't think they could, I thought it was only clockwork clocks that went mad."

Colin took the timepiece from her and shook it. "You can't mend them by shaking them," she said. "Not this kind. I don't know what's happening. I can't understand it. The pictures keep falling off the walls."

"Our house is pretty much a wreck," Colin said. "The electrics have all gone wrong. Well, you know."

"My house plants are dying."

"Yes, ours too."

Florence looked flushed and aggrieved. "Do you know," she said, "I hardly had time to take my coat off before she was yelling for me. I walk in here at five-thirty, and Sylvia's off like a shot. And where've *you* been? Would you like a cup of tea?"

"Better go up to her."

"Yes, if you could sit with her for half an hour, it would be a help, I could just clean up in the kitchen. There's some broken glass in there, I don't know where it came from, I nearly trod in it."

"Leave her to me," Colin said soothingly. Inside, he screamed for morphine, brandy: for oblivion.

"Without that Blank woman I don't know what we'd do. She's been in with Sylvia this afternoon, turning her. She says she can handle old people."

"That's all to the good then."

"Yes, but I don't like her in my house."

"Why's that?"

"Well, Colin, she's so gross."

"I agree her personal appearance leaves something to be desired, but we should be thankful we've got her. Look, Florence, why don't you put your feet up for half an hour?"

"I don't know," Florence muttered. "Claimants all day, and then to come home to this. She's driving me mad, Colin. I don't know how much longer I can stand it."

"You know they said if it got really bad, they'd take her back. And then there's that holiday-beds scheme, to give you a break for six weeks."

"What's six weeks?" Florence's eyes were puffy from lack of sleep. "She could live another fifteen years."

Colin trailed upstairs. He could already hear his mother talking to herself in the dry peremptory voice she had affected since she rose from the dead. She seemed to be making preparations for her wedding in St. James's Palace Chapel, 6th July 1893. If only there were some chronological sense within her delusions, it would be easier to deal with her, but in the space of a few minutes she could get herself from her early engagement to the Duke of Clarence through to the coronation of George VI. He stopped to listen outside the door. "Victoria," she said. "Mary. Augusta. Louise. Olga. Pauline. Claudine. Agnes."

"Hello, Mum," Colin cried gaily, pushing the door open.

Mrs. Sidney glared at him. She was sitting bolt upright in bed. She tried nowadays to keep her spine straight. "Tell that footman to bring me my medicine," she said. "It's time."

The room was stuffy; the central heating had been turned up, and the curtains had been drawn since four o'clock. The fuzzy light from the streetlamp shone through them and illuminated Mrs. Sidney's bedside cabinet with its glass of barley water and array of pills. Colin tiptoed over and picked up some of the bottles and packets. He turned them about in the dim light and read their names. God knows what she was being given, but there was a lot of it. He went to the door.

"Florence!"

"What?"

"She says it's time for her pills. Which do I give her?"

"Give her what she fancies," Florence's wrathful voice came back. "Oh, hold on, I'm coming."

He imagined he could hear the sharp intake of breath as Florence levered herself to her feet. Now he heard her grumbling and gasping to herself as she came upstairs. She was not young herself; all this was too much for her. Now she was in the room, glaring at the invalid.

"I'm sorry. Sorry to fetch you up again. But I don't know what she should have. I don't want to poison her."

"Well, you say that with some conviction." Breathing hard, Florence went to the side of the bed and picked up a couple of the bottles. "How about these?" she enquired, rattling them under her mother's nose. "How does she know it's time for her tablets?" she flung over her shoulder. "She never gets the time right to within fifty years."

"We want the yellow ones," Mrs. Sidney said.

"The yellow ones are for your blood pressure. If you have too many you'll pop off."

"That is not a nice way to talk about us. We shall have them when you are out of the room."

"Better take them away," Colin said in alarm.

Florence replaced them firmly on the bedside table. "They can stay there." She met his eyes. "It's inconvenient for me to have her medicines strewn all over the house."

"But what if she—"

Florence snatched the bottle up and once more rattled the tablets, in a passion. "They're childproof," she said. "Childproof! She hasn't got the strength in her wrists." Noisily, she began to cry.

Colin felt helpless and embarrassed. He stood watching her from the foot of the bed, unable to comfort or even approach her. He was used to Sylvia, with her tears of temper, but he could not remember seeing his sister like this. She was obviously at the end of her tether, a woman appalled by her own thoughts. Under pressure, the violent side of her was emerging. It seemed absurd to think of Florence, with her cable-stitch woollies, having a violent side. But he knew from the newspapers that everyone has their depths. No one could be more ruthless in pursuit of his ends than a peace campaigner. In the United States, opponents of abortion had taken to dynamiting clinics. And Florence, so insistent on the sacred quality of human life; would it after all be so surprising if she felt that Mother were an exception to her general rule?

"Oh, come on, old lass," he said. He stretched his hand out. "Give me those."

With a spluttering sob, Florence put the bottle into his hand. Mother's eyes watched them, the little black pupils darting to and fro. "I'm sorry," Florence said. She got out her handkerchief, with its frill of cheap lace and its initial. "It's just that I didn't sleep a wink last night. She was shouting out every half hour. She wanted the Court and Social page, and that woman Blank had gone and thrown the paper away. What could I do? I couldn't go out and print it."

Colin put his arm around her shoulders. The feeling of unreality remained. Speech was painful, an effort. It was an effort to bring his mind to bear on what was happening. "We must talk to the doctor again. The GP, I mean. Tell him she needs something to make her sleep."

"I've got something. She spits it out. She just spits her pills out and asks for the yellow ones."

"Well, we'd better put him in the picture, hadn't we?"

Florence took a deep breath, mastering herself. "I'm not going to let it get to me, Colin. I never thought she would get me to this pitch. I never thought I would entertain such thoughts, about my own mother."

Colin squeezed her arm. "Go down and have a snooze. Go on. I'll stay with her for a while."

"All right. Perhaps I could get Sylvia to sleep in for the odd night. But then who will look after her during the day? We'll have to depend on that woman."

Colin sat down by his mother's bedside. He might as well be here as at home, and do Florence a bit of good. He might as well sit here with his thoughts, in the close semi-darkness and the smell of invalidity. He shut his eyes. Perhaps he could sleep. Sleep would be good for him. He might wake up and find that his conversation with Jim Ryan had receded a little, softened around the edges. Just now there were fragments of it that lay behind his eyes, like bits of broken glass.

Isabel was different from the other women he had known. She sat still, and spoke very little. He had attributed wisdom to her. "She keeps herself on a very tight rein." It wasn't wisdom that had stilled her; it was fear that froze her up.

I know, he thought—I suppose I know—that people who are so exercised about the human condition are often refusing to face problems of their own. Like Sylvia; she rushes down the road to do some good elsewhere. He had never thought to compare the two ladies before. No doubt if they could meet, they would have a lot to say to each other. They would be able to pluck out a few thoughts of their heart and run a little comparison survey. Men did not do that. He understood why Jim Ryan had been so undignified. How would it be if he walked into the staff room tomorrow and said, "Gentlemen, I need to talk to you, I need to unburden myself and hear your advice?" It was unthinkable. They'd make a dash for it and there he'd be, standing by the photocopier while they rang for an ambulance. Yet without some process like this, how could he know what other men felt? He thought of his colleagues; after the first flurry of excitement, putting a minute diamond on some girl's finger, were they ever again beset by the stirrings of romance? Never: in his view. Stirrings of lechery, perhaps; those passed. One woman was the same as the next to them. Marriage was a practical arrangement which they entered into for the sake of comfort, and which they left under protest when the standard of comfort declined too far. They were inert, his colleagues, collections of cells for copulating and eating pork chops and going to the municipal swimming pool on a Sunday afternoon.

It was with the notion of Isabel that he had conspired to avoid this fate; it was with his picture he conspired, with the far-seeing eyes and mandarin lips. Always he had believed that somehow, somewhere, and one of these days, he would place before her his confusions, his doubts, the great mass of unsatisfied needs that doubled and raged inside him like a convulsing child; and there would be one word, and she would say it, and with that word she would put his life to rights.

And now? There was no future, but that was not it. There was no past; something had reached back and changed it. Had she always been crazy? It was easy to believe. She would turn into one of those women who stumble about the streets, talking to themselves; who sit in bus shelters in bitter weather with bottles sticking out of their shopping bags. She would grow old, decrepit, insane; and he would be old too, and so would Sylvia, a touching old Darby and Joan; and there would be Isabel, legless in a flower bed when they went to get the sunshine in the park.

"His Majesty is not feeling up to much today," his mother said conversationally. "I think I shall have to tour the Empire alone." She watched him, nodding in the hard chair. "You aren't going to marry that woman?" she said sharply.

He jerked awake. "What woman?"

"That woman you're always thinking about. Mrs. Ernest Simpson, you know what woman."

"Oh, her. No," he said slowly, dazed. "No, it would be too fraught and complicated, wouldn't it? I don't think I'll bother. I don't know why I ever thought I could."

"Speculation is rife. You must put an end to it at once."

He rubbed his eyes. "Okay."

That night, Lizzie Blank went down to Gino's Club. It was Ladies' Half-Price Nite, and very crowded. There was a man who stood up on a stage and insulted the audience, and people laughed at him. She was amazed when she learned that he got a wage for it. She thought it was just one of those things that happen.

She had just got on the right side of her first Tequila Sunrise when Clyde appeared. He made a nuisance of himself all night, nursing a Brown Split, with his feet stuck out and getting in the way of the dancers. She could see him watching her, his lugubrious face splintered by the mirror ball into a thousand blood-shot eyes.

It was two o'clock when she left, slipping out of the back door. She thought in terms of an early night, although it was true that sleep didn't interest her like it did other people. For a time she had taken Lizzie Blank's clothes with her in a carrier bag when she went out at night, and changed in a ladies' lavatory somewhere, but the weather was getting a bit chilly for that, and she didn't expect to meet Mr. Kowalski on the stairs. And what if she did? She smiled absently to herself. She had just got some new boots, white leather ones with platform soles and very high heels. Clyde saw her from the knee downwards, as he blundered out of the strobe lights and into the dark.

It had been raining earlier; the air was still damp, and there were puddles underfoot. Clyde had a torch. Slicing through the clammy night, the beam buried itself in her new coney coat, nuzzling at the dark-brown fur. She saw her face in one of the puddles, a white moon, a globe. There was a smell of vomit and chicken curry. Cats cried like human babies from the wall of an old washhouse. She put her back to the plum-coloured brick, waiting for him to catch her up.

Clyde thought his luck was in. She could tell that from the way his long face split in an uncertain grin, and from the way he fumbled at his flies. He lowered the torch beam decorously. She reached forward and took the torch from him, tickling the back of his hand in a flirtatious way with her long nails. Her face downcast, she turned the beam full on Clyde's exposed genital equipment. Clyde darted back. "Shy?" she said; half challenging and very coy. She reached out with her right hand for what he had on offer. A thin wail rose to join the noise of the cats. For good measure, she hit him with the torch on the side of the head. It was surprisingly sturdy, she thought, for plastic; she would keep it as a souvenir. Clyde backed off, folding his long body in half and retching onto the cobblestones. He flailed his arms and upended a dustbin with a clatter. Its entrails spilled out across the yard. From inside the club, Sam-7 and the Alkali Inspectorate ground their rhythms into the smoky air; off the beat, Lizzie stamped on Clyde's fingers. From way across the town she could hear the sound of a train rattling across the points, the 1.10 A.M. sleeper from Manchester Piccadilly to London Euston. Fearing that the damp might bring Lizzie's hair out of curl, she took her chiffon scarf from her pocket and shook it out. She saw the stars through it, the fuzzy and rose-pink constellations, so lost and far away, all shot through with the Lurex in the weave. Her blood was up. She knotted it under her chin as she clicked along the street.

She was only a quarter of a mile from Napier Street when she met Mr. K.; and it was all over quickly. She was not surprised to see the familiar shape trundling along, enjoying the amenities of the small hours. For a moment she forgot that it was Lizzie who was out, and she almost called to him. They came face to face at the street corner. It was clear at once that he shared Clyde's misperceptions; he thought that she was an amenity herself. He raised his stubbly head, and she saw the loneliness and hunger in his eyes. Bugger this for a game of coconuts, she thought. He put out a hand, so she bit it. It was quickly and unreflectingly done; a few clumps with her doubled fist, while the torch beam blinded him. She was not stronger than other women, but quite free from their dread of inflicting pain. "*Mater Amabilis!*" he cried, as her platform sole seemed to displace his kneecap. He did not resist; it was as if he felt he had it coming. Refuge of Sinners, Health of the Sick. The red nails came at him out of the dazzle. Morning Star, Ark of the Covenant: at first her blows seemed to make no impact on his larded torso, but gradually his knees began to sag. Tower of Ivory, Cause of Our Joy: grunting with effort, she pounded the ribs in the region of his heart. Virgin Most Merciful, Mirror of Justice: he gagged and staggered up against the wall, hunching his spine and throwing his arms over his head. Queen of the Apostles, Gate of Heaven: soon she would stop, either from boredom or fatigue. But her stamina was remarkable. She was treading on his feet now, one two, one two, like a storm trooper. Singular Vessel of Devotion, Mystical Rose, Tower of David, Mother most pure, *ora pro nobis*; not quite at the Hour of Our Death, but now, please, while we are bleeding in the gutter and it can still do us some good.

Colin's dreams now lay in ruins; also, it was necessary for him to move his bank account. He called into one or two, picking up leaflets about mortgages and saving schemes, furtively eyeing the cashiers to see if they appeared libidinous. Standing in the High Street, he found himself clutching a sheaf of dark purple leaflets entitled "Our Executor Service." Hastily he stuffed them into a passing litter bin, looking round to see if he was being observed.

When he arrived home, Dr. Rudge was just leaving. Sylvia, bundled into her combat jacket, was seeing him off at Florence's gate. It was 4:30 P.M., blue and cold. He let himself in at the front door. Suzanne was hanging about in the hall, probably waiting for the phone to ring.

"Did Jim call you?" he asked.

"Yes, he called."

"So you know what happened?"

"Yes, so I know." Her voice was listless. She crossed her arms over her belly. "I can't follow all the—permutations. It tires me. My back aches."

"Have you told your mother?"

"No, what's the point? That's up to you."

"Yes . . . thanks."

"Only, if you start rowing, I'll have to leave. I can't stand it."

"I don't think that will arise."

"You're not going to tell her about Isabel?"

"She probably knows. I think she does. Oh, not the name . . . but that there was somebody. I'm not sure that Isabel being Jim's wife adds a new dimension to our problems. It seems to, when you first think about it, but . . . it's not incest or anything, is it?"

"No, it's not that. Well, I hope you can sort yourselves out." Suzanne nodded distantly, as if they were only slight acquaintances. It was good of her, he thought, not to take up a moral stance. "It's kind of weird," she added, as she lumbered away.

Sylvia came in, rubbing her blue hands. "Oh, there you are, Colin. I've had a rotten day."

"You look all in."

"She's shouted and raved for hours. You know what it is now? She keeps pointing at Lizzie and saying that her name's Wilmot. She says she's called Wilmot and she used to live next door."

"This is next door."

"I know that. I'd worked that out. There was never anybody called Wilmot living here, was there?"

"Not that I remember. I only remember the Axons. They lived here for years."

"Yes, Evelyn and what's her name, Muriel. You'd hardly mix those two up with anybody else. I never knew Evelyn's husband. What was he called?"

"Clifford. Clifford Axon. Florence would tell you."

"Perhaps he had a friend called Wilmot."

"I don't think so. He was an eccentric. He spent all his time in the garden shed. What did the doctor say, then?"

"I reminded him of what the hospital told us. That if we got desperate they'd offer her a bed. He wasn't very sympathetic. He didn't seem to think we were desperate." I have often been desperate, Colin thought, but no one ever offered me a bed. "He told me this awful story about some people he knows who've got a demented mother and a handicapped fourteen-year-old in a council flat on the eighth floor. He said, there are two of you ladies. I told him I had commitments. Do you know what he said? He said, 'Charity begins at home.' I could have choked him."

"Is Florence back? Is Mum on her own?"

"Just for a few minutes. It won't hurt her. He said we could get the children to help. Can you imagine? He doesn't know our children. I have to pay Lizzie to stay with her every time I go out to the CAB."

"Perhaps Francis could arrange the odd parish helper."

"Everyone's gone on the peace march," Sylvia said. "And here I am, stuck at home. Anyway, he's given her some more sedatives, he says they're strong." Her gaze slid away from Colin's face; it came to rest obliquely, at the side of his head. He took her arm.

"I expect we ought to talk some time, Sylvia. We can't continue like this, exchanging the occasional word wedged up behind the front door."

"I never have time to sit down. Your mother, and Suzanne—it's driven everything else out of my head." You need leisure for an unhappy marriage, she seemed to imply. "But I can't go on like this."

"No?"

"No. There are half a dozen community projects to be set in train."

"I'm worried about Florence," he said impulsively. "I think the strain's too much for her. I think she might—"

"What?"

"No. Nothing. Never mind."

Jim Ryan said to his wife: "I suppose we could adopt it?"

"Adopt it?" she said. "I'd rather drown it." She looked at him; her voice and expression suddenly altered. "Besides, there's no need now."

"What? What do you mean?"

"Come here. Feel."

"Feel what? What are you doing?"

Carefully she laid the flat of his hand against the front of her body, keeping it covered with her own.

"I thought it was my liver," she said. "But it can't be, can it?"

"How did it happen? After all this time?"

"I have no bloody idea."

"You'd better go to the doctor," Jim said. He was alarmed. He almost felt that it was not a natural occurrence.

"He'll tell me to stop drinking."

"You'll have to stop. You'll damage it."

Isabel smiled into his face, madly and slyly. "You never know," she said, "who'll be damaged most in the end."

Muriel met Sholto. He looked haggard; his feet were damp, and his clothes were wearing out. "Still holding down your job?" he asked. She nodded. "You're doing all right, Muriel. Still going in disguise?"

"Yes. But not for long now."

"You don't still hold this changeling crap?"

She said, "I'm lonely, Sholto, out here in the town. Sometimes I'd like to climb back into my head. I'd like to sit on my bed and double up, and slide right down my own throat. Do you understand?"

"I'm finished with Crisp," Sholto said, not listening. "He's turned criminal. And you—I don't want to know. You'll be taking babies out of prams at the supermarket."

"They don't have prams," Muriel said. "They strap them into

those buggy things, or carry them on their backs. When I look at Miss Suzanne, all the words get tangled up inside my head, all those words you showed me on that pot head. In my mother's day, Sholto, we had a special room in our house. In that room my mother said there were things would pick the flesh off your bones. Where did it go to, that flesh? It isn't dead. It must be somewhere."

"You murdered that poor old bugger at the hospital."

"It wasn't murder. It was an execution. He didn't do well by me, Sholto. I could have been a married wife by now. He did it all without a by-your-leave. He never gave me a bouquet. Single red roses, that's what you give a girl."

"Now you're driving that Polack mad; or whatever he is."

"I don't drive. They go by themselves. He says there are men on the streets with poisoned umbrellas. He says there are countries where women walk round with black curtains over their heads. And that there's a man called Castro, and they sent him exploding cigars. He says they have factories where they make diseases." She blinked. "I never told him any of that."

Sholto glowered at her, out of his little rat's face. "When I met you, Muriel, I asked you if you was mad, or stupid. You said you was both. It took us in."

"I'm all gone to nothing." She hit her fist against her ribs, bending over as if to muffle the hollow sound. "Those ghosties have sucked the life out of me. Mother set them on. I've stopped expecting her. I think they've sucked her up too. Now there's only the changeling left."

"What you are is wicked," Sholto said.

Behind her thick glasses, Muriel blinked again.

"Do you know," said Sylvia, as she poured her muesli, "that in the past two years, according to a recent opinion poll, one in four of the population visited a canal?"

"Really?" Colin yawned. "Any particular population? It can't be Venice, I suppose."

"You know what I mean. In England and Wales. In fact, twenty-seven per cent. That's more than one in four."

"Stranger than fiction," Colin said.

"Now of these people, seventy-one per cent went for a walk. Eight per cent went fishing. Seven per cent hired a boat."

"That still leaves a number unaccounted for. What were they doing?"

"One per cent went swimming," Sylvia offered.

"I wouldn't fancy that in our canal."

"Exactly the point," Sylvia said. "We're going to have a community canal clean-up."

Colin looked at her warily over the top of the newspaper, and sank down a little in his chair. He thought that his mother had tired her out, but she seemed to be getting a second wind. He heard her speak of sponsorship and job creation and government schemes, and how the probation service would bring along strong young recidivists, and the Sea Scouts and the Brownies would pick up the litter from the banks. He ducked his head well below the holidays page. Exclusive villa parties, he read, wind-surfing, houseparties on the water's edge. Barbados, Crete, the Algarve. Love Nest for Two by Sardinia's Sandy Beaches. Cheap flights. Cheap flights, free escapes. Cheap flights without leaving Coketown. *"Hard Times,"* he said to himself.

"Of course they are," Sylvia agreed. "But this stretch should have been done two years ago. It was scheduled. I've got to get on to the Inland Waterways Board. Of course, it's Francis's idea really, but he's got a lot on at the moment. There's this man picketing the church."

"Good God," Colin said. "Is he violent?"

"No, not so far, he's just a nuisance, but he does make threatening motions with his banner. He tries to stop people going in to Francis's services. You know when we had that Christians Against Rate-Capping meeting? He stood outside howling abuse. If it goes on Francis will have to get the police in, and that's against his principles."

"Yes, I see the problem." A November morning pressed its cold grey face against the kitchen window. No wonder he often felt that someone was looking over his shoulder. "Oh, well. It's not as bad as any of ours."

But Sylvia did not want to talk about the family. She did not mean to be deflected. Sylvia made progress; it was only his mind that went round and round endlessly, revolving the same problems. Isabel: my God, how miserable she must be. How frustrated, how agonised inside. Had he not some responsibility there? Supposing he had left his family all those years ago, would Isabel be different now? What if? And what if?

I could do with being two people really, he thought; people who could live quite alternative lives, and meet up from time to time to compare notes. I am incapable of a decision, and always have been; I wait for circumstances to make my decisions for me, and just as I pray for resolution, so I dread it. Act, and you might as well be dead. Action is the great abortionist. It wipes out freedom. It terminates desire.

"And then there was the chromium-plating plant," Sylvia was saying, "pumping out acids year after year. And the dye works. I can remember a time when there were weeds on the canal, but now there's just an inch of scum on the surface and that awful smell of rotten eggs. Francis says that there's no oxygen in it at all. The water doesn't move, and there's a couple of feet of poisonous mud at the bottom. The walls are collapsing in. It could be damaging our health. He says there could be literally anything at the bottom of that canal."

Since Dr. Rudge's visit, Mrs. Sidney had sunk into a twilit world, sleeping for twenty hours of the twenty-four, surfacing only occasionally to ask for the Lord Chamberlain. It was much more peaceful, but unfortunately—and perhaps because of her new sedatives—she had become doubly incontinent. Florence had rung the hospital, but they said that, with Christmas coming up, and the long-range weather forecast being what it was, they could hardly think of taking her in before next May. Since then, disaster had struck.

It had made the national news: FIRE HAS BROKEN OUT AT A GERI-ATRIC HOSPITAL IN THE MIDLANDS, TRAPPING STAFF AND PATIENTS IN A FIRST-FLOOR WARD. FIREMEN WHO EVACUATED VICTIMS FROM THE FORMER WORKHOUSE SAID THAT ESCAPE ROUTES WERE GROSSLY INADEQUATE. A PUBLIC INQUIRY HAS BEEN CALLED FOR.

When Florence heard, she went upstairs to her mother's room. She stood by the bed with her arms folded, watching the withered eyelids flutter in drugged sleep. "That could have been you," she whispered.

Dr. Rudge came by. "Lucky escape," he said.

"If you say so, Doctor."

"Oh, come come, Miss Sidney. You want your mother with you for some years yet." As he coiled his stethoscope into his bag, Dr. Rudge looked sharply at her expression. He was a bald, tubby man, who prided himself on being humane; but really, there were no geriatric beds, and that was that.

Florence had run downstairs after him and followed him into the street. "I can't go on," she wailed. "Dr. Rudge, listen to me."

Dr. Rudge stopped in surprise, bouncing his car keys on his palm. "But you've got the district nurse, Miss Sidney. Be thankful for small mercies."

"But I can't manage! The smell! And the way she wakes up and thinks she's at Marlborough House! It frightens me!"

"You have domestic help, I understand."

"She keeps abusing her! She says she's the daughter of the woman who used to live next door. She accuses her of holding seances. It's horrible. It's worse than May of Teck. She's totally and completely mad."

"Really, pull yourself together," said Dr. Rudge. "You know we're promised a geriatric unit for 1990. Go in, Miss Sidney, it's starting to rain. And I do have other calls to make."

"But I can't go on." Florence's voice rose into the damp after-noon. "Don't you understand? We can't take any more, any of us." Two women, coming back from the Parade, rested their shopping baskets on a low wall and watched attentively. The Deakins, elderly people from down the road, were peeping out from their porch. Dr. Rudge cursed under his breath, and felt in his overcoat pockets for his prescription pad. He scribbled on it and ripped the page off.

"Try this to calm you down, Miss Sidney." He thrust the prescription at her. Florence crumpled it in her fist and threw it after him. It struck him smartly on the neck as he jumped into his Volvo. He slammed the door and drove away.

"Old Aunt Flo," said Suzanne now, coming into the kitchen. "Making a scene like that in the street. All the neighbours will be talking about it."

"We're beyond caring what the neighbours say," Sylvia said. "We have to be."

Suzanne manoeuvred herself into a chair. "I've come to tell you. I'm moving out when the baby's born."

Sylvia regarded her sadly. "I can't stop you. Where are you planning to go?"

"I've got this friend, Edwina. She's got this flat."

"Unusual name," Colin said.

"She'll let me stay with her till Jim sorts himself out."

"Jim will never be sorted out. You know that, Suzanne."

"Don't tell me what I know. Who are you to advise anybody?"

"How will Edwina like having a baby around?" Sylvia said. "She'll soon get tired of it."

"I've got other friends. I can move on."

"You're not a bloody gypsy. Babies can't do with that sort of life. They have to be settled. They need a routine. They need to be kept warm."

"Don't think I'm staying here." Suzanne's voice quivered, on the edge of hysteria. "You've all let me down. This house is horrible. Nothing works. There's no hot water. The lightbulb's gone in my room and I daren't stand on a chair. It's like the Black Hole of Calcutta. If I stand on a chair I'll go dizzy and I'll fall off and have a miscarriage and then Jim will never marry me."

"I think you're getting things out of proportion," Sylvia said, with a restraint that Colin could only commend. "You ought to calm down. Ask Aunt Florence to give you one of your grandmother's pills."

"I can't have pills," Suzanne said, blubbering. Colin handed her his handkerchief. "I'll give birth to a monster. I suppose I will anyway. What can you expect, coming from a family like this?"

Colin and Sylvia exchanged a glance, each beaten and weary face eyeing the other. Colin understood that cleaning up the canal was a diversion for his wife, just as pining for the lost girl who was now Isabel Ryan was a diversion for him. They were like a pair of felons roped together, singing to pass the time on their trip to Tyburn. Suzanne blew her nose into his handkerchief and gave it back to him. Her chin drooped. She looked eleven months gone.

CHAPTER 8

Christmas was celebrated quietly at Buckingham Avenue. In the morning, Francis and Hermione called round between services to have a glass of sherry. Their general air was far from festive. Austin had turned down a place on the Youth Training Scheme, saying that he was self-employed as a satanist, and had failed that week to keep an appointment with his probation officer.

"Of course, young people must rebel," Francis said. "But why Satanism? Why has this spirit of vicious irrationality got abroad? Tell me that, Colin."

Sylvia went to and fro, carrying a wine box. She seemed dazed. A smell of burning carrots came from the kitchen. She had aged, Colin thought: deep lines from nose to chin.

"I asked you much the same," he said to Francis. "I asked you why I found teeth in my front garden. Something's happening round here. Did you see that advert in *The Times* for the Koestler Chair of Parapsychology?"

"I don't read *The Times*, I'm afraid."

"I read it in the staff room. It said you have to have an interest in the way some individuals interacted with the environment other than by normal channels. I'm sure somebody's interacting in this house."

"It's true," Sylvia said. "We keep getting these electrical faults, but we've had the wiring checked. The milk keeps turning sour. Things go missing."

"I'm disappointed in you," the vicar said.

"Have you thought of trying Unigate?" Hermione put in. "You can get low-fat yoghurt as well."

"We read a book about it," Sylvia said. "We thought it might be Suzanne. Her amassed discontent finding expression."

"I'm surprised you don't want an exorcism."

"That might not be a bad idea."

"What about this woman Blank? If objects are missing, you probably need look no further. Have you checked her credentials?"

"She doesn't have credentials," Sylvia said sulkily. "She's a cleaning woman."

"I think it's our unhappiness that does it," Colin said. "It's the accumulated misery, bouncing off the walls."

"Are you unhappy, Colin?" the vicar asked. "I didn't know."

Florence arrived just as Francis and his wife were leaving; reporting in as usual for Christmas dinner. "I've given her double pills," she said. "It should keep her quiet for an hour or two."

"You have to watch dosages, with the elderly," Francis warned. Florence scowled at him.

"I didn't like your sermon. People want the ox and the ass, not the National Coal Board. I agree with that man who stands outside with the placard."

Suzanne, swaying around in the kitchen, upset a pan of sprouts and scalded her feet. Alistair lay on his bed, the door locked and his eyes closed, breathing raggedly with the breathing of the room. Karen locked herself into the bathroom and squeezed her spots till her face flared with scarlet patches. Claire put on her Brownie uniform. "Enjoy your day," Sylvia said at the door. "Christmas is no holiday for me," the vicar replied.

The Ryans had begun the day late. Jim had long ago given up taking Isabel to see his family, and this year there was no need to go to the hospital. Christmas dinner was a silent affair. Jim watched Isabel's face, waiting for the wine to enter her bloodstream and make her voluble. First, she would fling accusations at him; second, she would cry into the bread sauce. After a while she would talk about concentration camps. Later still she would collapse. He would drag her onto the sofa and throw a rug over her, and go for a walk round the park.

At Mr. K.'s house, Mrs. Wilmot and Miss Anaemia sat with their landlord at the kitchen table. Although it was now some time since Mr. K. had been beaten up by the woman in the street, he still bore traces of his injuries; patches of greenish discoloration showed on his face where his bruises were fading. As for the dismay, fright, and humiliation, it might be years before he recovered from those.

"That was no woman," he said, for the third time that morning. Gloomily he adjusted the yellow paper hat that Miss Anaemia had insisted that he wear. "That was a man in disguise."

"A Transylvanian," said Miss Anaemia. "Leave it out, Mr. K. Your dinner's getting cold."

They had decided to incorporate the traditional Christmas trimmings—crackers, a game of pass the parcel—with the kind of food each of them liked best. "After all," Miss Anaemia said, "we're three loners, we've only ourselves to please." Pickled cucumbers were put on the table, and dumplings with caraway seeds, and All-Bran; tinned ravioli, and chocolate digestive biscuits. Wheezing as he moved across the room, Mr. Kowalski produced from the cool pantry some bottled beer. He squeezed out a few tears, thinking of carp on Christmas Eve, of his little sister with new hair ribbons, of candles burning in the windows to light them home from midnight Mass. He did not know whether it was his own past he was grieving for, or other people's; the images flickered and ticked behind his retina like shots from silent films. Miss Anaemia thought of growing up in Burton-on-Trent. Poor Mrs. Wilmot thought of nothing at all, for she had no past to remember; but she shook with silent mirth when she read the mottoes in the crackers. After dinner had been cleared away, the presents were exchanged. Mrs. Wilmot and Mr. K. each gave the other mufflers and miniature bottles of whisky; they both gave bath salts to Miss Anaemia. They knew that she would never take a bath, because the rusty trickle of warm water that ran from the antiquated pipes would not bathe a flea; but she agreed with them about the air of ease and luxury the bottles would lend to her dressing table. Then the cards were taken out, and they played Happy Families, and ate chocolates. Mr. Kowalski grew excitable, and insisted on getting them to their feet for a lively traditional dance that involved clapping rhythmically and standing on one leg. Mrs. Wilmot fell over a good deal. Mr. K. threw an extra scuttle of coal on the kitchen range, and soon they were enveloped in a pleasant warm fug, doors tightly shut against the elements, the windows sealed. Mr. K. seized his young lodger's hand. The bottled beer had gone to his head. He put his hands around her waist and whirled her off her feet, rumbling out the refrain in his rib-heaving bass and stamping his left foot. "My dear young thing," he said, breaking off his chorus, "won't you join me in holy matrimony?"

"Then I'd never get my giro back," Miss Anaemia said. "You'd have to keep me. 'He that hath wife and children hath given hostages to fortune,' or words to that effect."

"No need for children," Mr. K. said. "Rubber goods can be obtained."

But Miss Anaemia shook her head. Two spots of scarlet flamed on her cheeks. The kettle sang merrily on the range. Mr. K. roared and stomped, and held his arms in a tree shape above his head. Poor Mrs. Wilmot staggered exhausted to the kitchen table. She hugged her belly, and swayed, and gave a mute bellow of laughter; she licked her pale lips, and the steam from the kettle misted up her glasses.

The smell of the roasting turkey woke Alistair from his lassitude. He got up, groaning, and ventured out onto the landing. "There's sumfin growing on my wall," he said. "Fungus or sumfin." Next door Mrs. Sidney stirred in her sleep, and mumbled; she had caught the note of the festivities, and thought she was at Balmoral.

Evening came. Lizzie Blank had arranged to take Sholto and Emmanuel to Gino's Club for the Christmas Nite Special. I want to be a special fantasia, she thought, with gold paint on my nails and a tinsel crown; she was buggered if she was going to do that in a WC. Miss Anaemia and Mr. K. were sleeping off the afternoon's excitement; what did it matter if the click-click of her stilettos on the stairs entered their dreams? It was 8:30 P.M.; she gave her lipstick a final coat of gloss, patted her curls, and departed.

But as she reached the foot of the stairs, the kitchen door opened; there stood Mr. K. in his vest and braces. He rubbed his eyes, itching from the smoke of the kitchen; there was a poker in his fist. His jaw dropped. "In my own house," he cried. She sprang for the door.

At the Ryans' house, Isabel was asleep on the sofa. Her book lay face-down on the carpet; not the book she was reading, but the book she was writing, her loose-leaf collection of scruffy typed sheets. Jim didn't believe in her book. He didn't believe that she would ever finish it, or that anyone would care to publish it if she did. But she was determined, in her drunken way. She was guilty, and she must have something to be guilty of; she must be properly accused. Her body heaved in sleep, her skin grew damp, her face emptied of pleasure or hope. Her many pulses beat.

Mr. Kowalski fell back against the door frame, gagging in panic. The fire iron trembled, clutched against his chest. Ole King Cole, Muriel sang on the street. She could feel the faculties clattering inside her skull, the lines clashing and meshing like railway sidings; she could feel the words twisting together, the separate letters intertwining, the bs with the ps with the ks, all lashing and plaiting their tails. CALCULATION was twisting in her cranium, HUMAN NATURE battered at the bone, at the fissures and the sagittal suture, at the tentorium, at the parietal arch. Ole King Cole, with his frantic black soul; and he called for his fiddlers, ME.

New Year.

Miss Anaemia went down to see the DHSS. "I'm pregnant," she said. "Rehouse me."

"We would require confirmation of that."

"I'll confirm it. I'm telling you, aren't I?"

"Medical confirmation."

"Oh, I see. What if I had an elderly dependant?"

"Are you saying you have an elderly dependant?"

"What if, I'm saying."

"And you are pregnant as well?"

"Look, you had a tip-off, didn't you? You came and looked at my sheets. You said I was going with a giant. If I've got a man I could be pregnant. What do you have a man for?"

The woman put her pencil down. "According to our Rotherham office, you turned up there to claim benefit, giving a false address and stating that your name was Lady Margaret Hall. You do realise that we could prosecute you for attempted fraud?"

"Supposing I brought you a baby?" Miss Anaemia said. "Would you pay out then?"

Muriel leaned over Mrs. Sidney. "Yellow ones?" she enquired. She shook the bottle and held it tantalisingly out of reach. Mrs. Sidney croaked faintly. Her features were drawn already, corpse-like. Muriel unscrewed the bottle and dropped the pills into her palm. "Open wide," she said. Mrs. Sidney's jaw quivered, and she parted her lips. Muriel fed her the pills one by one, slipping some in from the other bottles when she felt like it. It took a long time. She held Mrs. Sidney's jaw shut to make sure she swallowed. She had seen it done at Fulmers Moor.

Sylvia was out at a meeting of the Canal Clean-up Co-operative. Florence was out at work. Lizzie Blank was in sole charge; that was how they trusted her. She left the old lady to it and went next door to clean the bathroom. She put her feet up for an hour in Sylvia's living room and read magazines, and ate the caramel toffees she had brought with her. When she went next door to check on Mrs. Sidney the old lady was still breathing, so she pulled a pillow from beneath her head and held it over her face until she was confident that she had expired.

It did not escape her, going downstairs, that by disposing of Mrs. Sidney she might be helping the family rather than hindering them. The break-up of their family life, the increasing dereliction of the family home, was happening around her, but perhaps not at her behest; it was not she who had arranged for Jim Ryan to impregnate Suzanne. Life just arranges itself, usually for the worst, and chance is not blind at all; it has as many eyes as a fly on the wall.

Even if the death did not incommode them in the long term, she could not resist it. She wanted to see their faces. She needed to see how they displayed strong emotion, so that she could copy them, and have something to feed on.

She had reset her features, and was making herself a cup of coffee, when Suzanne came to join her. "Want one?" Lizzie said. "How are things?"

"I'm staying till it's born," Suzanne said. "When it's born I'm getting out."

"And will you be coming to my place?" Her tone was bright; but it worried her. She could see snags. If Suzanne came to stay at Mr. K.'s house, Poor Mrs. Wilmot would have to move out. She could not trust Crisp with her personal effects; he might sell them, and give the money to the poor. "Why not stay at home?" she said coaxingly. "Just for the first week or two. Give us all a chance to get to know the baby."

"No, I'm going to Edwina's. Or I might go to Sean's. Or I might go back to Manchester to that squat I told you about, only they've had a lot of trouble with the police coming round and they might have to move out. I don't know where I'll be. Can I use your address?"

"All right."

"Then if I'm moving around, I can use it for getting my giro. And I can give it to Jim, because there isn't a phone at the squat, and when he wants to get in touch he can write to me there and you'll save it for me, okay?" Her eyes flickered away. "He will want to get in touch, won't he? Don't you think so? He'll want to see the baby, won't he?"

"Oh yes," Lizzie said. "He'll take an interest. It'll come out in the wash, you'll see."

"Okay, so you'll save me any post that comes? I don't trust Mum to pass my letters on."

"Or I could mind the baby for you," Lizzie said. "I could, you know. I wouldn't mind, if you had business. Or if you wanted a night out. You're bound to want a night out when you get over having it. You could get Jim to take you to a club."

"I know you'd help me out," Suzanne said emotionally. "That's what I like about you, Lizzie, you're a Real Person. You don't fill people up with empty promises." Sadly, Suzanne turned to leave the kitchen, her coffee mug in her hand. "I shouldn't," she said, "it gives me indigestion." She was very big now. Soon she would lean backwards when she walked. She hadn't a clue what would happen to her or the baby. Things are coming to a head, Muriel thought. Soon I'll have my changeling back, soon I'll be a mother, I'll be perfectly fulfilled. Soon I'll be leaving here. There'll be a signal, and I'll go. She believed in signals. They were as good as anything.

"Come down our den, our Kari," Alistair said.

"What for?"

"Show you summat."

"What is it?"

"Dunno. Skeleton."

"Yah," said Kari, incredulous.

"Honest."

"Where'd you get it?"

"Canal. Claire found it. Her and her mates. Brownies."

"When?"

"Last Saturday."

"Full-size one?"

"Nah. Little."

"Murder," Kari said. "Let's have a look, will you?"

"Come down our den."

"What d'you want?" Kari said with suspicion.

"Fetch us some UHU."

"No."

"Aw, go on. You go in Fletcher's in your school uniform. Tell 'em you're gluing for your project."

"I might."

"And I tell you what, Kari, nick us a clothespeg."

"What for?"

"Sherwood's a Rasta and his plaits get in the glue."

"Nick one hisself."

"His mum don't do no washing." He paused. "Honest, Kari, fetch us some glue, you can share the skeleton."

Kari wavered. "All right," she said. "What size tube you want?"

When Sylvia came home from her meeting she let herself into Florence's house and went upstairs. She stuck her head around the door and saw the pillow lying on Mrs. Sidney's chest. Her impulse was to close the door again and pretend she had not seen it, and let Colin discover for himself what had happened, since it was his mother who was apparently dead, and his sister who had apparently made her that way; she had a nice sense of delicacy, and she did not believe that an outsider, even an in-law, should interfere in such a close family matter.

But leaving her scruples aside—because she did not trust Colin to have any common sense—she crossed the room and removed the pillow to a less remarkable position. She put the back of her hand against Mrs. Sidney's cheek. There was not much doubt about what had happened, but it was hard to tell just by looking; the features were not distorted, there had been no struggle. She opened the wardrobe and squashed the pillow onto the top shelf, above the pile of folded Witney blankets. The wardrobe door creaked; the smell of camphor crept out into the room. She had an impulse to open the window; but it was raining hard, and it might not be respectful. The original position of the pillow would be a private satisfaction to her. She would know, and Florence would know that she did. So when Flo got pious in future, she could catch her eye. The balance of terror within the family would be altered; and in her favour. She was not surprised to find out what Florence was capable of; but if I had been in her position, she thought, I would not have signalled my intentions so clearly. She touched Mother's cheek again, wondering how long she had been dead. Florence must have slipped out and done it in her teabreak. She went downstairs to ring Dr. Rudge to come and give them a death certificate. The rain was turning to sleet.

You had to hand it to Florence, she said later to Colin (and he agreed); that clutch at the throat, the doubled fist striking the door frame, the way the blood drained from her highly coloured features. Perhaps it was natural, though, at the sight of Dr. Rudge; his sardonic expression as he looked down at the bedside cabinet, and with a forefinger separated the empty pill bottles from the rest. Sylvia hadn't noticed that. It argued a degree of premeditation, she thought. She caught Colin's eye, turning down the corners of her mouth in a meaningful way.

"But I didn't give them to her!" Florence was good at the innocence outraged; the pop-eyes, the pewter complexion. "She must have taken them herself."

"I see," said Dr. Rudge nastily, "and all you did, eh, was to leave them close at hand and with the top off? We're not accusing you of choking her, Miss Sidney, we're not saying that you forced them down her throat one by one. We know she was fond of the yellow ones, don't we?"

"But I didn't! I'm careful with her medicines!"

"Come, come," said the doctor, smiling. "If I wanted to take the matter further, your neighbours would no doubt remember the scene you made in the street."

"What about Lizzie Blank?" Florence wailed. "Why wasn't she attending to her? She was left in charge!"

"That's a digression, Miss Sidney, if I may say so."

"Shall I phone the undertaker?" Sylvia said. "Oh, come on, Flo, we all know you did it."

"However," Dr. Rudge said, "I do call myself a compassionate man, and this is not the first time that a distressed relative in my practice has—as we call it—eased an elderly person out of a life of suffering—but in your case, Miss Sidney, I'm bound to say, it is very strange of you to try and pin the blame on the daily help."

"Strange?" Colin said. "It's monstrous. I'm not trying to take a moral stance, Florence, but honestly, you should have told us what you were up to."

"We always hope," Dr. Rudge said testily, "that we don't have to discuss the matter quite so openly."

"Prosecute me!" Florence said. "Call the police! Put me in the dock!"

"Don't be melodramatic," Sylvia said. "You're embarrassing us all. Think, Colin, I'll be able to cut down on Lizzie's hours now. I can go out in the evening again. I can take a more active part in the canal scheme."

"There won't be an inquest?" Colin asked.

"Not necessary," the doctor said.

"But of course there must be an inquest," Florence said. "I want my name cleared." She looked around at her brother, at her sister-in-law, at the doctor. Their faces were closed, smug, blank with careful discretion. "What will the neighbours say?" she asked. "They'll say I did it. They'll all be talking about me, right up Arlington Road."

"Better Arlington Road than the *News of the World*," Colin said. He left them and went downstairs. Murder now, he thought.

After the New Year, the cold weather set in. Every morning when the new term started Colin had to go out with a shovel at a quarter to eight and clear the drive of snow. Vehicles were abandoned by the side of the road, pipes froze up and burst, and sleet blew in whirlwinds and eddies across the motorway. The black branches of the trees on the Avenue bent under the weight of the winter; and then came a thaw, the gutters running with icy flood water.

Towards the end of February, Suzanne's baby—a girl—was born in hospital. She did not hear from Jim Ryan. When her mother and father visited her that evening she turned her face away from them and looked steadfastly at the wall. The baby, Gemma, slept by her bed in a plastic bubble. She entertained fantasies of walking up the Ryans' front path; of dropping in at the bank and laying the baby on Jim's desk amid the statements and paper clips.

"When people say they want a child," Colin explained, "when people say that, as Jim did to you, they may be speaking figuratively. They may be saying they want a second chance."

"She didn't think he was speaking figuratively," Sylvia said. "She saw herself walking up the aisle. That was no figure."

"I didn't think girls dreamed of their weddings any more," Colin said sadly. "I thought the world had changed."

"Oh no." Sylvia looked down at the child, the drift of dark hair, the formless undersea face. Her expression softened. "I love babies," she said. "I always did."

"I don't love them," Suzanne said. "I don't have any feelings." Her mother patted her wrist. Suzanne twitched her arm away. "Why shouldn't people have second chances?" she demanded.

"I don't know," Colin said, "they just don't, these days. In the seventies, people had second chances. Ten years ago. Now it's all battening down the hatches, that sort of thing."

"You could put the baby up for adoption," Sylvia said. "That is, we could adopt it. I'd be willing."

"Is there no stopping you?" Colin said. He eyed her sideways. She was planning to stay around then.

"You have your life to make," Sylvia told her daughter. "You've made a mistake, but you don't have to go on paying for it."

"Of course she does," Colin said. "Go on paying is what people do. Ask Jim."

Sylvia regarded him, unblinking. "I know why you are so bitter," she said. "I don't know the details, but I know the gist of it. I really think it's time you grew up." She turned to Suzanne. "Don't listen to your father. I'd be more than willing. You could finish your course." She was coaxing, trying to cajole the baby out of her daughter. "It's the least we can do."

Suzanne turned her face away again. "I'll never give her to you," she said. "God knows what you'd do to her. I shan't be coming home."

"I see." Sylvia walked over to the window, her hands thrust deep into the pockets of her jacket. She looked down into the hospital car park, sucking her lip. "Leave us your address then. Edwina's, or wherever."

"Get it from Lizzie Blank," Suzanne said.

When Colin arrived home, there was a parcel waiting for him. It was wrapped up in brown paper and inscribed "TO GRANDAD, FROM ALISTAIR AND OSTIN."

"Goodness," Colin said, "a pressie." He picked it up, applied his ear to it, and rattled it.

"You are childish," Sylvia said. He sat down with it on the sofa and began to pick at the string. "We've had the bill from the undertaker," she said.

"I saw it. It's too much."

"It's not the sort of thing you can haggle over."

"I don't see why not. They wouldn't dig her up, would they?"

"Give it to Florence," Sylvia suggested. "We wouldn't be faced with it if it weren't for her."

"If I tell her that she'll have an apoplexy."

"Let her."

"Then we'll have to pay for her funeral."

"Well, don't tell her then. Don't mention it. Just leave it discreetly on the telephone table."

"Like a visiting card."

"She'll know what it is. Do you want the scissors?"

"Yes, please."

"Why don't you go and get them then?"

"I can't find them."

"You haven't looked."

"No point. I can never find the scissors. It's one of the eternal verities. Something to cling to amid the vicissitudes of daily life."

"It wears me out," Sylvia said, "when you are so unrelentingly fatuous."

With a conspicuous grunt of effort she got to her feet, and went into the kitchen. She was pleased with "fatuous"; or did she mean facetious? That was possible. She rummaged in a drawer, thinking about Suzanne; thinking about Colin and his ten-year-old love affair, thinking about the undertaker's bill. It had been distasteful, having Colin make jokes about gun carriages and lying in state. She knew he was doing it to cover his shock; his shock at finding out what people were capable of. Looking sideways at Florence, snivelling in her pew, she had thought: how can she? It was touching how Francis, who had no particular belief in an afterlife, had subdued his natural militancy and tried to come up with comforting and appropriate texts. She had felt a sharp impulse to lay the matter at his feet, but stifled it. She was sure he would approve of mercy killing; but Mother didn't want to die. She was quite happy with her round of royal duties. She did not see how Florence could be so heartless, just for the sake of her career at the DHSS, but then she knew what her own first thought had been; no more trailing up and down the stairs, up and down the stairs. It took weight off—six calories a minute—but it wearied her.

But what would Francis say? He would like to agonise over it, if they had Hermione's mother become incontinent in their spare room. He would like to wrestle with his conscience. That was the proper way. She had not wrestled with hers. She was not sure if she had a conscience. It was the kind of thing Colin talked about. Who knew if, over the years, Francis's talk of it might become as tedious as Colin's? That was men: scant regard for practicalities. Probably she was not good enough for Francis; he would find her wanting. She had dusted her hands off—mentally—and gone downstairs to ring the Elliot Bros., Funeral Directors, 24-Hour Service, Chapel of Rest. All she had thought of was what, since she was so large, Suzanne could possibly wear to the funeral. She took the scissors out of the drawer; I haven't much imagination, she thought. Thank God.

"There you go," she said, coming back into the living room and handing the scissors to her husband. He had succeeded in getting his parcel half-undone. Now he opened the cardboard box inside the wrapping paper.

"Good Lord," he said. "It's a phrenologist's head. I've always wanted one of these."

He took it out and put it on the coffee table. He knelt before it and traced its lines with his forefinger: Faculty of Conjugality, Faculty of Self-esteem. "I wonder where they got it. Stole it, probably. Still, it's not the sort of thing you nick from Woolworth's, they must have gone to trouble."

"It's no laughing matter."

"Oh, there are worse crimes in the family."

"I don't like it, it's sinister."

"Faculty of Progenitiveness," Colin said. "Come here, Sylvia, let me feel your head." He fitted his fingers around her forehead and squeezed.

"Get off," she bellowed angrily. "My God, Colin, you're easily diverted. Your own daughter lying in a hospital bed, threatening to leave home, your son's a delinquent, and all you can do is mess about with toys."

"It's not a toy. Suzanne's just given birth, so where else would she be? And I understand she's left home already." He turned the head about. "Faculty of Combativeness."

"It's rubbish anyway," Sylvia said. "It's discredited."

"Oh, I don't know." Colin felt his skull above his left ear. "Opportunities for self-knowledge are so limited. It doesn't do to be dogmatic. I wonder what I'd find if I read Florence's bumps?"

"I think I'd rather not know. I'd rather not know more than I do."

" 'Where ignorance is bliss, 'tis folly to be wise.' "

"Another quotation," Sylvia said. "It's like Christmas every day, living with you. Out come the mottoes and the silly jokes, and the coloured plastic distractions, all the penny whistles and cheap novelties. And when the day's over, what happens? All the trash is left under the table, for me to clear up."

He didn't answer. Surprised by the fluency of her outburst, he sat on the sofa, his eyes indignantly wide, staring at the phrenological head. Sylvia went into the kitchen. He heard the fridge door open and shut, and the clink of glasses. She whipped back into the room, ignoring him, and began to rummage around in the drinks cupboard.

"Oh, are we drinking again?" he asked.

"I am. I need one, after that episode with Suzanne. Have you ever known anybody so ungrateful? What more does she think I can offer her?"

"Pour me one." He sounded forlorn.

"I'm having vodka."

"That'll do. Don't put anything silly in it."

Her voice floated through from the kitchen: "What do you call silly?" The telephone rang. Sylvia nipped back, dumped the glasses, picked it up; she thought it was Suzanne, changing her mind about things. He saw her back stiffen. "Yes," she said carefully. "Yes, it is. Yes, he is." She lowered the receiver, muffling it against her left breast. "It's Mrs. Ryan. She wants to know if she can speak to you. If it's convenient."

Colin leaned forward and took up his head. The pottery bones were cool and firm beneath his palms. "She being sarcastic?" he asked.

"Just hold on," Sylvia said into the receiver. To him, "What?"

"When she said 'If it's convenient?' I mean, does convenience enter into it?"

"Hold on, Mrs. Ryan." Sylvia put her hand over the mouthpiece. "Are you going to speak to her or not?"

"I mean, it's a pretty hollow concept, convenience," he said. "After ten years. She's known where I was, this past decade."

"What do you mean?"

"I mean I've been here, haven't I, at Buckingham Avenue? Where's she been? God only knows."

"You could have found out," Sylvia said. "I daresay it wouldn't have been beyond you. You could have made enquiries."

"Oh, I could." He upended the head and peered inside it. "But they might have led somewhere. Then I'd have had to take action. Then where would I be?"

"Mrs. Ryan," Sylvia said, "I don't think he wants to talk to you." There was a pause. "She says she must know from you." She held the receiver towards him. "I'll go out of the room if you like."

He shook his head.

"He shakes his head," Sylvia said.

"Oh, for God's sake." Colin banged the head down on the table. "There's nothing to say. There's nothing left. It was a delusion."

Sylvia bowed her head over the receiver, and like a confidential secretary repeated the message. She listened. "I'll tell him." She put the phone down gently, and watched it for a moment, as if she thought it might ring again. "She says to tell you, that's exactly as she supposed."

He knew, by the careful repetition of the phrase, that the words were Isabel's, exact; he knew, too, that they'd be the last she'd speak to him, directly or indirectly, the last ever. "Drink your drink," Sylvia said. "I don't mind if you have a cigarette. I know you've got some in your jacket pocket."

"I'm overwhelmed," he said.

He straightened up from the awkward posture he had assumed, crouching over the low table, and sat down at one end of the long sofa. Sylvia sat down at the other. She crossed her legs carefully, as if she expected to sit for some time. Both looked straight before them, like people in an airport lounge who fear that the journey ahead will be time enough for them to become acquainted.

Presently Sylvia shivered. "The central heating's gone off again," she said.

"There's something wrong with the time clock. I expect Alistair's been moving the tappets."

"He must be doing it by remote control then, he hasn't been in for days."

"No, I've not seen him either."

Their voices were carefully neutral and flat; polite people, feeling their way into conversation, thrown together in cramped accommodation by mere chance and the necessity of having to travel at all.

"Sometimes I think I'd like to run away," Sylvia said. "If kids can do it, why not parents? I can't cope with this place."

"Everything seems to be falling apart, doesn't it?"

"Did you know the washer's packed up altogether? The only thing to do is to go and leave it all behind. It's like, what do you call it? The House of Usher."

"It's like the house of Atreus," Colin said. "Now there's a coincidence for you. You eat this pie, and it just happens to contain your children."

Sylvia turned on him. "You're doing it again."

"You started it, with the House of Usher, I'm only putting a word in."

Sylvia jumped to her feet. Her face contorted with anger. She ran out of the room. Alarmed, he sped after her. He caught up with her at the foot of the stairs and threw his arms around her waist, swinging her round. The small effort put him out of breath; he would be no good these days on the squash court. Sylvia struggled; he lifted her almost off her feet and dumped her down on the third stair. "Don't move," he said. "Let's have this out. If we don't straighten it out now then we never will." He took her left wrist in a secure grip and sat down beside her. It was a tight fit. Sylvia had been expanding lately. They were red in the face; emotion and the moment's struggle had knocked the breath out of them both.

"You know the House of Usher?" Sylvia said, when she recovered herself. "I saw it on TV. It's better than TV, living here."

"No licence fee, only the mortgage. No adverts to interrupt you."

"I'd be glad of interruption at times."

"Did you throw out my photograph?" Colin said.

"Yes."

"I suppose you think you did it for my own good."

"No. I did it for my own."

"Thanks a million."

"That was her, wasn't it? It's all the same woman."

"Yes, I've often thought that."

"I'm not stupid," Sylvia said. "I can put two and two together."

"I don't see how."

"I have my sources of information."

"You didn't say anything."

"What would have been the point?"

"That's that," he said. "Ten years of mental agony."

"It can't have been. Not ten years solid. There must have been bright spots."

"She's an alcoholic. Her husband told me."

"I'm sorry to hear that."

"*C'est la vie,*" Colin said. "I saw her coming out of the bank. I thought she was a figment of my imagination, some sort of mirage. So I let it go. There's a moment for everything and when that moment's passed you might as well strike camp and stamp out the bonfire—and get back to daily life. You've been away too long." He paused. "I've been thinking . . . I've something to tell you."

"Oh yes?"

"If you really want to run away . . . do you remember Frank O'Dwyer?"

"Could I forget him?" Alarm and dislike crossed Sylvia's face: it was an old colleague, whose dipsomaniac company she had never relished. "What about him? I thought you never saw him since he went to County Hall."

"Only occasionally. I mean, the Educational Advisors don't

come by that often. They might be contaminated by contact with the kids."

"And?"

"He's had an accident. He was over at the Forty Martyrs Comprehensive last week, and he'd been drinking whisky in the office—you know what the Brothers are like, very hospitable. Anyway, they couldn't find him. Thought he'd gone—then Brother Ambrose turned him up in the gym. He'd been on the equipment, you know, swinging from the trapeze and putting his feet through those rings that come down from the ceiling. Broken both legs."

"Oh, I shouldn't." Sylvia covered her mouth with her hand. "Oh, it's awful, laughing at people's misfortunes."

"Anyway, that's the last straw. He's had warnings. Early retirement. The point is, if you were willing to move, I could have his job."

"Are you sure?"

"It's unofficial. It'll have to be advertised, but I think I can swing it. Everybody says so. They'll want to appoint soon, for September."

"Do I want to move? Oh Colin, I can't tell you how I want to move."

"Two hours ago you wanted to adopt a baby."

"I want to move."

"We could look for a house."

"But September? That's months away. I can't see myself in September. I can't imagine it. Gemma will be seven months old. It'll be a different world. I can't imagine lasting out till then. Something awful will happen."

"Such as?"

"You'll change your mind about that woman. You'll be ringing her up. I expect you're planning right now to ring her up. You're only telling me all this to throw me off the scent."

He squeezed her wrist. "That hurts," she said.

"Get the book. The telephone book."

"What?"

"Look up some estate agents and ring them up first thing tomorrow morning. Let's do it, Sylvia, quick. Ask them for details of a nice house—three bed, Claire and Karen can share—modern, big windows, plenty light, nothing with a past; a nice jerry-built house like the one we used to have, with all the flaws built in."

"The houses are all right, Colin. It's us the flaws are built into."

"Not any more. I'm being positive, I'm laying plans." He paused, momentarily amazed. It's easy once you start. The momentum carries you forward. "As soon as we find the house, we must move. I'll have to stay at school till the end of the summer term, but I can commute. I can come on the new link road. It'll only take me thirty minutes. If that."

"Do you really think we could? Just get away? Why didn't you say so before?"

"I was waiting for Frank to break his legs. A *deus ex machina*," he said. "Every home should have one."

"So that's it then?" She spoke with finality and with hope, and a look of exhaustion crossed her face, from the strain of keeping up such complex and contradictory emotions. Colin looked up at the ceiling of the hall, still stained dark from the kitchen fire.

"Do you think we'll sell this scrap heap?"

"I don't see why not. After all, it's not structurally defective, is it, except for that growth in Alistair's room? We'll have to scrape the walls and paint it with something. And in the hall, what you've got to do is keep the light off when people come. You wouldn't notice. You'd just think it was a nice beige shade. You wouldn't notice till you came to wash the walls down. Then it'd go all streaky."

"That's unscrupulous."

"They get what they see. What they don't see, that's their problem."

"That's settled then. Get somebody round to give us a valuation." He took her hand. "And what about Francis? What will he say?"

She looked down at her knees. "I don't know, what will he say?"

"I thought you had something going."

"Not really."

"I thought at one time he was going to leave Hermione."

"Leave Hermione?" she said scornfully. "She's a bishop's daughter. Anyway, do you know, I saw another side of him. When we were down at the night shelter—I didn't tell you, did I? These two poor old men came in, wanting soup. Well, I didn't recognise them, they were wearing balaclavas. They were having leek and potato. When Francis saw them he ran up and said, 'These are the bastards who've been causing me all the trouble.' He said he'd caught them laying a fire in the vestry. He kicked one of them quite hard—you know what big boots he wears. I was ashamed, I said, they were probably feeling the cold, you know what February is. He said, 'You don't set fire to cassocks, do you?' He said it was arson. He phoned the police."

"What happened to them?"

"They were taken into custody. They've been sent to a home."

"They'll probably be better off."

"Oh, no, Colin. They'll get institutionalised."

"Still, I can see why you were disillusioned. Does he know you've gone off him?"

"Probably." Sylvia dipped her head. A tear ran down her cheek, slow and singular, and quivered at the corner of her mouth. "He doesn't care. He's got other involvements."

"Oh yes?"

"There's this deaconess. Julie."

"The man's a philanderer! Well, never mind," Colin said cheerfully. "Never mind, you've done some good to the community between you, which I may say is more than Isabel Ryan and I ever did. We were great theorists, but I don't think we left anybody better off. How's the canal clean-up going?"

"Oh, it's going to be lovely." She sniffed, and wiped her face with the back of her hand. "We're going to have a nature trail.

Anyway, I'll tell you another thing about Francis. He has this fat crease in his ear."

"What?"

"It means he's going to have a coronary. Men with paunches and creases in their ears, they're At Risk. I read it somewhere."

"The *Beano*?"

"No, it's true."

"Have I got one?"

"I don't think so. I'm not sure if I'm looking in the right place."

"At least I know now why you keep staring at the side of my head."

"There's this new diet I've heard of. For the first two days you just eat apples. Any kind, but you mustn't mix them; if you have Golden Delicious for breakfast you can't have Cox's for lunch. Then for two days you eat only cheese—if you have Edam for breakfast you must—"

"No," Colin said. He shook his head. "No, I don't think so."

"No, somehow I don't think so either. I'll just get fat."

"That would be restful."

"Mrs. Ryan wasn't fat, was she?"

"Skin and bone."

"Colin?"

"Yes?"

"Do you think three beds will be enough?"

"I'm counting on Alistair going to Borstal before long. I think it's a fair bet."

"What if Suzanne decides to come home? Oh, you know, I can't forgive myself now for trying to talk her into an abortion. When I saw Gemma I thought—well, she's a lovely little thing, who would be without her? And if Suzanne wants—"

"She won't come home. She told you, she's got her own life now. So has Alistair, he'll be off soon, somewhere or other. They're nearly grown up, Sylvia. That part of our life is over. The other two will be off before you know it. It's they who have the future."

"And we have none?"

"There are worse things than no future." He put his arm across her shoulder, held her tight by the upper arm. "Cheer up. The excitement's over. Nothing will happen to us now."

Next day, when Lizzie Blank came in to clean, she found Colin's present sitting on the coffee table. She looked at it for a long time, without touching. Then she knelt before it, as Colin had done, and traced the faculties with her finger. I have got these now, she thought. All of them. I have got everything, except offspring. Carefully she lifted the head and dusted it, although it did not need dusting, and set it down in the dead centre of the table. She was perfectly sure that it was what she had waited for. She had last seen it in Sholto's shop; its arrival here could not help but tell her something. It was a mysterious transportation; there would be others.

Sylvia came downstairs. She was still in her dressing gown, and she smiled secretly to herself, and hummed as she went into the kitchen. Lizzie followed her.

"Mr. Sidney get his leg over, then?" she enquired.

"Lizzie!" Sylvia glared at her. "You can stop it, you know, or I'll have to give you notice. I can't have the children hearing you talk like that."

"The little lambkins," Lizzie said sarcastically. " 'Hearing you talk like that.' We've got very snooty, haven't we?"

Sylvia looked at her daily woman with barely concealed dislike. Since the incident with the photograph she had become increasingly familiar and cutting, and she was definitely skimping on her work, claiming that the breakdown of most of the electrical appliances was making cleaning impossible, that she was tired out and worn to the bone. She looked far from bone, Sylvia thought, her white unhealthy-looking flesh oozing out of her clothes. She had flesh, and to spare.

"I'll be straight with you, Lizzie," she said. "I believe in straight talking."

"Oh yes?"

"I don't like you, Lizzie. There's something about you I never have liked, and I resent you poking your nose into my daughter's business. I kept you on because when we had Colin's mother here you were a godsend, and I don't deny that, and I'll give you a reference, and you can read it."

"And now you're discharging me?" the woman said sullenly.

"We don't need you. We'll be moving soon."

"I can travel."

"Not that far."

Lizzie looked up. "And this house will be empty?"

"It will be on the market. As soon as I find somewhere, we'll be off."

"Well, I'll save you the trouble of firing me, Mrs. Sidney, madam. I was going to give in my notice anyway. I think you stink."

"That's as maybe," Sylvia said levelly.

"And you needn't worry I'll tell on Florence. I wouldn't soil my lips, I might tell on her if they still had capital punishment. If I thought she'd be hanged by the neck till she was dead."

"You monster," Sylvia burst out. "Get out of my house."

"Your house? Not for long."

"And give me my daughter's address before you go. Your address, I mean, it's the only one I've got for her. I'll send your wages on."

"I'd sooner have cash."

"I'm sure you would, but I haven't got it on me. You'll have to wait. I'll pay you for the week."

"Don't bankrupt yourself, will you?"

"If you don't go," Sylvia said, "I shall hit you. Here, write it down on this." She thrust at Lizzie the notepad she used for her shopping lists, and the stub of a pencil. "She's not with you, is she, Suzanne?"

"No, I've not seen her." Lizzie bent over the counter top, grasping the pencil awkwardly.

"If you do see her, tell her to come home. I can't bear to lose my children."

"You're very emotional, aren't you?" Lizzie looked up, and puckered her face. "Like this, you go."

"How dare you imitate me?"

"I've seen your old photographs. How dare you imitate me?"

"What? You've been through my drawers?"

"A lot of water's gone under the bridges since those days, Mrs. S."

"It's the last straw. Hurry up with that and go."

Laboriously, Lizzie set down Mr. Kowalski's address; wavering block capitals traced with much effort. She pushed it at Sylvia. "There you are."

"You can barely write." Sylvia took it from her and looked at it in astonishment. "Who wrote your application for you? I had a letter."

"My landlord wrote it. You didn't ask me if I could write."

"You're here under false pretences."

"If you like," Lizzie said grimly. She took her coat from the hook by the door and put it on.

"You can go out by the back door," said Sylvia, pointing. "You always do."

"Pardon me, Mrs. Sidney. I can go out the front."

On the way through the hall she paused and looked up the stairs. All the bedroom doors were closed; the stairhead was in darkness. The final straw, she thought. Four and twenty Sidneys, baked in a pie.

Isabel Ryan was blundering about in her kitchen, still in her dressing gown, though it was nearly midday. That's nothing, she thought. I can still be in it at four in the afternoon, I can still be in it at eight o'clock, and then it is time to get back into it and go to bed. Have I been to bed? she wondered. The house was very cold, though it barely registered with her. She did not think about what her body needed; it had its own life. She could not remember how much time had passed since she had rung up Sylvia Sidney; one night, or two, or many more. In a mist of grief and nausea, she clung to the edge of the kitchen sink, swaying gently.

Perhaps she should have been more persistent. The woman had sounded stiff and dangerous, as if she were going to snake down the wires and do her some damage. What had she thought, that she had rung up to claim Colin back? After all these years? It must have sounded like it. All she had wanted was information. What was the child like?

Is it some natural kind of child, she wondered, that looks like Jim, or like its mother? Or is it a mystery baby; and does it get solved? She ran her hand down over her body. If this was the solution, would she know it soon enough to put it in her exposé? It must come along quickly, because she had almost run out of typing paper; she couldn't get more unless she was sober, and if she was ever sober there was no saying what she might find out, and the task would be endless. She might even find out if she was pregnant or not. Would Jim stay with her, now she had contracted this mysterious swelling? He hadn't said.

She could feel resolution spreading inside her; another strange organic growth, beyond her control. I will get together some clothes, she thought, even if it takes me an hour to do it. I will go out and drive my car, even if I crash it. I will go upstairs and find that letter that Miss Suzanne Sidney has written to my husband. Then I will take the address and look at my street map, and taking the letter, I will shred it up finely and flush it down the lavatory. Then I will go round and see her. I will wait outside her house and watch her come and go. I will just look on. I shall just show myself, walk down the street. Then she will see what it is like to be Jim's wife. She will profit by my example; and I will profit by hers.

Or else I have lost everything, she thought. Jim Ryan, Colin Sidney; and my whisky glass as well.

Less than a mile away from Buckingham Avenue, lying to either side of a narrow and little-used road called Turner's Lane, there was a tract of open ground. It was surprising that houses had not been built there, but the residents of Lauderdale Road, whose gardens backed onto it, regarded it as an amenity, and had fought with vigour the various schemes for its use which had been put forward over the years. And so it had been unchanged for as long as they remembered; a few desolate acres of tussocky grass, stagnant marshy pools, and little thickets of prickly bushes. The residents never went there; there were houses on three sides of it, and on the fourth side only the old canal. They left it to stray dogs and cats, to the odd exhibitionist, to the passing rabbit and urban fox; and to their children.

It was in one of these prickly thickets that Alistair Sidney and his friends had set up their den. When they had reached school-leaving age, and the winter came on, they had thought they would leave dens behind. But their homes were not congenial to them, and they found that they needed it more than ever. They had a clean dirt floor, swept and compacted; branches curved densely above them, making their shelter almost as wind- and weather-proof as a conventional tent. It was not quite high enough for standing, but you could manage a crouch. The thorns left long pink scratches and puncture marks, which sometimes went septic; but Sherwood had stolen a first-aid kit recently, so that was all right. A dense undergrowth protected them from observation; in spring, as Austin said, they'd be practically invisible. If it had only had video games it would have been perfect.

The children had passed many happy hours here, playing with the skeleton that the Brownies had found by the canal.

"They want to do their karate badge, them Brownies," Austin said. "Then they could of protected it from us."

"Kari reckons it's a rabbit anyway," Alistair said. "She does biology. Don't you, pimpleface?"

"Nar," Austin said. "It's human, that."

"It could be a mix."

"A chimera," said Karen.

"A wot?"

"A chimera. A mix-up. A bit of this and a bit of that. A monster. A thing of hybrid character."

"Yer," said Austin judiciously. "Could be."

Since Christmas, they had occupied themselves in trying to arrange the bones in an intelligent order, and they were immersed in this, one sunless afternoon at half-term, when the sound of crunching wood and vegetation alerted them to an imminent invasion.

"Christ, it's my dad," Austin said. "Nobody else has boots like that. Quick, boil-head, get the bones back in the box."

Karen leaped up and began to shovel the skeleton into the Tesco box in which they kept it between jigsaw sessions. The sound of crashing and scrunching came closer, punctuated by damning and blasting in a powerful male voice. "It is my dad!" Austin hissed. "Quick, get it out of the way. I'm off. He's bloody violent. He can cripple you with one kick."

Heavy breathing warned them that the intruder was almost upon them. Austin fled, bent double, through the back exit. Karen shoved the box after him and, grasping the springy twigs and branches, attempted to cover the signs of his retreat. Her hands bled; she fell to her knees and shovelled dead leaves into a mound, banking them against the entrance to the bolt hole. Before she had time to scramble to her feet the intruder was upon them; not the Reverend Teller, but a wild youth, brawny and stubble-headed, wearing boots the equal of the vicar's, and with leather thongs binding each wrist.

"Jesus," Alistair breathed. He sized up the lad and knew he was no match. They were at his mercy. Do something, Scab, he thought, distract him, offer him your body. "We weren't doing no harm, mister," he said in a whining voice. "Don't beat us up, we'll leave peaceable, honest." Karen, still crouching, stared up at the youth, holding up hands finely beaded with blood.

The youth's beefy chest heaved. He reached forward; Alistair was taken up by the front of his zipper jacket and held, skull to hairless skull.

"Where's that friggin' Austin?" the youth demanded.

"Never saw 'im," Alistair said gamely. "Who are you? Aw, gerrof, don't torture me."

216

"Me?" said the youth. He breathed into Alistair's putty face. "I'm his friggin' probation officer."

A month later, after Austin had been sent down—burglary, retail premises—the remnants of the gang had met to discuss their problem. They had to face the fact that their den was no longer secure; if they wanted to keep their skeleton, they would have to find a safer place for it.

"Can't keep it at our house," Karen said. "We're moving. Anyway, if you had a box, my mum would look in it."

Alistair thought. "She would if it was yours," he said, after some effort.

"She would if it was yours too."

"You can't keep it at my house," Sherwood said. "My mammy would pawn it."

"Nar, you couldn't pawn a skeleton."

"She pawn anything. Or, come Friday night, start stewing, curry bones, mm-mm, delicious, old family recipe from Montego Bay."

"You Rastafarian git," Alistair murmured. "Your mammy goes down the chip shop, I've seen her."

Karen giggled. "I bet Lizzie Blank would eat stewed bones. She used to eat everything Claire gave her when she was doing her cookery badge, and some of it was absolutely disgusting."

"I wish you'd shut it," Alistair grumbled. "And give me some peace while I'm trying to think." He squatted, cradling his head between his hands. Suddenly he looked up, his features clearing. "Got it in one," he said. "What a piece of fucking brilliance."

"What? What is it?"

"Look, you know our lot. You know what they do. Sleep around, knock off old ladies, receiving stolen goods. But what's the one thing they don't do? Mess about with other people's post."

"How do you mean?"

"Well, all right, suppose a letter come addressed to Dad. Mum would want to open it, she'd be tempted, she'd feel it around to see if there was anything inside it, but she wouldn't actually open it, oh no, she'd be ashamed. After he'd come home and opened it, she'd sneak it away and read it, but that's different, according to her." He tapped his head. "That's psychology, Sherwood."

"So?"

"So, Lizzie Blank."

"We had this daily," Kari explained. "But she's left."

"So, we go down Fletcher's, nick some brown paper and string, and we do up the bones in a nice parcel. Then we put her name on it, and our address, and leave it in our hall. Like it's come through the post. Nobody'll interfere with it."

"But what when she comes?" Sherwood said. "She'll take it away, open it up; oh my my!"

"She won't collect it, dumbo, because she's left, hasn't she, she'll never come back."

"What when we move?"

"That'll be weeks. Months."

"But then Mum might throw it away."

"Look, I can't solve everything at one go, give us a chance. We'll cross that bridge when we come to it."

"It sounds feasible," Kari said cautiously.

"Could try it, man," Sherwood said.

Alistair pointed to his chest. "Nobel Prize for Being a Clever Bugger."

"Get the news this morning?" Miss Anaemia asked.

Hardly likely. Mr. K. looked up, fearful, his jaw sagging a little. Nothing came from his radio except strange blips and crackles, and police messages; even when he tuned into "Big Band Special" they were there again when he next switched on.

"There's this man," Miss Anaemia continued, seating herself by the kitchen range. "There's this man knocked off his wife. He's gone driving round the countryside, pretending to be somewhere else—"

"An alias, is an expression," said Mr. K.

"Then he's gone off to the Lake District and dumped her body in a deep lake, and ten years pass, and he thinks he's got away with it. Then—guess what?"

"But I can't guess," Mr. K. said. "Secret murder come to light?"

"There are the police, looking for some other body completely, and what do they find? This chap's wife, all preserved, just as good as when she went in. And if he'd rowed his boat out twenty feet further, she'd have gone into the deepest part of the lake and they'd never have found her at all."

"For the want of a nail a shoe was lost," Mr. K. observed.

"I don't know about that, but now he's in gaol. Horrible, innit? What do you think, Mrs. Wilmot?"

But Mrs. Wilmot had slipped off, melted away, as if into the wall.

Two days later, when Sylvia entered the house, she almost tripped over the large cardboard box in the hall. "Damn, what's this?" she said, scrabbling on the floor for the letters she had dropped. "Karen, are you there? What's this?"

Karen came out of the kitchen, eating a chocolate biscuit. "Dunno," she said. "A man brought it."

"What man?"

"Dunno." She shrugged. "Postman?"

"Put the light on, will you?"

"Bulb's gone again."

"Damn this house." Sylvia bent down and peered at the box. "I can't see any postage on it. It's addressed to Lizzie. Fancy that."

"Maybe it was a friend of hers," Karen said, carefully. "This man who brought it."

"Well, I don't know what she wants to have her post sent here for. I'd be very annoyed if I thought she'd been giving this address to people. Anyway, if she thinks I'm trailing round after her, she's mistaken. She can just come and collect it. I'll phone her up."

"Oh, I wouldn't bother," Karen said. "It's probably nothing."

"It's a big box. I wonder what it is?" Sylvia took it in both hands. "Not heavy." She shook it. "Rattles a bit."

"Probably something from mail order," Karen suggested.

"Probably. Must be some cowboy outfit. Don't even run to printed labels."

"Well, you know how it is," Karen said. "You send for something and it turns up weeks later when you've forgotten about it, right?"

"Or unsolicited goods," Sylvia said. "She's not obliged to return them. I'll tell her her Rights."

"I wouldn't bother."

"Of course I must. I've got her number somewhere."

Karen quailed. They had not thought of this. It had been a case of out of sight, out of mind; they never expected to see Lizzie again, and they had not thought of Sylvia being able to trace her. A diversion was needed. "What's the post?" Karen said craftily.

"It's from the solicitor. Come in the kitchen where I can see." Kari followed her. Sylvia turned. Her face shone. "We've got it," she said. "We can move. Vacant possession."

"When?"

"It can't be soon enough for me. Your father's taking out a bridging loan. It'll probably bankrupt us, but I can't wait." She sat down abruptly on a kitchen chair, suddenly deflated, the smile wiped from her face. "Only what about Suzanne? I don't want to go off and leave her like this. She's my daughter, I love her. And the baby, I haven't seen Gemma since the hospital. It's cruel of Suzanne to break off contact like this, not even to ring up and let us know she's all right."

"Never mind, Mum. You've got me."

"Yes," Sylvia said without enthusiasm. She opened her bag and took out her address book. There was a loose sheet of paper inside.

"I've got Lizzie's number here," she said. "I can ask if she's heard from Suzanne. It comes to something, when you have to go to a scrubber like that for news of your only grandchild. Number 56, Napier Street. That's funny. I should have noticed before. I thought she lived at Eugene Terrace, at an Indian shop."

"Perhaps they evicted her."

"I wouldn't be surprised. Karen, do you have to eat your way through every packet of biscuits that comes into this house? Is it any wonder you've got spots?"

It would soon be Easter. The telephone rang often in Mr. Kowalski's hall. Sometimes he ignored it, sometimes he shook his fist at it and threatened to rip it out of the wall; what was it but a tool for criminals and a source of disease? Sometimes he lifted the receiver, and bellowed down it in one or other of his many languages.

Muriel intercepted the postman. There was another letter for Miss Blank. She opened it. Mrs. Sidney cast aspersions on my writing, she thought; but I can read perfectly well.

Dear Lizzie,

When I phoned up the number you gave me I got this man with an accent. I could not get any sense out of him so I am writing. I am at my friend Edwina's and this is the address, but do not give it to my mother. Can you baby-sit Gemma next Wednesday? Ring me up and tell me if you can. She is no trouble, she sleeps a lot. We are all going up to Manchester to see about the squat, because it looks as if it might be on again. Sean has reconnected the electricity, and we have met this geophysicist who does a lot of plumbing, it is known as the black economy. I don't want to take Gemma with me because of the cold, you know what April is, the cruellest month, so please I hope you can. I will be back for teatime and I can pay you.

Love, Suzanne.

Enclosed was a scrap of paper with Edwina's address and telephone number. "It falls into your lap," Mrs. Wilmot observed to her landlord.

"What?" Mr. K. dropped back. He was edgy these days.

"No, I mean, opportunity knocks. It's an expression, Mr. K."

"You poor old Wilmot," Mr. K. said sorrowfully. "When the ship sinks, we will be like drowned rats. You, I, Miss Anaemia, all shall go down in the shipwreck of my fortunes, unless our Blessed Lady smiles on us. Those," he added with some satisfaction, "are expressions too."

"Well, I hope you've been saying your litany," Mrs. Wilmot said. "Course, I don't know any litanies, I'm a Metho."

"We need more than prayers, we need revolvers," Mr. K. said. "Mantraps, Molotov cocktails. You see new woman in the street, watching out of a car? Always watching, watching, seeing who comes and goes. Always silent, silent, silent like the grave."

"Don't get carried away," Mrs. Wilmot said. "You make me shudder with your prognostications."

"Soon I will lay about me," Mr. K. promised. "I cannot longer endure the agony of mind. My nerve is twisted to such a pitch—" He picked up a fork from the kitchen table, one of only two he had, and taking it in both hands, bent it until the handle was twisted and the tines drooped. "Like that," he said. The sweat started out on his forehead. "Like that."

It seemed to Colin, light-headed in the severe spring weather, that for once things were going his way. His appointment was confirmed, and he was counting off the weeks till the end of the summer term. He had sent Frank a get-well card and a basket of fruit. His colleagues said he was just the man for Frank's job, and he knew it was true. He hugged himself, mentally, when he went into his office every morning. No more shillings, no more pence, no more sitting on the old school fence, No more geography, no more sums, no more beating on us bums. He had made a resolve that on the last day of term he would go home and turn out every one of his pockets, and blow out the chalk dust for ever, and never never let it back. He would never touch a stick of chalk again, or even engage with the school computer; he would never walk into a classroom again, except as a strict noncombatant. He would be a serious professional man, not a registered child minder, and he would impress his colleagues old and new with his suave, considered, and practical advice. He would be the History Advisor; he would be given the best chair in staff rooms throughout the county, and he would enjoy single malts—though not too many—with an obsequious Brother Ambrose.

Of course, there were many weeks to get through first; but they would be moving in a few days, and then, in part, he would be free. Free of Florence, with her wearisome protestations of innocence, for she never let the subject drop; free of ten years at Buckingham Avenue. At a stroke, he would sever his wife from the canal scheme, his son from his gang, and his youngest daughter from the Brownies; and who knew whether the change of air would not improve Karen's spots? Whether Suzanne came back or not, no doubt the family survivors could begin to put together some sort of life.

Sylvia was behaving herself, he thought. She seemed content, wrapping newspaper round such crockery as remained, making inventories of their possessions. She was too busy to rake up the past. The telephone stayed silent. Or it rang; but not for him.

Wednesday came. Muriel had set the alarm early, but she woke up without it and turned it off. Just like the old days; as if Mother were standing over her and shaking her.

She pulled the covers up to her chin and lay there, thinking. Emmanuel had explained it to her, or tried to, before they took him back to Fulmers Moor. The unbaptised child is the lodge of the devil; and wasn't it the Devil in person whom Mother had feared, taking a turn on the landing, peering at them down the stairs? Baptism drives the Devil out; the child gets contented and grows fat. The bad child you put in the canal and the good child you get out are the same one, but the Devil is out, and God is in.

That can make a lot of difference. It's only baptism; a bit more drastic and risky than what you get at the parish church, but there are some babies that are hard cases.

Of course, that was only his theory. He was on the bottle at the time. "Where's this resurrection you promised?" she asked him. He looked pious. "Easter, of course." And here it was. Give or take a few days.

Now the house was very quiet; before Jim got up, Isabel was wrapping her parcel. The exposé had turned quite bulky. She couldn't get it in an envelope. Strange that failure should take up so much space; that foolishness and ineptitude should need so many stamps. Finishing the narrative had not brought her the release she had expected. The more she wrote, the less clear it had become. What were those writing tips she had been given, at the evening class where she had met Colin? But that was as unclear as all the rest, all the events of her life up to now muddied and confused by her fear and sickness in the Axons' spare room. The strange bulk under her clothes sighed softly, shuffled, and disposed itself.

She sat at the kitchen table, fumbling with her string. She was glad in one way that she had written it. Whatever happened, it would be a sort of testimony. That day, she was going to find Suzanne, for sure; she would give up the futile observation, and go and knock on the door. She would find her, and talk. Suzanne could not harm her, she could not murder her, could she? Why was she so afraid? She would have a little drink, just a small tumbler of whisky to steady her. She addressed her parcel; she would post it on the way.

Would they be able to follow it, at the *Sunday Enquirer*? They wouldn't mind, they would print anything. Would they want proof, some sort of circumstantial evidence? There was the file, of course; the file on Muriel Axon. She had kept that. It had been easier to account for its disappearance, than to account for its contents. But the file did not tell the end of the story. The old woman was dead. The baby was dead too. The baby's mother was locked away somewhere, a person or persons unknown. Was that the phrase? It didn't seem quite right. Her hand shook as she poured her drink. "MANY YEARS LATER," she said to herself, "THE FACTS OF THE CASE CAME TO LIGHT."

Perhaps it would not make sense to the reader. But sense was not her requirement.

She pictured her parcel, travelling in a van along Fleet Street. She imagined the people in the offices of the *Enquirer*, opening her parcel. Now when people pointed at her in the town, they would have something to point about. Now when they talked, they would have something to say. When she poured her drink, she noticed, she had poured far more than she meant to. She was not going to put it back.

Seven o'clock struck. Jim was running the bath taps. The day had begun. She caught sight of her white face in the dark kitchen window; peaked, blurred, with formless swimming eyes.

And now Muriel was out of bed. She was on her feet, regarding herself in the spotted mirror of the dressing table; the carefully shuttered expression, the drooping lids. She reached out and picked up Lizzie's wig from its stand. Her high-heeled boots were under the bed, her leopard-skin coat was in the wardrobe. It was the last time she would need them.

Miss Anaemia came in from the street, her teeth chattering. "That woman," she complained, standing in the kitchen. "It's her, you know, Mr. K., the one with the hollow face. These DHSS get worse and worse. I know she watches me, but she's never *done* anything before. I was just going to the post box, trying to catch the first post with my appeal form, and there she was, squashing a great big parcel into the slot. It gave me a shock, I can tell you. I've never seen her out of the car before."

"And so? What did she do?" Mr. K. asked fearfully. So early in the morning, alarms before his oat flakes.

"So she caught hold of me and pinched my arm. She says, where's the baby? I say, what baby? I said, I wish I had one, I could get rehoused. She says, don't try to pull the wool over my eyes, Suzanne. Suzanne? Who's she?"

"Related to this Blank, no doubt," Mr. Kowalski said with a sneer. "Related to Snoopers, related to the giant who brought the bread that day. A woman phones up constantly, asking for Blank. I try everything, sing down the receiver, rude noises."

"Have you tried leaving it off the hook?"

"But my precious, how shall I follow their tricks? No, we must face it, Anaemia, our number is up. This woman who accosts you, she is the one who looks—so—with the staring eyes, the ghoul?"

"That's her. The pale one."

Mr. K. shuddered. "Have you seen Wilmot?" he asked.

"Not come out this morning."

"She must be given her orders. It is a siege. Please to stay on the upper storey till further notice."

"You won't catch me going out there again. That woman's bonkers. They can insult you, but they're not allowed to pinch your arm. It's mistaken identity. I'll sue them." She hurried off, rubbing her sore arm. "There's tribunals."

Left to himself, Mr. Kowalski lumbered into the hall and drew the big bolts on the front door. He went back to the kitchen and locked himself in. Five minutes later Lizzie Blank came downstairs, carrying her boots. For once, she wasn't bothered about giving him any frights. He was getting a bit unpredictable, she sensed. By leaning hard on the inside of the door, you could get sufficient play to draw back the bolts without making a noise. This she did; and, in her finery, stepped into the street.

Mr. K. tipped half a scuttle of coal into the range. He might as well be comfortable now. I could have a hearty breakfast, he reflected; except that he had neglected to procure the essentials for one. But truly, he had no stomach for it. He was sick when he thought of dying; sick and cold. But I will defend it to the last, he thought: hearth and home.

From between the worn cushions of his fireside chair he

extracted his book of idioms. He picked up his pen, and was overwhelmed by a rush of feeling so violent that his hand shook and he was forced to put it down again and recover himself. All the horrors of the last months flooded back; the voices of strange women, the heavy footsteps overhead. The beating in the street, the blonde impostor on his own stairs; the giant, limping off round the corner. Presently he calmed himself; but his hand still shook when he picked up his pen and wrote: Curtains, Swansong, Terminus: THE FINAL CHAPTER.

CHAPTER 9

It was a wild blustery day; tossing grey clouds, rain on the wind, outbreaks of sunshine. Muriel would have put her umbrella up, but she couldn't juggle both together; the umbrella and the cardboard box.

The baby, Gemma, had been sleeping when she arrived at Edwina's flat. She had left the empty box at the bottom of the stairs, gone up and rang the doorbell. There was no sign of the flat's owner, but Suzanne was waiting for her, in her boots and big sweater, ready to go.

"There you are, Lizzie, hello. She's asleep."

"That's good. And how are you, ducks?"

"Oh, I'm all right," Suzanne said, with a little laugh. She had been heavily pregnant when they had last seen each other; now she looked paler, hollow-eyed, inwardly collapsed. The flat—two rooms really—was dirty and neglected, a near-slum. There was a scrap of fraying carpet, then bare boards; windows were cracked and crisscrossed with tape. There were mattresses strewn over the floor. Somewhere a tap was dripping, tip-tap, tip-tap. Suzanne's possessions were in a heap inside the front door; a backpack, a sleeping bag, and a box of baby things. Her face had a bruised look, as if she hadn't slept.

"Heard from Jim?"

Suzanne shook her head. She brushed her hair out of her eyes. "Here are her things," she said, handing over a plastic carrier bag. "Her bottle and everything, disposable nappies, put cream on her when you change her, she's getting a rash. She can have a feed when she wakes up."

"How do you know?" Muriel said suddenly. "How do you know how to look after them?"

"It's only common sense. It's not the mystery that people make of it."

"It's cold here."

"The squat should be warmer. I hope it's all right. I'm taking most of my stuff over on the off chance. I'll pick her up about six o'clock, will that be okay?"

"I'll fetch her back."

"Oh, would you? Course, you could stay here with her"—she looked around doubtfully—"but it's a bit depressing."

"Better off at my place," Muriel said. "Be an outing for her, won't it?"

"I don't think she's old enough to appreciate an outing."

"She'll get the air, though. Where is she?"

Suzanne went into the other room and came back with a quilted bundle. She kissed the baby's fluffy head, and pulled up her hood around her face. "There, she'll be nice and warm," she said. "Can you manage? She's heavier than you think. Hold on, and I'll put her cot blanket round her. There. Okay?"

"Okay. Good luck then."

"Thanks, Lizzie. I'll pay you tonight. See you."

She followed them out onto the stairs. A keen draught whistled under the closed doors of the landing. Suzanne crossed her arms over her chest. She looked anxious.

"Sure you'll manage?"

"No problem." Muriel thought she was going to follow, hovering over them, until they were down in the street; but she paused at the top of the uncarpeted stairs and let them go down alone. Manoeuvring with her foot, Muriel pulled the front door behind

229

her, and it closed with a clatter. There was a tiny porch, long unglazed, the wood rotting. Her box was where she had left it, on the composition floor running with damp. She stooped and put the baby in. Gemma was a bigger bundle than she had expected, encased in her snug quilting. She was asleep, and dreaming; Muriel saw the movement of her eyes under the tender skin of the lids.

She took up the box in her arms. At some point before she reached home, Gemma was sure to wake up, and then she would cry and attract attention. For this reason, it would be better not to fold over the flaps of the box; it would look odd. It was true that Mother had done it, but her own infant had been past crying, and moving only faintly, moving only feebly, like something burrowing underground. If anyone stops us, she thought, I'll say I'm her godmother. She stepped into the street.

No one stopped them. No one noticed them hurrying by; the big fleshy woman plastered with make-up, strutting along in her high-heeled boots; and her box from the Pick 'N' Save. The bottom edge of the box dug into her chest. She had no gloves, and her nails were drops of blood against the cardboard. The townspeople passed them, bending in the wind, their faces screwed up and their collars pulled about their ears. In their concrete bunkers in the shopping centre, the saplings lashed in the gust, whipping the moist air with their half-fledged green. There was mud and broken glass on the pavements, the polystyrene cartons from the hamburger shop bowled down the street. Birds fled shrieking from wire to wire.

At ten o'clock the woman rang up again; the woman with the harsh, strange, threatening voice. She said, was Lizzie Blank there? This was the third time she'd rung, she said.

"No Blank is here," Mr. K. said. "You are under a mistake."

"Look," Sylvia said, "will you tell her, please, that I have this box for her?"

"Specify contents," said Mr. K. gruffly. High explosive, he thought.

"How would I know what's in it? All I know is that it's been cluttering up my hall for weeks past. Tell her: if she doesn't collect it right now, I don't know how she'll get it, because I'm moving today. The house will be all locked up."

She was a persistent, headstrong woman, this; he would not like to meet her in the dark. It seemed a bad mistake to inform her quarry over the telephone about what was in store; but no doubt, like him, she was a veteran of intrigue and destruction, and like him had long forgotten whose side she was on. Someone, somewhere, would be taping the call. It was all over the papers, about telephone tappers. Sooner or later the box would turn up; the parcel, the mystery, the infernal machine. He would be ready for it.

"Right," said Florence, straightening up. "Anything else I can do for you?" She sneezed twice, and blew her nose in a businesslike fashion.

Her face, when she took the handkerchief away, was sulky and woebegone. She had taken exception to their moving; was thinking about selling up herself and getting a flat. Colin could not imagine her leaving the district, but she said that people were talking about her. She said they had got wind of it, about Mother, and that when she walked along Lauderdale Road, people exchanged glances, and talked out of the side of their mouths, and hurried in, slamming their front doors.

"No, I think that's about it," Colin said to her. "Thanks, Florence, it was good of you to take time off. I think they're just about finished on the van." He went to the front door and looked out into the road. The removal men were just securing the tailgate. "That's it," he said.

The house was empty; even the carpets were taken up. They had come down far enough on the purchase price, Sylvia said, without throwing in soft furnishings. There were pale marks on the walls where the pictures had been; buttons and small coins, shaken out of the furniture, lay on the floorboards for the new owner to sweep up. At the top of the stairs, all the doors were wedged open, and an unaccustomed white light lay across the banisters and the bare landing. There was something about the house in its present state that discomfited him extremely; like an old woman stripped naked. He couldn't wait to leave.

Florence pulled on her gloves. "Better get back to the office. I've got to go out and see a claimant."

"Don't be too hard on him."

"Her. It's a woman. I don't know why you think I'm such a tyrant. It's the taxpayer's money, you know. Well, Colin . . . so this is it."

"Yes. I hope the children won't be a nuisance when they come home from school. I'll be over for them mid-evening."

"They will be a nuisance, but by now I'm reconciled. Where's Alistair today?"

"God knows. I expect he'll turn up; like a homing rat or something."

For a moment he thought she was going to offer him her hand. "We've been neighbours ten years, Colin. I shall miss you."

"We'll miss you, too."

"I hope you will be very happy," she said formally, as she set off down the path.

Anyone would think I were getting married, Colin thought, as he watched her go. It still gave him a pang to think of Isabel; but now that he had become such a decision-maker, he was discovering an ability, a happy knack, of not thinking about her at all. The obsessions that had once alarmed him were attenuated now, washed-up little ghosts, trailing their spectral images through his brain when he was on the verge of sleep. He was not so vulnerable now, in waking hours. It was a man's life; an open countenance, a shuttered heart. It was just as the Prime Minister always said: There Is No Alternative. And that was a comfort too.

Sylvia came down the stairs, her feet clattering on the bare treads.

"What a day!" she said. "We could have picked a finer day for it."

"Looks as if it might clear, to me."

"Let's hope. Ready?"

"Yes."

Sylvia came to a halt, stubbing her toe on the cardboard box that still lay in the hall. "Oh, this blasted box," she said. "What am I to do with it?"

"Leave it."

"I rang up again. That bloke's foreign, who always answers. I can't get any sense out of him."

"You've got the right number?"

"She gave it me herself. Anyway, the address must be right, because that's where I sent her wages, and if she hadn't got them she'd have been round like a shot."

"I could take it," Colin offered. "I could drop it off."

"No, I'll do it. You follow the removers. Here you are." She took out of her shoulder bag the keys to the new house, with the estate agent's tag still on them. She dropped them into his hand. "You go and open up, and I'll drop the box off at Napier Street and follow you in the Mini."

"But I don't know where you want the furniture."

"Never mind." She smiled. "Whatever I decide now, I'll want it changed next week, I know I will. Off you go, then, I'll be right with you." She kissed him on the cheek.

Colin went down the path, swinging the keys. "My old man said follow the van," he sang. "And don't dilly dally on the way." He jumped into the Toyota and revved up the engine, ready for a sporty start. "Off went the van with me home packed in it—" He sped away from the kerb, waving gaily as he approached the corner, though his wife was no longer in sight.

Leaving the front door ajar, so that the squally rain blew in through the crack, Sylvia turned and clip-clopped down the hall. Just a final check, she thought. In the kitchen the smell of pine disinfectant rose to meet her. She had given the worktops a good going-over that morning, and washed the floor. There had to be some

233

mess, when carpets were taken up, but she wanted the purchasers to know that she was clean.

She opened the cupboards one by one. All empty; the groceries were in the back of the car. Inside the last cupboard, by the hinge, there was a smear of something red. Tomato sauce, she thought. Those kids again, eating, eating, always eating. Pulling her abdomen in, she looked around. There was nothing to wipe it up with, no cloth or anything. Not even a tissue in her pocket. With an expression of distaste, she clicked the door shut and left the kitchen behind.

Strange how the living room looked smaller with all the furniture gone. You'd think it would be the other way round. On the mantel-piece sat Colin's head. Much to his disgust, and to Alistair's, she had insisted it should be left behind. A horrible thing, she thought it, with its blind white eyes. She walked over to it, touched the tip of the nose, then the cold lips. The porcelain was yellowish and crazed at the base. Faculty of Benevolence. Faculty of Hope.

She climbed the stairs and checked the bedrooms, opening the doors of the built-in wardrobes and easing out the drawers. In Alistair's room she stood by the window for a moment, looking out over the dank garden, into the tangle of grey branches that fenced it off. In summer it would be an impenetrable wall of green, but of course she would not be here to see it. She laid the palm of her hand flat against the wall. It felt damp, but there was no trace of the fungus now. Colin had done a good job on it. Perhaps there was hope for him yet. The growths would be back, naturally; but that was the next tenant's problem.

The sun was struggling out as she left Alistair's room, and shining through the narrow window onto the landing. It seemed to make everything look worse; illuminating the stains on the wallpaper, the cracks in the floorboards, even the brushmarks in the paintwork; a scouring, bleaching April sun. She hesitated, then turned back and drew closed the door of Alistair's room. Softly, in turn, she closed the other doors. Her face half in shadow, she went downstairs. She picked up the box, surprised again by how light it was. "Lost me way and don't know where to roam," she hummed. The front door clicked shut after her. She took the keys out of her pocket and posted them back through the letter box.

As soon as Muriel turned the corner—she felt the baby stirring within the box—she saw the car parked by the kerb; hello, she thought, Miss Isabel Field. She was parked a few houses along, on the other side of the road, and she was watching Mr. K.'s gate. Muriel saw the upturned white oval of her face; then sunlight struck across the windscreen, and wiped it from her view.

Miss Field was not somebody who understood life. She had not grasped how things work. She had not grasped it ten years ago; almost under her nose, she and Mother had toddled off to the canal. Muriel had an impulse to cross the road, the box in her arms, and pass the time of day.

But there was a need to hurry. It was necessary to get herself back upstairs and change into her own clothes. She couldn't take the baby to the canal wearing Lizzie's white boots, it would be unsuitable. Besides, why should the changeling emerge, unless it recognised its mother?

She turned in at the gate. She saw it, in her own mind, the murky waters parting as the human baby sank. She looked down at Gemma; pity, she thought, you could get fond of it. Slowly, trailing green weed, her own skeletal child swam to the bank. "Resurrection is a fact," she whispered. She drew the child from the water; rigid, but not with cold. With damp and bony fingers, the changeling reached for her face.

She was putting the key in the lock when she heard hurried footsteps behind her. She turned, holding the box between herself and her pursuer.

"What's that?" Miss Field demanded. She peered into the box.

"That's little Gemma," Muriel said calmly. "That's little Gemma Ryan."

"And who the hell are you?"

"Just the baby-sitter."

"Where's Suzanne?"

"Upstairs." She nodded towards the front door. "Coming?" Isabel followed her inside, leaving the front door ajar. Muriel put down the box on the hall table. There was no one around; the doors were all closed. Isabel looked down at the child. "She doesn't look like anybody," she said. "Just a baby. Why is she in a box?"

"Ask her mother." Muriel led the way upstairs.

Outside on Napier Street, the Mini was crawling along. It had begun to rain again, quite hard, and visibility was poor. This must be close enough, Sylvia thought. She pulled up, and took the box from the passenger seat. She left the car unlocked; I'll only be a minute, she thought. Here it is, number 54, number 56. I could leave it outside. But it was wet on the front step, and she could see that the parcel would get ruined. The door was off the latch, so she opened it a fraction more, and peeped in. Her curiosity got the better of her; she intruded her head. "Hello, anybody home?" Some kind of rooming house, she thought, pretty sordid. There must be someone around. "Hello?" I've come this far, I may as well deliver it properly. She stepped inside, closing the door to the street.

Inside the hall, on a small table, was another box. Sylvia looked into it; to her amazement it contained a baby, a tiny wrapped-up baby with a pink healthy skin. As she watched it, it yawned and blinked, and waved a hand at her. Sylvia put her parcel down at her feet. She bent over the baby. It looked a well-cared-for mite, happy and plump, but what was it doing in a cardboard box? The waving, plucking fingers were caught in the open weave of its blanket. Gently and expertly, Sylvia began to free them. She straightened up and looked around her. There was not a sound. She grew alarmed, and ventured up the stairs. "Hello!" she called. "Lizzie? Are you there?"

But Lizzie was no longer there at all. On the first landing, she paused, to let Miss Field catch her up. This was Mr. K.'s floor, but apart from his bedroom, these rooms were empty, and kept locked. She had keys, of course; and about her person.

"Where is she?" Isabel asked, reaching the top of the stairs. "You can take me to her. I won't do anything. I only want to find out where we stand." Muriel caught a whiff of the whisky on her breath.

She unlocked the door, and they stepped inside. A smell of dampness and decay rushed out. The narrow window, uncurtained, looked out onto a brick wall. The paper was peeling from the walls, a spider's web hung in the corner. Miss Field turned, her eyes suddenly bright with terror, the only light in the dark room. Muriel reached up and removed her wig. Miss Field screamed.

Sylvia stopped dead. *What was that?* I don't like it, she thought; a baby in a cardboard box, and some woman—a battered wife perhaps—shrieking in terror overhead. Whoever these people were, they were certainly in need of the attentions of Social Services, if not of the police. She took a deep breath, and ran up the first flight of stairs. She stopped on the landing and looked around. Quite a big place, she thought, bigger than it looked from the outside; and dirt everywhere. Where had the noise come from? Suddenly, she felt herself seized from behind. A brawny arm locked across her throat, and her assailant forced her backwards. Her knees buckled, and she was dragged along. She kicked out behind her, clawed at the imprisoning arm, but the breath was being squeezed out of her, and she was weak with shock. Somewhere, the woman was still screaming. A door was thrust open and she was propelled through it. A blow between her shoulder blades sent her crashing forward. She landed on all fours, at the screamer's feet. She heard the door close. She raised her head. "Hello, Mrs.

Ryan," she said. "What are you doing here?" At once she noticed that Mrs. Ryan was expecting. The whole thing had surprised her, of course, but she was not as astonished as she might have been. She felt she had been travelling for years to get here; as the key turned behind her in the lock, she knew that she had finally arrived.

When the woman had stopped screaming and the house was quiet again, Miss Anaemia left her room and went downstairs. If Mr. K. had done a murder—and she could see things going that way—she would just have to say she knew nothing about it; but she was not, repeat not, going to be in when that woman arrived, wanting to look at the bedsheets again. She pulled her raincoat on as she went through the hall, and wondered if Poor Mrs. Wilmot would mind if she borrowed her telescopic umbrella from the stand by the front door.

What's this? she said to herself. Another delivery for Mr. K.? As another strange face loomed over her, Gemma began to cry. Miss Anaemia opened her eyes wide, reached into the box, and lifted the baby out. She held the quilted head against her cheek, rocking, making soothing noises in her throat. "Don't cry, sweetheart," she said. "What are you doing in a cardboard box then? Have they left you all on your own? Never mind, don't cry, precious. You and me are off to the housing office."

She dropped the empty box on the floor, swaddled the baby in her blanket, hitched her onto her shoulder, and set off out of the front door. It was still drizzling, but the wind had dropped a bit. Miss Anaemia felt exalted, defiant; as if she were going to make people eat their words. Patches of scarlet flared in her cheeks. She crossed the road, clucking to the baby, quickening her step; and turned the corner by the post box. At once she spotted the person she was looking for; there she is, she thought, that fat old cow Miss Sidney from the DHSS, Snoopers herself, wielding her black umbrella, and looking in at everyone's windows as she advances purposefully up the street.

"Hi there!" she called. "Coming to see me, were you? Told you I'd got a baby, didn't I? Who's a liar now?" Miss Sidney checked her stride, and stared.

When the cries of the infant subsided, Mr. Kowalski emerged from the kitchen. It was a fake, he had no doubt, a tape recording, a lure to draw him out. It was a cry from the past; the infants mewling in the burned-out ruins, the mothers bleeding in the city streets.

The box was the first thing he saw. He picked it up, put it on the hall table, and read the address: To Lizzie Blank, 2 Buckingham Avenue. The house had long ago run out of his control. Locking doors had no effect; he knew that now. From upstairs he heard voices raised, the voices of strange women. I will do or die for Poor Mrs. Wilmot, he thought; touch not a hair of that old grey head. He rattled the box. Curiosity killed the cat, is an expression. He touched the metal bulge of the Luger in his deep trouser pocket. Death was in the air of the damp old house. He could smell it, and he knew. He was a professional. He had burned his bridges; there was nothing to lose. He tore at the wrapping paper.

Muriel put on her boots; Muriel's own boots, stout and thick-soled, ready for the mud on Turner's Fields. She put on her big wool overcoat, and knotted her check scarf on the point of her chin. All over the house—in the empty room where the women were imprisoned, and in the kitchen where Mr. Kowalski was loading his gun—they could hear her feet stamping on the stairs, one two, one two: Terror Comes to Town.

And now for little Diddums. She turned, from the foot of the stairs, and gaped. Sweetie Pie had altered; altered out of all recognition. Displayed on the hall table, neat and sweet and perfectly articulated, was a skeleton; fine and tiny, and set together with a deft and knowing hand. If there were an odd number of fingers, and something animal about the skull, she did not notice it. She had never torn the living apart, to study the bones within. With a forefinger, she probed the empty ribs. She shuddered. Bones can be clothed. It was a miraculous transportation; and an hour saved, of her valuable time. One by one she picked up the little bones and placed them in an orderly fashion back inside the box. Only when she had done this did she notice that it was a different box from the one she had carried Gemma in. A different box, with one of her names on it: TO LIZZIE BLANK, inscribed there by the hand of God.

I'm here first, Colin thought, pulling up in his new drive. Here I am for my ten-year NHBC guarantee; my split-level living area, my open aspect to rear. The small estate was on high ground; a golf course fell away below him, hidden now by the steady rain and a belt of young trees.

They should have taken the motorway, he thought, as he fumbled for the keys and prepared to dash for shelter. They'll have got snarled up in the traffic going across the bridge; I should have told them about the road works. He looked at his watch. Thirty minutes; not bad. He let himself into the empty house. Well, you've dallied and dillied, haven't you, he would say to the men when they arrived. He wondered if Sylvia would have the sense to use the motorway. Smiling to himself, he went through to the kitchen to turn the electricity on.

Muriel was at home. She was at home at last; Buckingham Avenue. Holding her box, she wandered through the empty rooms. The Sidneys had gone, and the house was returning to itself; their occupation had been a temporary thing, the blink of an eye, a memory erased as soon as the door closed on them. The dimness was gathering, hanging in clots from the ceiling; the air itself was thickening, and the floors exuded the cold and secret smell of earth. She would take a few minutes; enjoy herself. Then she would go upstairs to the spare room, sit down; arrange the bones, and wait.

Mr. Kowalski went upstairs. He heard them; chattering, their voices on the edge of hysteria. Telephone Voice was one of them; the other was Ghoul.

It seemed that hours had passed. The women heard the key turn in the lock. They stood together, arms intertwined. He faced them, a squat bristling bully, yelling in Rumanian and waving a gun. He motioned them apart. They obeyed, their eyes staring, licking their dry lips in fear. Mr. K. pointed the gun at Sylvia. She lifted her head and glared at him as she dropped back against the wall. He swung round to Isabel. Her fists were clenched at her sides, tensed for the explosion. "I know an expression," he said. "Eeny, meemy, miny, mo—" Both together, the ladies screamed.

The furniture was all in place. Well, you say in place; as Sylvia said, it would be all changed by this time next week. If he could find the kettle, he might be able to make some coffee. They had brought quite a lot of stuff over last night. He looked at his watch again. Where the devil had she got to? She couldn't have taken the motorway after all.

He surveyed the pile of boxes and tea-chests stacked up in the living room. Where to start? He wished she would come. Had the Mini broken down again? It often gave trouble in wet weather. Francis said it was the condenser; but what would a bloody vicar know? "You can't trust these Specials like an old-time copper—" he sang. The telephone rang.

Warily—because he was not expecting a call, and yet he was always expecting one—Colin raised his head and listened. Just where was the telephone? He followed the sound. "When you can't find your way home," he sang. Kitchen; wall phone, very modish. "Hello?" He had to read the number off the dial. "Five-one-two-eight-six?"

There was no answer, just the sound of breathing; quiet and steady.

"Sylvia, is that you?" No answer. He sighed impatiently. "If you want the Broadbents, they've moved. They went yesterday. I've got their address somewhere, I can give it to you if you ring back later tonight." Imbecile vendors; why hadn't they left their new number to hand, as he had done? He paused. "Who is that?"

He felt the hairs rise, prickling, at the nape of his neck. Funny, he'd always imagined that was a figure of speech. The line was open: a meaningless hum, a static crackle. "Mr. Sidney?"

That was not a voice he knew. It seemed to come from very far away. It pricked at his memory with an evil familiarity, like an old habit, an old crime. Again he heard the sound of breathing: heavier, almost laboured, hoarse. At first it seemed that the caller was choking back laughter, gloating laughter long suppressed; but then the note changed, as if a term had been set to the merriment, by a hand around the throat. What could he do, alone in the cold and empty house? He turned his head, hunched his shoulders, as if he felt that the walls had moved in on him; the matt emulsion, the cork notice-board, making their approach. There was something else on the line: the chant of dubiously human voices, a subdued and gathering roar. Was someone throwing a party? He could hear the clink of crystal, the popping of corks; the discreet firm contact of flesh upon flesh. Was someone mourning? Had somebody died? Colin listened, his mouth gaping a little, his hand tight on the receiver: the chuckling, the gasping, the sniggering, the struggle for air. He could not be sure what he heard any more, terminal jubilee, bodily harm; the act of laughter, the art of dying. Rain spattered against the uncurtained windows; the wind got up, and already, by mid-afternoon, it was quite dark.